# ACCLAIM FOR BETH WISEMAN

## The Bookseller's Promise

"*The Bookseller's Promise* beautifully illustrates the power of love, family bonds, and the good news of the gospel . . . A captivating story of discovering faith and finding hope in the midst of despair."

—Jennifer Beckstrand, author of The Matchmakers of Huckleberry Hill series

## A Season of Change

"A beautiful story about love, forgiveness, and finding family in an unexpected place."

—Kathleen Fuller, *USA TODAY* bestselling author

## An Unlikely Match

"With multiple vibrant story lines, Wiseman's excellent tale will have readers anticipating the next. Any fan of Amish romance will love this."

—*Publishers Weekly* on *An Unlikely Match*

"This was such a sweet story. I cheered on Evelyn and Jayce the whole way. Jayce is having issues with his difficult father, who's brought a Hollywood crew to Amish country to film a scene in a nearby cave. Evelyn has a strong, supportive family, so she feels for Jayce immediately. As they grow closer and help each other overcome fears and phobias, they know this can't last. But God, and two persnickety Amish sisters, Lizzie and Esther, have other plans. Can a Hollywood boy fall for an Amish girl and make it work? Find out. Read this delightful, heartwarming story!"

—Lenora Worth, author of *Their Amish Reunion*

"Beth Wiseman's *An Unlikely Match* will keep you turning the pages as you are pulled into this heartwarming and unpredictable Amish romance story about Evelyn and Jayce, two interesting and compelling characters. Beth doesn't disappoint keeping you guessing as to how this story will end."

Molly Jebber, bestselling Amish inspirational historical romance author

## A Picture of Love

"This is a warm story of romance and second chances with some great characters that fans of the genre will love."

—*Parkersburg News & Sentinel*

"Beth Wiseman's *A Picture of Love* will delight readers of Amish fiction. Naomi and Amos's romance is a heartfelt story of love, forgiveness, and second chances. This book has everything readers love about a Beth Wiseman story—an authentic portrait of the Amish community, humor, the power of grace and hope and, above all, faith in God's Word and His promises."

—Amy Clipston, bestselling author of *The Coffee Corner*

## A Beautiful Arrangement

"*A Beautiful Arrangement* has everything you want in an escape novel."

—*Amish Heartland*

"Wiseman's delightful third installment of the Amish Journey series centers on the struggles and unexpected joys of a marriage of convenience . . . Series devotees and newcomers alike will find this engrossing romance hard to put down."

—*Publishers Weekly*

"*A Beautiful Arrangement* has so much heart, you won't want to put it down until you've read the last page. I love second-chance love stories, and Lydia and Samuel's story is heartbreaking and sweet with unexpected twists and turns that make their journey to love all the more satisfying. Beth's fans will cherish this book."

—Jennifer Beckstrand, author of The Petersheim Brothers series

## Listening to Love

"Wiseman is at her best in this surprising tale of love and faith."

—*Publishers Weekly*

"I always find Beth Wiseman's books to be both tenderly romantic and thought provoking. She has a way of setting a scene that makes me feel like I'm part of an Amish community and visiting for supper. I loved the title of this book, the message about faith and God, and the heartfelt romance between Lucas and Natalie. *Listening to Love* has everything I love in a Beth Wiseman novel—a strong faith message, a touching romance, and a beautiful sense of place. Beth is such an incredibly gifted storyteller."

—Shelley Shepard Gray, bestselling author

"*Listening to Love* is vintage Beth Wiseman . . . Clear your calendar because you're going to want to read this one in a single sitting."

—Vannetta Chapman, author of Shipshewana Amish Mystery series

## Hearts in Harmony

"This is a sweet story, not only of romance, but of older generations and younger generations coming together in friendship. It's a tearjerker as well as an uplifting story."

—*Parkersburg News & Sentinel*

"Beth Wiseman has penned a poignant story of friendship, faith, and love that is sure to touch readers' hearts."

—Kathleen Fuller, *USA TODAY* bestselling author

"Beth Wiseman's *Hearts in Harmony* is a lyrical hymn. Mary and Levi are heartwarming, lovable characters who instantly feel like dear friends. Once readers open this book, they won't put it down until they've reached the last page."

—Amy Clipston, bestselling author of *A Seat by the Hearth*

# *The* BOOKSELLER'S PROMISE

# Other Books by Beth Wiseman

The Amish Inn Novels

*A Picture of Love*

*An Unlikely Match*

*A Season of Change*

The Amish Journey Novels

*Hearts in Harmony*

*Listening to Love*

*A Beautiful Arrangement*

The Amish Secrets Novels

*Her Brother's Keeper*

*Love Bears All Things*

*Home All Along*

The Land of Canaan Novels

*Seek Me with All Your Heart*

*The Wonder of Your Love*

*His Love Endures Forever*

The Daughters of the Promise Novels

*Plain Perfect*

*Plain Pursuit*

*Plain Promise*

*Plain Paradise*

*Plain Proposal*

*Plain Peace*

Other Novels

*Need You Now*

*The House That Love Built*

*The Promise*

Story Collections

*An Amish Year*

*Amish Celebrations*

Stories

*A Choice to Forgive* included in *An Amish Christmas*

*A Change of Heart* included in *An Amish Gathering*

*Healing Hearts* included in *An Amish Love*

*A Perfect Plan* included in *An Amish Wedding*

*A Recipe for Hope* included in *An Amish Kitchen*

*Always Beautiful* included in *An Amish Miracle*

*Rooted in Love* included in *An Amish Garden*

*When Christmas Comes Again* included in *An Amish Second Christmas*

*In His Father's Arms* included in *An Amish Cradle*

*A Cup Half Full* included in *An Amish Home*

*The Cedar Chest* included in *An Amish Heirloom*

*When Love Returns* included in *An Amish Homecoming*

*A Reunion of Hearts* included in *An Amish Reunion*

*Loaves of Love* included in *An Amish Christmas Bakery*

# *The* BOOKSELLER'S PROMISE

AN AMISH BOOKSTORE NOVEL

BETH WISEMAN

ZONDERVAN

*The Bookseller's Promise*



Requests for information should be addressed to:

Zondervan, *3900 Sparks Dr. SE, Grand Rapids, Michigan 49546*

Library of Congress Cataloging-in-Publication Data
Names: Wiseman, Beth, 1962- author.
Title: The bookseller's promise / Beth Wiseman.
Description: Grand Rapids, Michigan : Zondervan, [2022] | Series: An Amish bookstore novel | Summary: "In the first novel of Beth Wiseman's new Amish Bookstore series, a rare, old book may hold answers to a present-day romance"-- Provided by publisher.
Identifiers: LCCN 2021046145 (print) | LCCN 2021046146 (ebook) | ISBN 9780310365532 (paperback) | ISBN 9780310365624 (library binding) | ISBN 9780310365549 (epub) | ISBN 9780310365556
Classification: LCC PS3623.I83 B66 2022 (print) | LCC PS3623.I83 (ebook) | DDC 813/.6--dc23
LC record available at https://lccn.loc.gov/2021046145
LC ebook record available at https://lccn.loc.gov/2021046146

Publisher's Note: This novel is a work of fiction. Names, characters, places, and incidents are either products of the author's imagination or used fictitiously. All characters are fictional, and any similarity to people living or dead is purely coincidental.



Zondervan titles may be purchased in bulk for educational, business, fundraising, or sales promotional use. For information, please email SpecialMarkets@Zondervan.com.

*Printed in the United States of America*

22 23 24 25 26 LSC 10 9 8 7 6 5 4 3 2 1

*To Mother and Daddy, together again.*
*I love and miss you both.*

# GLOSSARY

*ab im kopp:* crazy, off in the head
*ach:* oh
*bruder:* brother
*danki:* thank you
*Deitsch:* Dutch
*dochder:* daughter
*Englisch:* those who are not Amish folk; the English language
*er dutt mir leed:* I'm sorry
*fraa:* wife
*Gott:* God
*grossdaadi:* grandfather
*gut:* good
*kaffi:* coffee
*kind/kinner:* child/children
*lieb:* love
*maedel:* young woman
*mamm:* mom
*mei:* my

*mudder:* mother

*nee:* no

*rumschpringe:* adolescent rite of passage

*schweschder:* sister

*sohn:* son

*urgrossvadder:* great-grandfather

*Wie bischt:* Hello, how are you?

*ya:* yes

# CHAPTER 1

Yvonne reread for the third time the letter she'd received from Jake Lantz. Parts of his correspondence included words she wasn't familiar with. She didn't know much about the Amish, but after a quick Google search, she'd learned they spoke Pennsylvania Dutch and English. But even before she'd looked on the internet, Mr. Lantz's words had registered, and Yvonne's disappointment had quickly turned to anger as fury almost choked her.

Dear Mrs. Wilson,

I am in receipt of your letter dated May 2nd, and I must tell you that the book you inquired about is not for sale. *Er dutt mir leed*, and I wish you all of *Gott*'s blessings.

Sincerely,

Jake Lantz

With trembling hands, Yvonne handed the letter to Trevor, not even looking at him as she paced the living room, shaking her head. "Who does that? Who turns down a hundred grand?" After groaning, she threw her hands into the air. "I've spent months trying to find that book. And George is paying me a thirty percent commission, which is unheard of."

Trevor set the letter on the coffee table in front of him as he lifted himself off the couch. By the time he wrapped his arms around Yvonne, she shook even more. He kissed her on the cheek and pulled her closer. "I told you to give up on that project a long time ago. We don't need the money."

Yvonne rolled her eyes. "Apparently, neither does Jake Lantz." She let Trevor hold her for a few more seconds before she eased away, recognizing the familiar smell of cherry cough drop on his breath. He ate them like candy, citing a tickle in his throat that seemed to be terminal, he often joked. Yvonne had gotten used to the imitation breath mints a long time ago.

"I read up on the Amish, just a little, and they seem to live simple lives." She shook her head again. "But no one turns down that kind of money, Amish or not."

"I see he addresses you as *Mrs.* Wilson." Trevor grinned as he tucked her shoulder-length brown hair behind her ears. "Soon enough, you'll be Mrs. Trevor Adams."

Yvonne forced a smile even though she was angry enough to spit nails at a guy named Jake Lantz, a man she'd never met. "That money would have gone a long way toward wedding expenses, a bigger house, or even a new car."

Trevor cupped her cheeks before he tenderly kissed her lips, lingering there for what he probably presumed was long enough to calm her down. "The wedding is paid for. We've been looking at houses, and I'll buy you any car you want."

Yvonne took a deep breath. Trevor was the most generous human being she'd ever known. He was kind, good looking, successful, and had never met a stranger. She was lucky to be engaged to him. But unlike Yvonne, Trevor had been born into a family that had money. Not to say Trevor didn't work hard. He did. But the value of a dollar didn't mean the same to both of them. Yvonne had always made her own way. The house they were standing in, soon to be put on the market, was the biggest purchase she'd ever made. Modest as it was, she'd never been prouder than the day she'd closed on the property. After she married Trevor in the fall, they'd move into his larger home—unless they found something even bigger first. They were both in their early thirties and anxious to start a family soon. But she would miss her first house.

"I love you for wanting to take care of me, but . . ." She trailed off and shrugged.

"I know." He sighed as he ran a hand through his dark hair, his temples sprinkled with gray. "You want to take care of yourself. And I get that." Now he was the one shaking his head. "But you've worked hard all your life. And you've been on a wild-goose chase for that book George wants. Just let it go. We'll go rent a house at the beach or something for a long weekend. If George wants it so bad, then he can travel to Indiana and try to talk the guy into selling it."

Yvonne felt a surge of adrenaline rush through her veins. "That's it. I'll go to Indiana. I'll get the guy to sell it."

"Not everything is for sale." Trevor walked around the coffee table and sat on Yvonne's powder-blue couch. Everything in her living room was styled in outdated pastels, but she hadn't been able to bring herself to redecorate. What was the point now—unless maybe it would help the house to sell sooner? Her stomach clenched at the thought of someone else living in her home.

"Yes, everything *is* for sale. George will offer more money." Yvonne was pacing again, her mind spinning. "I won't tell him about the letter. I'll just go to Indiana, convince the guy to sell, but then if he doesn't, I'll explain to George while I'm there."

Trevor frowned as he lifted his socked feet up onto the coffee table. "I can go with you for a long weekend, but I've got those men from corporate coming in from New York next week, so—"

"No, no. You don't need to go." Yvonne avoided his eyes, knowing she'd spoken too quickly. She loved Trevor and looked forward to being his wife, but this might be her last time to do something totally on her own. She'd watched too many of her friends go from self-reliant women to subservient wives in barely the blink of an eye. Maybe it wouldn't be that way with Trevor. She didn't expect to have to change after she was married, especially when Trevor always said he admired her independence. But still, the thought lingered in the back of her mind.

"I don't *need* to go, or you don't *want* me to go?" Trevor held up a hand when she opened her mouth to speak. "You know how delicate my feelings are." He spoke so overdramatically that she almost laughed. "It's okay to want some time to yourself and to tackle this project on your own." Grinning, he patted the spot beside him on the couch. "So, come give me a little love, beautiful, before you jet off to Small Town, Indiana."

She sat on the couch and curled up in his arms.

He kissed her on the forehead and gave her a gentle squeeze. "Even though I wish you would let the whole thing go. It's had you tied up in knots." He twisted to face her until their eyes locked. "But I don't want to be that kind of husband. We're not always going to agree on everything, and I'm not ever going to try to change you. I can tell buying the book is important to you."

This time it was Yvonne who initiated the kiss, wondering if Trevor could read her mind.

Despite their close connection and the love they felt for each other, she couldn't help but wonder if their intimacy would always be infused with such passion. She was thirty-two and had held out for the perfect man. And she'd found everything she longed for in Trevor. But the closer they got to the date of their wedding in September, the more impossible it was not to feel a little nervous. How could anyone really be sure they would love one person for the rest of their lives?

"How long will you be gone?" Trevor kissed the pulsing hollow at the base of her throat, sending a delightful shiver up her spine. She would miss this—miss Trevor—while she was away. But Jake Lantz had presented her with the biggest challenge of her career. And George was her biggest client. She didn't want to let him down.

"However long it takes to get that Amish man to sell the book." She leaned in for another kiss before he could argue.

---

Jake turned the key in the lock and opened the front door, breathing in the familiar smell of the old building. He'd owned the small bookstore since his grandfather left it to him four years ago. Jake had grown up at his grandfather's side and had spent more time at the bookstore than at home. He'd known the business inside and out by the time he was twelve. Thirteen years later, not much had changed, even though his grandfather had told Jake repeatedly to redecorate or adjust things to suit himself. Jake had chosen to leave everything exactly as it had been. The only thing he'd done after his grandfather died was to hire help. Eva Graber had been working for him for four years. He'd hired her when she was fifteen, and she'd been a quick study. She was a book lover, like he was, and a whiz with numbers. These days, she took care of all the accounting and ordering, kept the coffee bar stocked, and made sure the place was always clean.

"*Wie bischt.*" Eva walked in toting a basket on her arm. To Jake, it looked like a mini picnic basket, and he was always glad to see her carrying it into the bookstore. It meant she'd brought tasty treats.

He breathed in the aroma as she walked closer to the counter he was standing behind. "*Wie bischt.*" He sniffed the air. "Cinnamon rolls?"

Eva smiled. "*Ya.*" She scooted past the counter. "I'm going to put them in the back room, then get the coffee percolating."

There was a makeshift kitchen in the back, which was the one thing Jake knew he should probably upgrade. Although there was room for a propane oven, they were still using a propane burner atop the small counter. Reheating things on the burner wasn't convenient. Of course, they didn't have a microwave, either, or any electricity at all. Some shop owners had succumbed to more modern conveniences when the bishop approved it, but Jake liked things the way they were. Although a small propane oven would make things easier for Eva.

Jake had watched Eva grow into a beautiful young woman. She was six years his junior at nineteen, and he knew he'd soon lose her to a lucky man. Most likely John Yoder. John had been smitten with Eva for a long time, and he'd confessed his feelings to Jake about a year ago. In fact,

Jake was pretty sure the entire town knew how John felt about Eva. But if Eva was aware of John's feelings, she'd never let on, and she had yet to go on a date with him as far as Jake knew. He wasn't sure if Eva had gone on a date with anyone.

Jake had grown up with John, a man two years younger than him. John had planned things out meticulously. He'd told Jake that first he wanted to land a good job. Then he wanted to build a house. When that was accomplished, he would court Eva and ask her to marry him. John had a good job with a local construction company now, and he was putting the finishing touches on his house. It probably wouldn't be long until he and Eva started to date. Personally, Jake thought it was risky for John not to ask Eva out sooner, for fear someone else would beat him to it. But perhaps potential suitors didn't want to get in the way of John's plan. John had certainly mentioned his intentions to most of the eligible men in their district.

Jake had to admit they would make a fine-looking couple, even though the thought left him feeling unsettled sometimes. After Eva married, Jake would be forced to find her replacement. She'd have a full-time job taking care of her husband and running their household.

*As it should be.*

He sighed as he wondered if he would ever have that life—a wife along with a houseful of children. He'd dated on and off, but he'd yet to find the woman he wanted to plan his future with.

He pushed the button on the cash register and began loading the slots with money he carted to and from the store each day. The task reminded him of his grandfather. Thoughts of Jeremiah Lantz brought fond memories these days, but back when his grandfather died, Jake hadn't been sure how he'd get up each morning. Jake's grandmother had died when he was four or five, and he didn't remember much about her. Losing his grandfather had been the first time he'd experienced real grief.

But at least he had his grandfather's bookstore and the home that had been in his family for generations. Jake's parents had moved to the smaller house on the family's property—the *daadi haus*—after his grandfather died, leaving Jake to run the farm and reside in the big house. His mother had been insistent about it, obviously anxious for Jake to get married and start a family.

As Jake was an only child, his father still helped out when he could, but a tractor accident years ago had left him with a bad back that had gotten worse over the past few years. It was a small farm, though, and manageable. The only time the bookstore and the farm competed for Jake's time was during planting season and throughout the harvest.

Eva came around the corner carrying two cups of coffee. The skylight directly above the counter filtered the early-morning rays and was always the first spot brightened each morning. As the sun rose, the rest of the skylights welcomed the incoming light, each one gaining in brightness slowly until the natural hues of the sun shone on a new day throughout the store.

"*Danki*," he said when Eva handed him his cup of coffee—always in the same white mug, perfectly percolated, and with one teaspoon of sugar. As he took a sip, he peeked over the edge of his cup and wondered for the hundredth time if Eva had any idea how gorgeous she was. Her light brown hair framed a delicate face, and she had a smile that lit up a room. Jake had watched visitors in the store—Amish and non-Amish—stare at her in awe. She'd become a woman overnight, it seemed, dainty yet strong in her convictions.

Eva had yet to give any single men her attention. Jake was selfishly glad about that since he'd lose her as an employee. But he wanted her to find the perfect man and be happy. She deserved that. Maybe she was secretly waiting on John Yoder.

Eva walked around the counter and sidled up to Jake, breathing in the sandalwood soap he used, mingled with his minty mouthwash. "Do you want me to make selections from the catalog, or do you want to have a go at it?"

Jake chuckled. "The last time I had 'a go at it,' we ended up returning a lot of inventory. I think you have a better feel for what our customers want." He dug through a pile of paperwork on the counter, then handed her two publishers' catalogs. One was tailored toward commercial fiction and the other toward books more biblical in nature. Jake had carried on his grandfather's wishes by stocking only clean and wholesome fiction, which—luckily for the shop—was gobbled up by Amish and English readers alike. The English women were particularly fond of love stories about the Amish, although plenty of Amish women purchased the novels too. The bishop wasn't keen about members of his district reading about romantic interludes, no matter how clean and wholesome they might be. But he tended to look the other way, according to what his wife had told Jake years ago.

"Your account is holding steady. Do you want me to order around the same number of books as we have been lately?" Eva's heart beat a little faster, the way it always did when she was close to Jake. "And several gift items were popular and sold quickly. I can reorder those."

Jake nodded as he turned to her and smiled. "I trust you to order whatever we need."

What she needed was for Jake to notice her as the woman she'd become, not the fifteen-year-old girl he'd hired four years ago. But every time she tried to insert herself into his life as more than an employee, he didn't even seem to notice her efforts. Or maybe he just didn't find her attractive.

"Here." He reached for a cell phone he kept in his pocket. Prior to a couple of months ago, Jake had held out on getting a mobile device. But nearly everyone in the community had a phone, with the bishop's blessing as long as it was for emergencies or business use. Eva had a phone, too, but she didn't flaunt it. Her father wasn't fond of mobile phones, and as long as she was under her parents' roof, she tried to abide by the rules. Most of them. Her three brothers had phones, too, but they also tried to be respectful of their father's wishes by at least keeping the devices out of sight. Her mother didn't seem to mind the phones, citing them as a necessity for their work. Josh, David, and Amos all worked at a local lumberyard. Their work didn't necessarily require a phone, but keeping in contact with their girlfriends did.

Eva had been on the phone placing orders for about fifteen minutes when another call came in. She let it go to voice mail, then handed the phone to Jake when he came out from the back room. "Someone called and left a message."

He looked at the number of the missed call and shrugged before he began to listen to the message. After he'd clicked the phone off, he set it on the counter and scratched his cheek.

"Everything okay?"

Jake sat down on the stool behind the counter. "*Ya*, I guess."

Eva bit her bottom lip, tempted to push for more information but unwilling to pry. Although as Jake sighed and shook his head, she couldn't help but wonder who had left the message. Finally, he looked at her, blinking his eyes as if bewildered.

"The message was from a woman who wrote me a letter not long ago. She was wanting to purchase a book I have in my inventory." He paused, shifting his eyes away from hers a moment before he looked at her again. "I wrote her back and told her the book wasn't for sale." It was hard to miss the irritation in his voice.

Eva sat on the other stool and faced him. "It's a bookstore. Aren't all the books for sale?"

He twisted his mouth back and forth, the way he did sometimes when he was in heavy thought. "Not the one she wants."

"Which book?" Eva couldn't imagine any of the inventory being unavailable for sale.

"It's not out on the shelf." He stood up and walked around the counter, then began pacing the small area near the front door, his thumbs looped beneath his suspenders. "She offered an absurd amount of money."

Eva wondered what Jake considered an absurd amount. *A hundred dollars? Maybe two hundred?* Currently, they didn't have any books that were priced higher than thirty-five dollars—at least none she was aware of. The store sold mostly paperbacks—fiction and nonfiction—along with a few hardbacks Eva had ordered during a sale or discount by the publisher.

"I'm wondering how she got *mei* phone number." He stopped pacing, took off his hat, and scratched his head, frowning. Then he grumbled. "*Ach*, I ran some advertisements and used *mei* mobile phone number. Maybe that was it. But she isn't local. She lives in Texas."

Eva still wondered which book the woman had offered

to buy and why it wasn't for sale. "Why would a woman in Texas want to buy a book from your small bookstore in Montgomery, Indiana?"

He shook his head, scowling. "I don't know. But she was willing to pay a lot of money for it."

Eva held her breath but finally couldn't stand it. "Over a hundred dollars?"

Jake locked eyes with her, then laughed. "*Ya*, you could say that. She wanted to buy it for a hundred *thousand* dollars."

Eva placed her hands firmly on the counter when she almost fell off her stool. After she picked up her jaw, she thought for a few moments. "I read in the newspaper that people make calls that aren't real. They call them scam calls. Maybe it wasn't a real offer?" *It couldn't be.*

"She didn't offer the money over the phone the first time. She sent a letter and said she would pay that much."

Eva took a deep breath as she tried to sort things out. "Did she make the same offer again when she left a message just now?"

Jake nodded. "*Ya*, she did. She's very pushy."

Eva stood up, walked around the counter, and leaned against it, watching Jake start to pace again. "That can't be a real offer. What book could possibly be worth that much money?" She hoped he would tell her. And on the off chance it was a genuine offer, why in the world wouldn't Jake sell the woman the book? For a long time, he had wanted to paint the entire building. It also needed a new roof. The building could stand to be leveled. And there was plenty more that needed to be done to the old structure. But Jake didn't have time, and Eva sensed he didn't have enough money, even in his personal accounts, to hire someone to make the repairs.

Their people lived simple lives, but homes and businesses still needed repairs. Eva was sure the community would come together to assist Jake with the structural repairs, but when she'd brought up the subject before, he'd shunned the idea, citing the fact everyone was too busy to take on extra projects. She reminded him of the barn raisings they were able to accomplish in one to two days, but Jake didn't want to ask for help. Pride was frowned upon, but they were human, and the emotion was evident in their community just like everywhere else.

Jake seemed to be thinking about the money too. "When *mei grossdaadi* left me the bookstore, he told me to make any changes I wanted to, that it was my store." He glanced at her. "That was when he first fell ill. But I liked things the way they were. Still do." He pointed upward. "We need a new roof. And other work. But I chose to keep the interior mostly the same."

Eva liked when he said "we" when referring to the bookstore. "Jake, I don't want to overstep." She paused and waited for him to look at her. "But a hundred thousand dollars would put a new roof on the store and also take care of a lot of the repairs you've mentioned before."

"*Ya, ya*. I know." Sighing, he leaned up against the

counter next to her. "There was one stipulation *mei grossdaadi* made when he gave me the store. I could do anything I wanted, but I was never to sell a certain book." He lowered his head, shaking it, then looked at her. "That's the book this woman wants to buy, and no amount of money will tempt me to break that promise."

"Do you know why your *grossdaadi* made you promise not to sell the book?" Eva's arm brushed against his as they stood side by side, causing a tingling in the pit of her stomach.

He shook his head. "*Nee*, I have no idea. At the time, I didn't think much about it. I assumed it had some sort of sentimental value, and maybe it does."

Eva thought she might burst if Jake didn't tell her about the book, but she clamped her mouth closed.

Grinning, he turned toward her. "It's crazy, isn't it? I never thought about the book having a monetary value."

Eva wasn't sure what was crazier—the woman's definitely absurd offer or Jake's refusal to sell the book. But she believed in keeping promises, and the fact that Jake would turn down that kind of money solidified what Eva had always known. The man she was in love with was a genuine and honest person.

She nodded.

"And do you want to know what's even crazier?" He stopped smiling, and his expression shifted to one of worry, the lines between his eyebrows forming a *V* as he scowled. "That woman left a message saying she was coming here to discuss purchase of the book."

Eva's eye widened. "All the way from Texas? She must really want you to sell." Her curiosity rose another notch. *What book?*

"It will be a wasted trip for her. I'm not selling it." Jake sighed.

Eva was going to self-combust if he didn't tell her about this book soon, but instead of querying him further, she said, "When will this woman be here?"

His dreamy blue eyes hardened. "Day after tomorrow." After he held the expression for a few seconds, he walked away, unlocked the basement door, and headed down the stairs.

Eva had never understood why the basement door was always locked. But now she wondered—was the book in the basement? *What else is down there?*

# CHAPTER 2

Yvonne stepped out of the car she'd rented at the Indianapolis airport. She'd opted for a small SUV with four-wheel drive since she'd read that most people in the southern part of the state owned vehicles with four-wheel drive. She wasn't sure why. Her two-hour trip had consisted of mostly freeway driving until she'd almost reached her destination. Then she'd found herself in a rural area with a lot of farms on both sides of the two-lane roads, some of them not even paved. She'd seen her first Amish buggies when she'd gotten close to Montgomery—a small, picturesque town. If there were Amish in Texas, she'd never come across any. It was fascinating to see people dressed as pioneers driving the black buggies, especially since some of the drivers didn't look old enough to operate a car.

She put a hand to her forehead to block the morning sun, hoping she hadn't arrived too early. There wasn't a listing for the bookstore on the internet, so she didn't know the hours of operation. After studying the small building, which was actually larger than she had imagined, she walked up a narrow sidewalk. She was greeted by a lovely window box filled with colorful blooms set against a dark red exterior that surrounded the huge windows lining the front of the building. A bell chimed when she opened the door, and the wood floor creaked beneath her feet. A red candle on the counter caught her attention, along with the aroma of cinnamon wafting up her nose. The first word that came to her mind was *quaint*. Perhaps *quaint* and *charming*—two words that described this unique bookstore to a *T*.

A young woman behind the counter lifted her head and smiled. "Hello. Are you looking for anything in particular, or would you just like to browse?"

Yvonne struggled not to stare. She'd seen only a few Amish people up close, and that had been during her quest for the book she needed Jake Lantz to part with. This woman was lovely, even without any makeup on. She had brown doe eyes with thick dark eyelashes, and her rosy cheeks dimpled as she smiled. The woman wore a white head covering, and a black apron sat atop a maroon-colored dress.

Yvonne blinked her eyes a few times, then moved forward, the heels on her boots clicking against the wood floor. She'd chosen a dressy pair of jeans with a hint of bling and boots that were more fashionable than cowgirl boots, with a decent heel to boost her five-foot-four stance. Trevor always said dark blue was her power color, so she'd opted for a button-up dark blue blouse that hung loose just below her waistline. Professional but not too fancy.

"I'm here to see Jake Lantz." She set her black purse on the counter. "Is he in?"

"*Ya,* he is. May I tell him your name?" The woman continued to smile, but her dimples diminished after Yvonne said who she was. After tucking her chin, the clerk nodded, then left her spot and disappeared around the corner.

Yvonne glanced around, surprised by how lit up the place was from all the skylights. She wondered what they did when it wasn't a sunny day outside. There were a lot of windows, but perusing the books on a cloudy day had to be difficult.

To her left marched rows of bookshelves. To her right stood the small counter with two stools behind it and a very old cash register. As she moved a little farther into the room, she saw spiral notebooks, pencils, file folders, and other office and school supplies. There was also a section with trinkets and gift items. Yvonne picked up a snow globe that had an Amish buggy with a family inside. As she shook it and snow filled the round orb, she heard voices.

"*Ya*, that's the lady from Texas." A male made the statement in a disgruntled voice.

Yvonne tried to tiptoe in her boots back toward the front of the store. She kept the snow globe, deciding to buy it as a gesture of goodwill. And because she loved the intricate details. It would be her souvenir to go along with her thirty-thousand-dollar check when she convinced Jake Lantz to sell her the book she needed.

She had just placed the globe on the counter when a man came around the corner, followed by the young woman. *Wow.* Her eyes widened as she took in the tall and incredibly handsome guy coming toward her. His semicropped bangs were swept to one side beneath a straw hat that did nothing to take away from his athletic physique, and when his compelling blue eyes locked with hers, Yvonne worried she had overestimated her ability to charm the owner of the store out of the book. She hadn't been sure how Jake Lantz would project himself, but she hadn't been prepared for the person standing before her. She'd expected someone more . . . simple. This man oozed confidence and strength, and he barely offered her a smile as his jaw visibly tensed.

The woman sidled up beside him on the other side of the counter, and Yvonne swallowed hard, feeling a bit self-conscious. She was at least ten years older than the other woman, whose face was void of the beginnings of crow's-feet. Yvonne scrutinized the tiny lines on her own face daily in the mirror and had been doing so ever since she'd slid past thirty over two years ago. The Amish lady radiated natural beauty and youth.

"I-I'm Yvonne Wilson. I sent you a letter, and I also left you a message." She paused, waiting for a response, but the man merely raised an eyebrow. The woman's dimples had returned. Yvonne wondered if they were a couple.

"I'm Jake Lantz. I'm afraid you made a trip for nothing.

As I told you, the book you want is not for sale." He stared at her for several long seconds before he glanced at the globe on the counter.

"Oh, yeah . . . I'd like to buy that." She nodded toward the snow globe and realized her goodwill gesture wasn't going to win her any points with this guy. "I'd also respectfully ask you to reconsider my client's generous offer for the book. If it's a matter of money—"

"It's not," he said quickly. "I promised *mei* grandfather that I would never sell the book."

Yvonne tipped her head to one side as she considered what he was saying. "You promised your grandfather? That's why you're turning down a hundred thousand dollars?" She hadn't meant for the indignity in her voice to shine through as much as it obviously had.

Jake frowned. "*Ya*, that's right. A promise. One that I intend to keep." He folded his arms across his chest. His beautiful sidekick did the same thing. It would have been kind of cute if thirty thousand dollars wasn't on the line.

Yvonne sighed, put a hand to her forehead, then lowered it slowly. "Can I ask you what is so important about this book that my client is willing to pay so much for it? And why would your grandfather make you promise not to sell it?" It hadn't mattered much about the content in the book prior to this moment. She knew it was a rare edition of a religious book, that it was written in 1875, and that only a hundred copies were in print. Yvonne had been able to track down only this one.

"I have no idea." Jake continued to face off with her, but the young woman had lowered her arms and was now biting her bottom lip as if she might feel a tad sorry for Yvonne. "There isn't anything you can say to make me change *mei* mind."

Yvonne had picked up on their accent, which might also have been charming if so much wasn't riding on this deal. "I can call my client and see how high he is willing to go to buy the book."

"It won't matter." Jake's grin showed a touch of arrogance, which should have evoked irritation, but an unwelcome surge of attraction assaulted her instead.

*I'm engaged.* She'd never had eyes for anyone but Trevor, but this guy was melting her resolve and causing her pulse to pick up. She was unprepared for this. She'd assumed she would win over a simple man with her charm. This was not the person she had planned to go up against.

She cleared her throat, knowing she needed to go somewhere and come up with a better plan. After digging around in her purse, she found her wallet. "Here. I still want the globe." She handed him a credit card, which he promptly passed to the woman standing next to him, the smug grin still on his face.

"Thirty-five dollars and twenty-two cents." Jake's employee, girlfriend, wife—whoever she was—slipped the Visa into a type of credit card imprinter Yvonne hadn't seen since she'd gone shopping with her mother as a child. After the woman swiped the device across the card, she passed it back to Yvonne and handed her a pen. "Just sign here, please."

Yvonne did, taking her time, pondering if there was anything more she could say to at least have Jake thinking about her offer. He was a young guy, maybe a few years younger than herself, hovering around twenty-five or twenty-six, she thought.

After Yvonne laid the pen on the counter, the woman wrapped the globe in several layers of tissue paper and put it in a bag.

"Again, I'm sorry that you made the trip for no reason." Jake's grin faded as his expression turned taut and derisive.

Yvonne picked up the bag, then met Jake's challenging eyes. "Can I at least *see* the book?"

"*Nee.*" He tipped the rim of his hat before he turned to leave. "Safe travels," he said over his shoulder before he stalked off and disappeared out of sight.

Yvonne turned to the woman, who winced. "I'm sorry for your troubles," she said with her chin once again tucked.

Maybe Yvonne needed an ally, or at least more information. "I didn't get your name."

"I'm Eva." She folded her hands in front of her as she cautiously lifted her gaze.

Yvonne set the bag and her purse back on the counter. "Nice to meet you, Eva. Do you have any idea why your boss . . . I'm sorry, or is that your boyfriend or husband?"

Eva's rosy cheeks turned a bright shade of red. "I just work for him."

"Sorry to be so nosy, but I'm confused. Do you have any idea why your boss won't sell that book? It can't be just because of a promise he made to his grandfather." She paused, cringing. "Can it?"

"I believe that truly is the reason." Eva shrugged. "I don't think you will be able to change his mind. I haven't even seen the book."

"The whole thing is odd." Sighing, Yvonne lifted her purse to her shoulder and picked up the bag.

"Will you be flying back to Texas now?" Eva raised both eyebrows a bit too enthusiastically.

"No. I'm not going home without that book, which means I need a place to stay."

Eva stared at the floor a moment before she looked up at Yvonne. "I think you might as well move here, then. He won't change his mind. But if you need lodging, I can recommend several places."

"That would be great. Normally I would have booked somewhere in advance, but I kind of wanted to check out the area and then decide."

"*Ach*, let's see . . . There is The Peony Inn. It's a lovely bed-and-breakfast run by two sweet older women." She tapped one finger to another. "And there is also the Gasthof Village Inn. It has a restaurant on-site, along with a gift shop and a lake. Both are nearby. And there are several *regular* hotels not too far away."

Yvonne stifled a smile at the derogatory way the woman referred to *regular* hotels. "I'm guessing my best choices are the places you mentioned?"

"In my opinion." Eva grinned. "Both serve excellent meals. Although there is no electricity at The Peony Inn. Depending on what you're used to, you might prefer accommodations with air-conditioning."

Yvonne chuckled. "It's already eighty degrees in Texas, so your weather feels wonderful to me, and not as humid." Her phone had showed sixty-eight degrees when she'd landed at the airport. "But I think I'll opt for the Gasthof Village with the on-site restaurant. I'm not much for scheduled meals. Especially after traveling. I'll probably sleep in."

Eva nodded, but now there was no smile, not even a grin or hint of a dimple. "I'm guessing we will see you again."

"Yes. For sure." Yvonne gave a quick wave, fought a yawn, and left the bookstore.

---

Eva watched the English woman drive away as her stomach churned. There was something about the way Yvonne Wilson had looked at Jake, and while her boss might not like Yvonne's interest in the book, she thought she'd seen a sparkle in his eyes as well.

Jake came from the back room with a cinnamon roll in his hand. "*Ach*, glad she's gone. Some *Englisch* with a lot of money think they can buy anything they want."

"I think she's trying to buy it for someone else," Eva said, keeping her eyes on Jake, watching for any reaction that might indicate he was attracted to the woman. She'd been fancy. Surely Jake wouldn't be taken in by someone like that.

"*Ya*, I know. She refers to herself as a book broker. I'm not sure I've heard of that occupation before." He took a large bite of the cinnamon roll as he sat down on the stool next to where Eva stood.

"She's very pretty." Eva sat next to him, placed her hands on the wooden countertop, and took in a slow, deep breath.

"*Ya*, she is." He nudged Eva with his shoulder as he smirked. "In an *Englisch* sort of way. But I'm glad she's gone."

Eva sighed. "She isn't exactly gone. She said she wasn't leaving without that book, and she will be staying at Gasthof Village."

"She's wasting her time and money." Jake shoved the last of the roll into his mouth.

"Um . . . do you really not know why the book was so important to your *grossdaadi*?" She twisted slightly to face him, tapping her finger to her chin, admiring his profile and longing to run her finger down the side of his ruggedly handsome face.

"I really don't know. And, I admit, I'm intrigued that someone would offer that kind of money for the book. *Mei grossdaadi* must have known something about the book that he never shared with me." She startled when he abruptly turned to face her. "But I'll never break *mei* promise. I've never even shown the book to anyone. All I know is that it's about three hundred pages . . . and old."

Eva reached for the string on her prayer covering and twisted it around her finger. She wanted so badly to see this mysterious book. She'd always wondered what was in the basement and why Jake kept the door locked. Maybe he kept more rare books down there. Or other valuable items. It wasn't their nature to collect expensive artifacts, though.

"You're dying to see it, aren't you?" Jake tapped her gently under her chin until she met his gaze. There wasn't anything romantic about the gesture; it was more playful as he winked at her. Jake liked her, for sure. But she wanted more than just friendship from him. Much more.

"I admit . . ." She braced herself and looked back at him. "I would like to see it." She'd love to be the only person Jake had ever let see the book. That would feel special, something only the two of them shared.

He stood up and waved an arm. "Come on. I'll show you."

She gasped as she rose also, her heart thumping in her chest. "Really?"

"*Ya*, sure."

Eva followed him to the back room and stood behind him when they reached the basement door. He reached for keys in his pocket, fumbled them between his fingers, then chose a really old-looking one and slipped it into the lock, which was also vintage.

"How long has this building been here?" She peered over his shoulder as he bent over, wiggling the key in the lock.

"I'm not sure. A long time." He smiled when the lock clicked open. "It might be cold down here," he said as he pushed the door wide. "And be careful on the stairs. They're steep. Hold the handrail on the left side." He reached for a flashlight hanging just inside on the wall, flicked it on, and shone it at his feet. Eva stayed close behind him.

At the bottom of the stairs, Jake reached for a lantern on a nearby table. After it was lit, he turned up the flame and held it higher. "Welcome to the basement."

Eva glanced around, surprised at how neat and orderly things were. At her house, the basement contained old furniture, boxes filled with things they'd probably never use, and other odds and ends in disarray. The only organized space was her mother's shelves of canned goods, all labeled and dated.

In Jake's basement, a mahogany rolltop desk sat against one wall with a high-back leather chair. Two walls were lined with bookshelves, both filled to capacity. There was also a twin-sized bed in the corner with a bedside table and another lantern.

Jake handed her a flashlight he took from atop the desk. "Here. Look around."

She wanted to see the mysterious book, but she did as told. As she gingerly ran her hand along a row of books, she was amazed to see she didn't pull back a speck of dust. "You must come down here a lot. Everything is so tidy." She glanced over her shoulder. Jake had sat down in the high-back chair. "Do you spend the night here sometimes?" she asked.

He shrugged. "I come down here at least once a week. Everything is how my *grossdaadi* left it, and I keep it clean. But I don't sleep here." He paused as he cocked his head to one side. "*Ach*, I did spend the night here once, but that was a long time ago. I wasn't feeling *gut*, and I didn't want to drive the buggy home. It was nice weather, so I left *mei* horse tethered outside with food and water. I remember *Grossdaadi* taking naps down here, though, especially as he got older."

"Are all of these books keepsakes? Or valuable like the one the *Englisch* woman wants to buy?" Eva glanced around at the hundreds of books on the shelves.

"Some are first editions. Others were just some of *mei grossdaadi's* favorites. I don't think any of them are collector's items or anything like that." He spun around in the chair, grinning. "I can remember spinning around in this chair as a kid."

Jake had always reminisced fondly about his grandfather. Maybe he kept the basement locked because this was a special place to him. Or was it solely because the book was stored here? "*Danki* for bringing me down here. I've always wondered why you keep it locked. I guess it's because of that book?" She looked around again, unsure what she'd been expecting. Perhaps a glass case enclosing the rare volume?

"*Nee*, the lock doesn't have anything to do with the book." He took off his hat and set it in his lap, revealing dark hair flattened on top. It contrasted with his blue eyes twinkling from the light of the lantern. His bangs were in need of a trim, she noticed. She briefly wondered if she should offer to cut his hair, but it felt too intimate somehow.

Jake continued. "*Mei grossdaadi* caught some teenagers down here one day. I'm not sure they would have stolen anything. He actually caught them kissing. And he kept the basement locked ever after. I just kept doing the same thing so no one could sneak down here when I wasn't looking."

"Were they Amish, the young couple?" Eva swallowed hard just thinking about kissing Jake in this place that was obviously special to him. His blue eyes gleamed again as the light from the lantern illuminated his features.

"*Ya*, they were." He chuckled. "I was probably twelve or thirteen when *mei grossdaadi* caught them down here. He gave them a good talking to. I remember that. Him telling them that being by themselves and intimate was inappropriate at their age—or any age without being married."

"He must have been very conservative. I think all couples kiss before they get married." Eva was glad it was fairly dark in the basement. Hopefully, Jake couldn't see her blushing. She could feel her cheeks burning.

"He was old school." He rubbed his hands together and raised both eyebrows as he flashed a mischievous look. "So, are you ready to see the hundred-thousand-dollar book?"

Eva's stomach swirled with excitement as she moved closer to him. "*Ya*, I am."

He lifted the rolltop cover on the desk, revealing several slotted compartments filled with envelopes and various papers. On the flat surface sat a large book with a weathered brown cover. Putting his hat on the desk, he eased out the book. He set it in his lap, then shined his flashlight at the title.

Slowly, he looked up at her. "I'm embarrassed to say . . . I've never read it. Something that obviously meant so much to *mei grossdaadi*, and . . ." His voice was soft, barely above a whisper as it trailed off. "Here." He cleared his throat and carefully picked up the book and handed it to her. She aimed the flashlight she was carrying across the cover and brushed a hand gently across the surface of the leather-bound casing. The coloring had faded, and the title appeared to have been gold at one time, now worn down to a musty yellow that spelled out "*Walk with Me* by Jerry Lance."

"Have you ever *wanted* to read it?" She slowly lifted her eyes to Jake's, having heard the regret in his voice. He stared somewhere past her, his eyes having lost the sparkle she'd seen earlier.

"I actually tried to once. I got to page ten or eleven. The, um . . ." He cleared his throat again, avoiding her eyes. "It's hard to read. I mean the words, and . . . um . . ."

Eva had run across plenty of books that had been difficult for her to understand. Their people only went to school through the eighth grade. For generations the elders had believed that was enough education, but Eva had always wondered if that was really true. "We could read it together. Out loud."

His eyes widened. "Do you know how long it would take to read that entire book aloud?"

"Not so long." She shrugged. "We could read for an hour or two each evening after we close the store." Eva could think of nothing better than spending extra time with Jake. Maybe he would take notice of her as more than the young girl he'd hired four years ago.

He tipped his head to one side, lowering his eyebrows in a frown. "Don't you have things to do at home? Don't you have to lend a hand with supper or have other chores you have to do?"

"*Mamm* always has supper ready when I get home from work." Eva always cleaned the kitchen right after they ate. She wondered how her mother would feel about leaving a sink full of dishes for Eva to clean when she got home. "I'll just explain to her what we're doing and that it's temporary. I think she'll understand."

Jake grinned. "Are you really that interested in the contents of this book, or are you just doing this for me?"

Eva wanted to tell him she'd read the phone book with him if it meant time spent together. She smiled. "A little of both."

"Then I guess we have a date every night until we get through three hundred pages?"

"I guess we do. Starting tomorrow. I'll talk to *mei*

*mamm* this evening." Eva tried to speak with a calmness she didn't feel. She wondered if he noticed. But he was looking at her differently than he usually did, studying her in a way that felt unfamiliar, as if seeing her for the first time.

She didn't look away, and for a moment she thought Jake could see inside her soul, interpret her feelings. But the connection was lost when the bell from the upstairs door chimed.

"Customer," she said as she handed the book carefully back to him. She pointed the flashlight toward the stairs and hurriedly began shuffling her way up the steps. When she reached the basement door, she looked over her shoulder. Jake was staring at the book that was back in his lap. Eva gave him time to look up at her as she slowly inched the door open, the hinge squeaking as she did so. But he never lifted his eyes.

Maybe they hadn't had a moment after all.

# CHAPTER 3

Yvonne crossed her legs underneath her on the bed, put her phone on speaker, and waited for Trevor to answer as she ran a comb through her wet hair.

"Hello, beautiful. Did you get that shower you were craving?" he asked after he answered.

"Ah, yes, I did. Traveling just makes me feel yucky, and it's been a long day." She gave the comb a final swipe through her hair and set it on the nightstand. "And not a very productive day, as I explained earlier. Although I did get a little sightseeing done." After fluffing her pillows, she leaned back, straightened her legs, and crossed her ankles. "The Amish guy is going to be a tough nut to crack."

"Well, you like a challenge." Trevor chuckled.

"To a point. But I've looked for this book for so long. I'm ready to be done with it, get my money, and move on." She stifled a yawn. "But before I allow myself to fall asleep,

I'm going to figure out a way to win over Jake Lantz. And I'm wondering if the way to Mr. Lantz might be through the Amish girl who works for him. Her loyalty lies to him, for sure. She looks at him all dreamy-eyed, but she seems to ooze sweetness, so maybe she's my way in. I could tell she wasn't thrilled that I wasn't hightailing it back to Texas, but she was still nice enough to recommend places for me to stay."

"Speaking of . . . Your voice mail earlier said you were staying at the Gasthof Village Inn. How is it?"

Yvonne glanced around her room. "It's quaint. Nice. It feels like a cross between a bed-and-breakfast and a hotel." She ran her hand across the red-and-white floral bedspread. "It's clean and cozy, but not as sterile as a hotel, if you know what I mean. There are some shops on the property, a twenty-five-acre lake, and an awesome restaurant. After Jake Lantz's firm rejection, I drove around for a while before I checked in. It's just so weird seeing all these people driving around with those horses and buggies." She fought another yawn. "It's way too early to go to sleep, but I think the plane ride, my sightseeing, and that heavy meal I ate is weighing on me." She groaned. "Not to mention a heavy dose of ego deflation. I was sure I could talk that guy out of the book, but he was gone before I even got to pour on any charm." She recalled how underconfident she'd felt around the gorgeous Eva and the handsome Jake Lantz.

"Missing me yet?"

Yvonne smiled. "Not yet. Maybe in a couple of days."

"Ouch. You don't always have to be so honest."

Yvonne bit her bottom lip. If she was totally honest with the man she was going to marry, she'd tell him how attracted she'd been to someone else today. But that would serve no purpose, and it didn't matter. Both she and Trevor would be in contact with members of the opposite sex they found physically attractive. They wouldn't be normal otherwise. But they were in love, and nothing could come between them. Again, she wondered if such feelings lasted a lifetime.

"You know me. Always honest." It was true. Even in her work, she told the truth and was honest about her intentions. She'd never told a lie to purchase a book for a client. Sometimes she highlighted the perks of selling the book, which was almost always about the money. But she didn't offer up false information to make a sale. If Jake Lantz truly didn't care about the money, she was really going to have to strategize—without misleading or lying to the man. She wasn't going to sacrifice her integrity, even for George and the outlandish commission he was going to pay her when she closed this deal. Yvonne usually had at least two or three searches going on at the same time, but right now George was her only client.

"Well, I'll let you wind down and rest. Call me before you go to sleep later if you feel like it." Trevor usually went to sleep way before Yvonne, but he got up earlier too. She had the luxury of making her own hours.

"I'll call you before your bedtime." Grinning, she said, "Before nine."

"Ha-ha. You know I'm up until ten." He chuckled. "I'll talk to you later. I love you."

"I love you too."

After she hit End, she lowered the phone to her lap and pondered ways to get Jake Lantz to give up the goods. If money wasn't a factor, how else could she convince him to sell? It would behoove her if she knew more about the book. There was nothing online, no sign of it anywhere on the internet. She had a name and an author and knew that only a hundred copies existed. She'd tracked down Jake Lantz's copy through a stroke of luck. After months of trying to find the book, she'd found a man in an Amish bookstore in Ohio who said he knew about the book.

She paused her thoughts. *"And the healing powers it has for those who are spiritually lost."* She'd forgotten that tidbit of information the man had shared, until now.

She picked up her phone, went to her Notes app, and found the folder for *Walk with Me by Jerry Lance.* There were all kinds of notations that had led to nowhere, but she hadn't jotted down the man's quote about the book. At the time, it hadn't seemed important. All that had been relevant was that he thought a small bookstore in Montgomery, Indiana, had a copy. *Bingo!* She could still recall the feeling of success at that moment, after months of dead ends. But now the man's words were relevant. It was the only clue she had about the book.

*How can I use that information to make some headway with Jake Lantz?*

Sighing, she stared at her phone. No whirlwind of ideas wafted into her mind.

*Think, think, think.*

Maybe after a good night's sleep, it would come to her in the morning. But even after she landed on a movie to watch, her mind kept drifting back to the book. If she could just see it, maybe read a few pages, maybe the content could give her some insight as to what all the fuss was about.

Lost in thought, she forgot to call Trevor before ten.

Jake finished brushing his teeth, slipped on his shirt, and pulled his suspenders into place. He'd tossed and turned all night and even had dreams about his grandfather. It had been a long time since he'd dreamed of the man he had admired so much.

He smelled bacon cooking before he even opened his bedroom door. His mother still walked to the main house most mornings and cooked Jake something to eat.

"*Mamm*, I've told you that you don't have to cook *mei* meals." He walked into the kitchen and breathed in the welcoming aroma. He reminded her often that cooking for him wasn't necessary, but he had to admit he was disappointed on the mornings he woke up to an empty kitchen.

"*Ya*, well, then you'd better snag a *fraa*." She winked at him as she set a bowl of eggs on the kitchen table.

"I don't have time, *Mamm*. I'm always at the bookstore."

That was partly true, but there also just hadn't been a spark with any of the women Jake had asked out, which hadn't been a lot. It was a small town. Everyone knew everyone in their district. Unless someone new moved to the area, he didn't hold out much hope. Although he did want a wife and family, someone to share his life with, children to fill up this big house.

"Make time," his mother said as she placed a small platter of bacon on the table. "I'm not getting any younger, and you're our only hope for grandchildren."

Jake sat down, lowered his head in prayer, then filled his plate. "*Ach*, before I forget, if you don't see me home until a little later, it's because Eva and I will be staying at the bookstore for an hour or two after closing."

His mother's hand towel dropped to the floor as her eyes widened. "Finally, you are seeing that *maedel* for the beautiful person she is." She picked up the towel and flung it over her shoulder. "Your *daed* and I have been praying that the two of you would see you are perfect together."

Jake shook his head. "It's not like that, *Mamm*. Not at all . . ." He paused as he recalled an indefinable look he and Eva had shared the day before. It had been brief and unfamiliar. And confusing. "She's just a kid."

His mother put her hands on her hips. "Take a closer look." She smirked. "Eva has grown up, right under your nose, into a beautiful woman."

Once again Jake disliked the thought of Eva marrying someone and leaving the bookstore. He told himself it was because she was a wonderful employee whom he would have to replace. His mother was right, though. Eva had grown into a beautiful young woman. Stored in his memories were all the times he'd teased her, playfully tickled her, showed her how to pitch a decent curveball, and taught her as a teenager how to practically run the bookstore. But Eva wasn't that young girl anymore. "And she'll be a *gut fraa* for some lucky man. Probably John Yoder." He tried to keep the sarcasm out of his voice. Jake wanted Eva to be happy, and John was a great guy.

His mother rolled her eyes. "*Ya, ya.* I've heard those rumors—that John Yoder is smitten with Eva. He sure has a funny way of showing it. I don't think he's ever asked her out. One of the ladies in the quilting group would have mentioned it."

Jake thought about John's plans and how close he was to moving into his new house. "He's a little shy, but I'm sure he'll be asking her out soon."

"Well, if there are no romantic intentions, then why are you and Eva staying late at the bookstore?" His mother leaned against the kitchen cabinets and folded her arms across her chest.

"There's a book we want to read together." Jake took a bite of bacon as he wondered if his mother would question him about which book they were planning to read. He was pretty sure she wouldn't want him to break a promise to his grandfather, but he'd never heard either of his parents mention the book. And he didn't really want to tell his mother about the Texas woman wanting to buy it. Jake wanted to believe that his mother would understand the promise he'd made to his grandfather, his mother's father-in-law. But a hundred thousand dollars was a lot of money. He didn't want anyone, even his mother, tempting him to break his promise.

His mother smiled. "*Ya*, okay," she said, grinning.

Jake shook his head, scarfed down some eggs, then stood up with a slice of bacon in his hand. "You've got it wrong about me and Eva, but *danki* for breakfast, *Mamm*."

"You're welcome, *sohn*." She turned on the water in the sink, then glanced over her shoulder. "Have a *gut* day." She paused, smiling. "And night."

He sighed as he turned and walked out the door. That was the first time his mother had offered up hope that Jake and Eva would end up together. After he was on the road and had his horse in a steady trot, he recalled the way Eva looked at him sometimes. For the most part, they were friends who ran a business together, but occasionally he caught a gleam in her eyes hinting that perhaps she thought of him as more than a friend. He'd even returned the gaze yesterday. It had felt spontaneous but surprised him.

Maybe staying after work with her was a bad idea. He didn't want to lead her on in a romantic way. It felt dishonorable since he knew John's feelings for her. He wondered if things might be different between him and Eva had John not shared his plans with Jake. He shook his head and fought to clear the thoughts from his mind. If John asked out Eva and she turned him down, then perhaps Jake would act on that occasional spark he thought he saw between him and Eva. But for now he would keep things friendly between them.

By the time he pulled into the parking lot at the bookstore, he was still considering that maybe reading by the light of a lantern in the basement might not be such a good idea in case Eva had romantic disillusions. But all thoughts of Eva washed away when he saw the SUV that had been there the day before. Frowning, he pulled back on the reins until his horse came to a complete stop. The Texas woman was back.

Eva stood behind the counter chatting with the English lady when Jake walked in the door. "*Wie bischt*, Jake." She stood taller and took a deep breath. "You remember Ms. Wilson from yesterday, *ya*?"

Jake tried to mask his irritation with a fake smile. "Of course. What can I do for you, Mrs. Wilson?"

"Good morning." The woman gave a slight wave. She was dressed in dark blue slacks and a white blouse and was wearing a long silver necklace and earrings. Her brown hair curled slightly under just above her shoulders. She was a pretty woman with high cheek bones, flawless ivory skin, and enough makeup to enhance her features without being overbearing. But as she batted her eyes at Jake, he was sure the woman had plans to try and charm him out of the book she so desperately wanted to buy.

"I'd like to take you to breakfast," she said, her long, dark eyelashes fluttering above hazel eyes that gleamed with purpose.

Jake opened his mouth to tell her that he'd already eaten, but he reconsidered. Eva had told him that the woman wasn't leaving town without the book. This was an opportunity for him to privately reiterate to Yvonne that he would never sell the book. Her charm wasn't going to work on him, and if he had to be firm with her, he would.

He rubbed his chin as he glanced back and forth between the women. Eva appeared to be holding her breath. Yvonne had both eyebrows raised.

"*Ya*, sure. Breakfast would be *gut*." He focused on Eva. "Will you be okay here by yourself for a while?"

Eva's mouth parted in surprise, but then she nodded . . . without the hint of a smile on her face.

Jake handed her the money bag and walked back to the front door, the bell chiming as he pulled it wide. "After you."

Yvonne breezed by him, catching his eye as she did so, and flashing a smile she probably meant to be genuine. But Jake saw it as sly like a fox. This woman really did think she could charm him out of the book. Hmm . . . *She's met her match.*

Eva tried to corral the herd of emotions scrambling for space in her mind. Jake hadn't been happy yesterday that the English woman was staying in town, but he'd accepted her invitation for breakfast with little hesitation. Yvonne Wilson was beautiful, and Eva wanted to believe that Jake wouldn't be attracted to a fancy English woman, but she'd seen it happen—members of their district falling for outsiders. Still, it was impossible not to notice the large diamond ring Yvonne wore on her left ring finger. She was either married or engaged and should pose no threat.

Eva's logical side said that the reason for Yvonne's invitation was so she could try to convince Jake to sell the book. But what was Jake's reason for accepting the invite? Maybe he was just hungry. He'd definitely already told her the book wasn't for sale.

The bell chimed on the door before she could give it any more thought. They weren't even officially open for another hour, but Jake hadn't locked the door on his way out. When two men walked into the store, Eva wished he would have. They looked about Jake's age, midtwenties, but they weren't Amish.

"I'm sorry. We aren't actually open yet." Eva's heart pounded in her chest. Both men wore torn blue jeans, which Eva knew to be in style among some of the English. But these appeared more worn from wear. They had on T-shirts, one of them a red one, the other a white one with a brown jacket also. Their facial hair wasn't really beards, just scruffy and unkept. When the taller of the men gave her a lopsided smirk, it sent a shiver up Eva's spine.

"Uh, we're just looking for a gift." He pointed over his shoulder. "The sign says books, office supplies, and gifts."

"Um . . . *ya*, but we . . . don't open for another hour. If you wouldn't mind coming back, please. We are still getting the shop ready for business." She tried to put emphasis on "we" even though she was there alone. Her bottom lip trembled as she tried to force a smile.

The same man said, "We're already here." He glanced at his friend, then pointed to Eva's right, to the section that housed the keepsakes and gift-type items. "Over there."

"Sorry," the shorter and younger-looking fellow said. "We won't be long. It's a friend's birthday." He shrugged before he followed his companion.

Eva folded her hands together, hoping to keep them from trembling like her lip. Only one other time since she'd worked at the bookstore had she ever felt uneasy. A group of teenaged boys had come into the store reeking of alcohol. They had said provocative things to her, and she'd been almost in tears when Jake emerged from the back and ushered them out. But Jake wasn't here right now as Eva watched the men going up and down the aisles. She reminded herself that looks or what a person wore didn't define them, but her heart didn't stop hammering against her chest.

It wasn't a minute later when the taller man walked back toward her. "Sorry to bother you, but can you show me where the restroom is?"

Eva felt her throat close up as if someone had a hand around her neck. You had to go through the back room to get to the restroom, and Eva didn't want to be alone with either stranger in an area where she was out of sight. At least in front of the window, she felt visible and safer, even if no one was outside. She wasn't sure if denying a customer a trip to the bathroom was illegal or not. At the least, it might anger the man.

She stepped from around the counter to show the man the way as she wondered if his friend would follow as well. But she slowed her stride when she became aware of the unlocked cash register she was leaving behind. Instead of escorting him, she pointed. "If you go through that door, there will be another door to the restroom."

"Thanks." He gave her a two-fingered salute before he strolled off, his friend shuffling along behind him. Eva tried to think if there was anything worth stealing in the back room. Then she reminded herself again that a person's looks didn't convey what was inside.

It was only a few minutes later when both men returned to the front of the store. Eva stood behind the counter willing herself to keep her breathing steady, hoping not to appear as nervous as she felt.

"This will work." The taller man set a small angel figurine on the counter. It was part of a group of five that were almost always sold together, although they could be purchased separately.

Eva rang up the transaction. When the cash drawer popped open, she caught it with her hand, leaving it only an inch open, then remembered that Jake had handed her the bag of cash right before he left with Yvonne. It lay out of sight, and the register was empty. Eva let the drawer slide open in full view. "That will be $5.36," she said as she began to wrap the small angel in white paper.

The two men eyed the register and looked at each other. Then the taller man placed six dollars on the counter. "Keep the change," he said as he accepted the small bag when Eva handed it to him.

"Thank you." She hoped they didn't hear the tremble in her voice.

"Yeah, have a good day."

The men left without looking back and took off walking down the street.

Eva locked the door behind them, put a hand to her chest, and realized she had allowed herself to be frightened just by the looks of the two men. *Never judge a book by its cover.* It was a cliché but there just the same.

When her pulse slowed down, she loaded the money into the cash register. Even if the men had been robbers, they wouldn't have gotten away with more than a few hundred dollars, mostly in fives, tens, and twenties.

Thirty minutes later, she flipped the sign to *Open*, and her thoughts drifted back to Jake and Yvonne having breakfast together. There was absolutely no reason for Eva to feel jealous. Jake would never get involved with an English woman, no matter how pretty she was. And Yvonne had a ring on her finger.

*Then why do I feel worried?*

# CHAPTER 4

Yvonne made it a point not to bring up the book until after they'd had coffee and ordered breakfast at the small café. She'd opted for a toasted English muffin and some fruit. She was surprised when Jake ordered the same thing. He had a tall, athletic build. She'd expected him to order the Hungry Man's Special.

The ride to the eatery had been short and quiet, and Jake Lantz hadn't said much since they'd arrived. He was hard to read, his expressionless, clean-shaven face a mystery. He'd clearly not been happy when she'd spoken with him about the book yesterday, so she was surprised he had agreed to breakfast so willingly.

Yvonne ran a finger around the rim of her coffee cup. She had carried the short conversation in the car, mostly questioning him about landmarks they'd passed. He had answered directly but without elaboration.

He'd set his straw hat in the chair next to him when they'd first sat. She wondered if he knew how flat his dark hair was on the top of his head.

"Are you always this quiet?"

"Only when *mei* guard is up." He grinned a little, which caused Yvonne to smile.

"Hmm . . . Honesty. I like that in a man." She was careful to sound complimentary and not seductive. Good old-fashioned charm wasn't going to work on this guy. "But there's really no need for your guard to be up. I understand perfectly that you don't want to sell the book."

"But you're here to change *mei* mind." He took a sip of his coffee, his eyes staying on hers.

She slowly took a drink from her white mug, then set the cup back on the red-checkered tablecloth. The café reminded her of places she'd seen on TV from the fifties or sixties, and she and Jake were the only patrons except for an older gentleman sitting at the counter eating a donut as he read the newspaper. She had given a lot of thought as to how she would approach Jake this morning. Being pushy wasn't going to get what she needed. "I understand that you don't want to sell the book because you made a promise to your grandfather." She paused, found his eyes, and held his gaze. "I respect that."

"Then why are we here?" He smirked again as he leaned back in his chair.

"The Amish man in Ohio—the one who told me the book might be at your bookstore—said something that has me curious." She waited for a response, but Jake only raised an eyebrow. "He said that the book has healing powers for those who are spiritually lost. I wonder if that's what makes it so valuable to my client." Yvonne had no idea if George was a spiritual man. She'd only known him to be a collector of rare books. "I know that only a hundred copies were printed, but the contents must be extraordinary to demand such a price."

"I don't know of anything in the book that could make it worth the kind of money you're offering." He shrugged but avoided her eyes.

"You've read it, haven't you?" She hadn't meant to pose the question in a way that sounded accusatory, but she knew she had when he scowled.

"Not all of it," he said before he took his first bite of muffin.

Yvonne thought for a few moments. "So . . . do your people believe in magic or superstitions?" It seemed unlikely based on the little she knew about the Amish.

He swallowed then glowered at her. "*Ya*, some folks might be a little superstitious, but we don't believe in the kind of magic I think you're talking about. As far as healing powers, that comes from God through the power of prayer."

Yvonne was quiet. She needed to be careful and not get into a religious conversation, an area in which she had little expertise. Her question had simply been an attempt to learn more about the book.

She pinched off a piece of her muffin and put it in her

mouth. After she'd swallowed, she said, "What should I tell my client? That y'all don't want to sell because the book has healing powers? Or that you don't want to sell because you made a promise to your grandfather? Because I have to tell you, neither one of those reasons sounds good enough to turn down a hundred thousand dollars." She raised a palm when he opened his mouth to respond. "Wait. Sorry. I shouldn't have said that. I already said that I respect the fact that you want to honor your promise to your grandfather, but don't you think he would want you to let go of the book for that kind of money? Maybe it has sentimental value attached to it, and he meant for you not to sell it for thirty dollars or something."

"It doesn't matter the amount. I promised him I wouldn't sell it." Jake slathered extra butter on his muffin, then added more grape jelly. "I told you that you're wasting your time."

Yvonne wasn't authorized to offer more money, but she had to know if Jake was hiding behind the fact that he was smarter than he let on, holding out for more. "All right. I'll go a hundred twenty thousand." Her chest tightened as she wondered if George would go that high. She was pretty sure he would, but she'd never presented an offer without his approval.

His mouth twitched with apparent amusement. "Keep going."

She tipped her head to one side as she eyed him, sweat starting to pool at her temples. "Are you toying with me?"

"What reason would I have to do that?" His smile was more of a mischievous grin now.

She recalled the basic information she'd read about the Amish. They were religious, didn't use electricity, and rode around in buggies pulled by horses. At least that's all that had really stuck. But in her mind, she didn't see them as jokesters.

"A hundred and thirty," she said barely above a whisper. "Final offer." Nothing was ever final, but she needed to know where she stood with this guy. She already wondered how thin the ice was where George was concerned.

Jake stood up, walked to the counter, and took money from his wallet. When he returned, she said, "I invited you to breakfast, and I was going to pay."

He had a toothpick in his mouth, which reminded her of a couple of cowboys who hung out in the parking lot of the feedstore near her house. "I *was* toying with you, so we're even." He sat back down and nodded at her half-eaten muffin. "No rush, though. Finish your breakfast."

She bit off a small piece of the dry muffin, eying the butter and jelly. If she was going to fit in her wedding dress, she needed to be careful. And she needed to take her time eating as she plotted other ways to get this guy to budge.

"Okay, to be clear . . ." She paused, set down her muffin, and leaned back against her chair. "You're turning down a hundred and thirty thousand dollars for a book you haven't read because you are keeping a promise to your grandfather?"

His mouth thinned with displeasure. "We've already covered this."

A tense silence emerged. Yvonne needed to get this man talking . . . about something. "Okay, point taken. But I traveled a long way to get here, so I might as well consider it a mini vacation before I go home. What is there to do around here? Any specific sights I should see while I'm here?" She awkwardly cleared her throat.

Jake stared at her for a few seconds, then nodded at her muffin. "That would taste a lot better with butter and jelly on it."

Yvonne sighed. "Yep, it sure would. But I'm getting married in the fall and don't need to put on any weight." She stirred uneasily in the chair as he stared at her.

"I think you look just fine." One side of his mouth curled into a partial smile, which was both sexy and alarming. Alarming because the comment sent her insides swirling.

"Thank you." She put her hands in her lap so he wouldn't see her fidgeting, and she wondered if her face was as red as it felt.

The silence began to lengthen between them, and Yvonne was once again caught off guard by her feelings of inadequacy around this man. He exuded a confidence she hadn't expected, and for the first time she considered the possibility that she was going to fail at this mission.

She dabbed her mouth with her napkin. "Are you ready to go?" she asked as she rose.

Jake nodded and followed her to the car. It was a quiet

ride back to the bookstore, but Yvonne's mind was still awhirl as she tried to think up some reason to spend more time with Jake. Maybe he would soften up and reconsider her offer.

"You never did give me a list of things of things to see while I'm here." She wasn't interested in sightseeing, but it was her only reason to stick around and figure out another way to get the book.

He turned to her just as Yvonne was pulling in the parking lot at the bookstore. "I can give you the short list of things we recommend to tourists. There's not that much to do. We're still growing when it comes to touristy-type things."

"Sure. That would be great."

He regarded her quizzically as if he wasn't buying her faked enthusiasm.

"Maybe you could even take the day off and show me around?" She flashed him a big smile, which he shot down with a full-on frown.

Yvonne gulped. *Or not.*

Jake had way too much to do to spend his time entertaining an English woman he didn't know. She was easy on the eyes, but he didn't trust her, nor did he want her hanging around Montgomery for much longer. He was trying to think of a polite way to deny her request as he reached for the door handle. "Uh, I don't think . . ."

His voice trailed off when he saw Eva talking to someone inside. He glanced at the tethered horse and buggy to his right, then peered through the glass window into the store, straining to get a better look. Eva was smiling and talking to John Yoder. Jake swallowed hard as his stomach clenched. John had finally come around. He was asking Eva out.

"It's okay," Yvonne said. "I'm sure you don't have time to just take a day off on a whim."

Jake couldn't seem to pull his eyes from Eva and John. He was surprised how much it stung seeing them together.

He had one foot out the door when he turned back to Yvonne. "Uh, what? What did you say?"

Her head was down, and she sighed before she looked up at him with sad eyes. "I said I'm sure you don't have time to just take a day off to spend with me."

Jake glanced at Eva and John again, then back at the pitiful look on Yvonne's face. This was a no-win situation. Spend the day with the English woman he didn't trust. Or spend the afternoon with Eva pretending he wasn't bothered by the fact that she was officially being courted now.

"Actually . . ." He took a deep breath before he turned to Yvonne. "I think I can spare a day for you. It's the least I can do since you traveled all the way from Texas for nothing." He tried to smile when she did, but his eyes were drawn back to Eva and John. He finally swung the car door open. "Let me just go in and tell Eva."

Yvonne got out of her car and leaned against it. "I'll wait out here. I need to check my emails."

"To properly show you our area, I think we should probably take *mei* buggy. Is that all right with you?" He expected her to be unagreeable, but her eyes lit up.

"That would be great."

She kept punching buttons on her phone, and Jake walked with heavy steps up the sidewalk. When he entered the store, Eva stood behind the counter with John facing her from the other side. John looked over his shoulder, then smiled as he walked toward Jake and shook his hand.

"Where is the *Englisch* woman?" Eva brushed hair from her face as she looked around Jake. "*Ach*, there she is. Why is she standing in the parking lot?"

"I told her I'd take her sightseeing, but I just wanted to make sure you'd be okay by yourself for most of the day."

Eva opened her mouth but snapped it closed, then pinched her lips together.

"Did everything go okay while I was gone?" Jake rubbed his chin, wondering what was on Eva's mind. He also wondered how long John had been there.

"Uh . . . *ya*. Go ahead and have fun." Eva plastered on a big smile, but Jake had a sinking feeling in his stomach that she was lying, which wasn't like her.

"Are you sure everything is okay?" He decided not to mention their planned reading session later, even though he'd seen a container of what appeared to be chicken and dumplings in the refrigerator earlier. Those plans and the meal were before John had shown up, and he didn't want to interfere with anything John might be planning. Even though his heart constricted when he thought about John and Eva together. He'd always known it was a possibility, but he hadn't expected to react so strongly when the reality presented itself.

As he avoided Eva's eyes, he focused on John and pointed over his shoulder. "I'd better go."

Eva watched as Jake and Yvonne left in Jake's buggy. Breakfast must have gone well, she assumed. Yvonne was smiling from ear to ear, and Jake even grinned as he turned the buggy around and headed out. Perhaps Eva had been wrong to think her boss wouldn't fall for a fancy English woman. She wondered if maybe Yvonne had talked him out of the book. Maybe he'd agreed to sell it to her after he read it.

Eva had considered telling him about how frightened she had been when the two men came into the store earlier, but he might have felt like he couldn't leave her alone. She didn't want him to stay out of duty.

John smiled and waved a hand in front of her. "Earth to Eva. Are you okay?"

Eva quickly averted her eyes from the buggy leaving the parking lot and focused on John. "I'm sorry." She bit her lip. "I had a couple of men in here early this morning that made me nervous. I was trying to decide whether or not to tell Jake." She shrugged. "I'm sure they are long gone, and I didn't want him to feel like he couldn't leave me alone in the store."

John straightened, squaring his muscular shoulders as he frowned. "Did they threaten you or anything?" His eyebrows narrowed above dark eyes as a muscle in his jaw flickered slightly. John was incredibly good looking, and Eva had heard the rumors that he wanted to ask her out. She hoped that wasn't why he was here, but she feared it was since he'd never come into the bookstore before.

She shook her head. "*Nee*. They didn't cause any harm." She paused, sighing. "I think I judged them based on their looks, which is wrong, but there was just something about them that I found unsettling."

John rubbed his chin, his eyes still squinted. Prior to Jake showing up, they'd only engaged in small talk about the weather. Now John seemed to be contemplating something. Was it about the men she'd described, or was he about to ask her out?

"Do you feel safe? I'm on my way to pick up supplies for a job, but I can stay with you until Jake returns."

Eva shook her head. She'd grown up with John, and they often spoke at worship services and during the meals afterward, but this was the first time he'd come calling, and Eva wanted him to get to the point. She had been thinking about how she would respond to a date request since he first walked in the door, in case the rumors were true.

"I'll be fine. Really." She smiled at him as she pressed her palms against the counter. "Are you here for anything specific? A book? A gift for someone?"

John cleared his throat as his face took on a pinkish tint,

and Eva was sure this was it. He was going to ask her out. "I was wondering if you might want to have supper with me tonight or tomorrow night?" One corner of his mouth lifted, which made him even handsomer. Under different circumstances, she would have gladly accepted his invitation, but Eva's heart belonged to someone else. That someone just didn't know yet. And because of that, she couldn't exactly confess her feelings about Jake to John.

"*Ach*, John, that is so nice of you to ask me to supper." She forced herself to smile, hoping it might soften the blow. "But I committed to working overtime for Jake tonight, tomorrow night, and . . . I don't really know for how long."

John scratched his cheek as he stared into her eyes. Eva was pretty sure he didn't believe her. "*Ya*, okay. I understand."

She wanted to tell him that he didn't understand at all, that she needed to spend this extra time with Jake to see if he cared about her the way she cared about him. Reading by the dim light of a lantern in the basement would provide an intimate environment and deviance from their normal routine.

"Maybe I'll check with you in a few days, and maybe you'll be through working overtime?" John's smile was gone, replaced by the sadness of rejection. Eva felt badly about that, but she didn't have the heart to do anything but agree to his terms.

"I think that would be just fine."

"Great. *Gut*." He tipped his hat, the half smile returning.

"Then I'll see you in a couple of days or at worship service." He gave her a quick wave before he turned to leave, and she responded with a smile and wave.

After he left, Eva rushed toward the back of the store to use the bathroom, but she hesitated as she passed the basement. She went to the large wooden door and turned the handle. As always, it was locked, so she continued on to the back room, envisioning Jake and her reading together by the light of the lantern later. Somehow, she had to get Jake to see her as a mature woman, someone who had deep feelings for him. Or was it too late? Had the English woman suddenly dug her hooks into him? And, if so, why? Was it all an effort to get him to sell the book, or were her intentions shifting the more she was around Eva's handsome boss?

Jake had expected Yvonne to be hot and miserable during the bouncy ride in the buggy, but the woman was all smiles, a far cry from the serious persona she'd displayed since her arrival. Every few minutes, she'd lean her head back, the breeze blowing her brown hair across her face, wearing a smile that was contagious. Her eyes were hidden behind a pair of black sunglasses, but the rising sun beaming down on them didn't seem to bother her. It was almost enough to keep Jake from stewing about Eva and John.

As Jake kept the horse in a slow trot, the animal decided to do his business. Yvonne turned to him and pinched her nose closed with her fingers. She laughed. "Trade hazard, I guess."

When she wasn't being pushy about buying the book, she was quite pleasant to look at and be around. When she smiled, it seemed to transform her personality as a more childlike enthusiasm took over. Maybe she was exactly what he needed today—a distraction.

"I'm not sure where to take you, but there is the school for our district." He pointed to the one-room schoolhouse to his left, and she quickly snapped a picture with her phone, which she'd been doing a lot of since they'd left. "The horse can only go around twenty miles, so we are a little limited as far as sightseeing. I just wanted you to have the whole sightseeing package, buggy ride included." In truth, Jake had thought she drove a little too fast in a vehicle she wasn't familiar with.

She tossed her head back again before she looked at him. "I think this is great, just driving around the countryside. It's so different from where I live."

"Do you live in a big city?" Jake had been to Indianapolis, Bloomington, and some of the larger cities in Indiana. He didn't like any of them. Too many people, everyone in a hurry, always traffic, and a general sense that the world had more people than it could handle.

"I live on the outskirts of Houston, so I'm not right in the middle of the hustle and bustle, but it's a far cry from the peace and serenity here. It's hotter in Texas too."

He turned onto a side street and slowed down. "That's

the library for our district." He pointed to the tiny structure that stood next to a shop that sold fabrics, kitchenware, and other odds and ends. The door was open, and inside sat a little boy and a small dog.

She gasped. "I've seen closets bigger than that. Wow." She turned to him, grinning. "It's not bigger than *my* closet. I don't have a very big house."

Jake recalled her saying she was getting married. "Will you move in with the man you are engaged to after you're married, or will you be purchasing a new house together?"

She snapped her fingers. "Ah, and that is the million-dollar question. We're not sure."

Jake tried to picture the type of fellow Yvonne might be marrying, even though he didn't know the woman at all. "What does your future husband do for a living?"

"Well, in his words, he'll tell you that he dillydallies in a bunch of different things, but that's because he's modest. He gathers investors for projects he's passionate about. Right now, he's working to build a gym for underprivileged children. Don't get me wrong, he makes money, but everything he does benefits our community."

"He sounds like a *gut* man." Jake was seeing a softer side of Yvonne.

She turned to him, her face aglow. "He really is, but . . ." She shook her head a couple of quick times. "Never mind. You're right. He is a good man. I guess I'm just nervous about getting married." She squinted her eyes at him. "That's normal, don't you think?"

"*Ya*, probably. I've never come close to getting married." Jake heard the regret in his voice, so he was sure she did too.

"Can I ask you something? It's kind of nosy." She cringed a little.

Jake put the reins in one hand and scratched his nose. "*Nee*, maybe don't." He grinned. "I think I like you better like this. Not nosy or pushy, just having a *gut* time."

"Hey!" She playfully slapped him on the arm, which made him chuckle.

"I'm just kidding. What would you like to know?" He held his breath and silently prayed it wasn't about the book.

"You said you've never come close to getting married. You must be . . . twenty-four? Twenty-five?" She paused, frowning. "I read online that your people usually get married fairly young, some even as young as seventeen. Why aren't you married?"

"Ah, a tourist who has done her research." He nodded as he turned down a street that would take her past some of the prettiest farms in their area. "I'm twenty-five, and I just haven't found the right person."

"Hmm . . ." She turned her face away from him. Jake couldn't see her expression.

"What does that mean . . . 'hmm'?"

She was quiet for a few moments. "Nothing. Just acknowledging what you said—that you haven't found the right person. I must admit . . ." She looked his way and dropped her sunglasses down on her nose, revealing hazel eyes that twinkled in the sunlight. "I assumed there was something between you and your employee, Eva."

This was the second time someone had inferred that he and Eva should or might be a couple. First his mother, now a stranger. "What makes you say that?"

She shrugged. "Just by the way she looks at you. And she is stunningly gorgeous."

Jake couldn't argue that point as he fought the vision of Eva and John together. "Eva is great, and I agree that she is very pretty. But . . ." He shrugged, trying to make light of a situation that was brewing as he spoke. "That fellow that was inside talking to her at the bookstore is John Yoder, and I've known for a while that he planned to ask Eva out."

Yvonne's sunglasses were still down on her nose as she peered over the rims. "Does that mean you're out of the running?"

Jake was pretty sure he was. Stepping aside was the honorable thing to do. "We're just friends, and she's a great employee." He wanted to change the subject. "How long have you known your fiancé?"

She pushed her sunglasses back up her nose. "Three years. We had our first date the same day we met. I was in a library researching a book I was looking for, and he walked in to talk to the librarian about the children's area in the library. It was small, and he'd arranged to expand it, offering the children more seating and making it overall more kid friendly. I overheard them talking." She chuckled. "I knew nothing about library expansions, but this man intrigued me, so I interrupted their conversation and made a suggestion regarding the renovations." She laughed again. "It wasn't even a good suggestion, but we ended up going to dinner that night to discuss it, and the rest is history."

"And it took you three years to get engaged?" Jake looked her way.

"Yeah. I wasn't in a big hurry. I mean, I love Trevor, and I have for a long time, but it took me some time to wrap my mind around the fact that I'd be in a permanent partnership. Would I lose my independence? And how do you know you'll love the same person for the rest of your life?"

Jake waited, assuming the question was rhetorical, but when she didn't say anything else, he said, "I guess marriage is a leap of faith in some ways." He smirked. "Although I'm obviously not an expert. But I think when two people commit to each other, and the union is blessed by God via marriage, that love grows and evolves. Every married person I've ever known said it takes work."

"But should it? How much work should it take?" She frowned. "Don't get me wrong. I'm not going to bail on him or anything. I'm just . . . a little nervous, I guess."

"I think that's probably normal." He wasn't sure he was being honest. Wouldn't true love withstand a bout of nerves? *Shouldn't it?*

She turned his way, pushed her sunglasses up on her head, and cocked her head to one side as she peered at him. "I don't know why I'm telling you all this. I don't even know you, but you're easy to talk to. Even though you are totally ruining my career . . ." She grinned. "But I'm having a nice time."

"Far be it for me to ruin your career." He paused, sighing. "Can't you just pick out a different book?"

She burst out laughing. "So, the Amish have a sense of humor?"

"We try." Jake had always wondered why his people had been typecast a certain way in the eyes of some English—as serious all the time, never joking around, and with little personality.

"Well, thank you for offering to show me around." She took off her sunglasses and clutched them in her lap as she leaned her head back, the wind catching her hair again.

Jake took in her profile, the loose tendrils of hair blowing wildly in the wind, gently whipping color into her cheeks. Her full lips were sightly parted, and her eyes were closed. He was pretty sure she was a few years older than him, based on the way she presented herself—a maturity that came with age. He'd noticed the laugh lines fanning out from the corners of her eyes, even though they did nothing to deter from her looks.

"You're welcome," he said softly, surprised that he was also having a nice time, especially after seeing John in pursuit of Eva. "There's a place I'd like to show you, but it's a bit of a haul in the buggy. We'd probably have to stop a couple of times to let the horse rest."

She turned to face him. "I'm happy to go anywhere with you, anywhere you'd like to take me."

Jake forced a half smile as he nodded. His experience with women was limited, but based on the sultry sound of her voice, the way she batted her eyes at him, and the smile that stretched across her face . . . Jake was pretty sure the book broker was flirting with him.

# CHAPTER 5

Yvonne stepped out of the buggy when Jake did, hoping her comment hadn't been too over the top. Surprisingly, his sense of humor seemed to mesh with hers, and her playful tone of voice was meant to be just that—playful.

Her tour guide for the day retrieved a bucket from the back of the buggy, filled it with water from a gallon jug, then set it in front of the horse before gently rubbing the animal's muzzle. Putting a hand to her forehead, Yvonne took in her surroundings. They were on a dirt road that seemed to lead to nowhere. After passing some gorgeous farms earlier, they'd stopped at two small shops. Jake had tended to the horse while Yvonne went in each and looked around. They'd then stopped for lemonade at a small stand run by three precious Amish boys. Then they'd taken a side street and had followed this narrow path for about fifteen minutes. "Where exactly are we going?"

He let the horse finish drinking from the bucket, then straightened. "Why? You scared?" Grinning, he pushed back the tip of his straw hat before he hauled the bucket back to the back of the buggy. After he'd set it inside, he said, "Well?"

Yvonne folded her arms across her chest and eyed the handsome, and whimsical, Amish man. "Nope. Not scared." He was a bit mysterious, but now that she'd spent some time with him, Jake Lantz didn't make her nervous at all. She was surprised by how comfortable she felt around him. "Just curious."

He waved an arm for her to get back into the buggy. "Come on. I'll show you something you wouldn't see on any tourist trip, something a bit more off the beaten path."

"I'm intrigued." She climbed into the buggy. Even though she had heels on her boots, they were square and not very high. "I would have dressed more appropriately if I'd known I'd be going on an off-road adventure."

"I think you look just fine." He clicked his tongue and gave the horse a gentle flick of the reins, and they continued their trek to nowhere. Or somewhere. Yvonne was more focused on the fact that this nice Amish man had told her she looked just fine twice today. "Thanks," she said, almost under her breath as she lifted her chin and kept her eyes in front of her.

Just when she thought the path couldn't get any narrower, it did. She had to bend down to avoid getting slapped in the face with low-hanging branches.

"Sorry. I haven't been out here in years, and I had no idea how grown-over this place might be." He turned to her, his eyes brimming with genuine concern. "I think maybe we should turn back." He pulled back on the reins, slowing the horse.

"Wait." She twisted slightly in the seat to face him. "Is it worth the trip, whatever it is you want to show me?"

He sighed. "I don't know anymore. In fact, you might think it is dumb."

Yvonne loved anything mysterious, and this entire day was proving to be more fun than she could have anticipated. "You said you haven't been out here in years. So, it's somewhere you went as a kid?"

An eager look flashed in his eyes. "*Ya*, me and two other boys. We saw something, and . . ." He raised a shoulder and dropped it slowly, shaking his head. "Maybe we should turn around."

Yvonne grinned. "No way. We've come this far. I've got to see this place now."

The sun was just beginning its descent, but it felt later, darker than it was, with the trees forming a canopy over the road. "It feels a little creepy," she said as she nodded in front of them. "I'm all in for a little adventure."

Jake's eyes brightened. "Don't say I didn't warn you." He looked over his shoulder, then reached into the back seat of the topless buggy, pulling out a pair of rubber boots. "These will be huge on you, but you might want to wear them when we get there. I can't really see you walking in the woods in those shoes." He nodded to her black boots.

She swallowed hard as she began to rethink things. "Exactly how far will we be walking into the woods?"

"Not very far." He paused. "You can still change your mind."

Visions of scary movies flowed briefly through her mind—girls being led into the woods only to meet their demise by seemingly good guys. But there wasn't anything sinister about Jake. She was sure of it. "Let's do this."

He chuckled. "Okay. Here we go. Watch for low branches."

Yvonne's insides swirled with an excitement she hadn't felt in a long time as the buggy started to move a little faster.

Eva stirred the chicken and dumplings on the burner. She had flipped the sign on the front door to *Closed* right at five o'clock, expecting Jake to be back any minute. She glanced at the clock on the wall again. Almost six o'clock. A bitter jealousy stirred inside her, mingled with surprise that Jake had spent the entire day with the English woman. There wasn't that much to see in Montgomery.

After another few minutes her angst shifted to worry, and she wondered if something had happened to them. There weren't any windows in the back part of the building, only two skylights, so it was always a little dark in the room, but this time of year, it didn't get dark until close to nine. She wondered if a storm might be brewing.

After she turned off the burner, she walked to the front of the store. Even though the sun was starting to go down, it was a cloudless early evening. Weather wasn't an issue, which didn't alleviate her worries. Accidents happened in buggies more than any of them liked to admit. But even though she had safety concerns, jealousy still fueled her irritation.

Sighing, she went behind the counter and found the set of keys that Jake kept in a box out of sight. There were keys for the front door—which Eva had a copy of—and keys for the basement and back door. They rarely used the back door, and until now Eva had never had a reason to go into the basement. But she figured she could at least get things ready for their reading time, assuming that was still on.

She fumbled with the vintage lock until the door clicked open, then she reached for the flashlight hanging on the nail by the door. Carefully, she made her way down the steps and stood there, shining the flashlight in every direction. Would they sit on the bed with a lantern lit nearby? Or would that feel too intimate? They'd most likely sit near the desk on two chairs. Eva didn't really care where they sat, as long as they were together.

After a few minutes, she realized there wasn't really anything to get ready. They'd light lanterns, and that would be about it. She lifted the rolltop on the desk and eased the book out, tempted to thumb through it, but she'd wait on Jake. She trudged back up the stairs and went back to the front of the store, disappointed that Jake's buggy was still gone.

When she returned to the back room, she relit the burner and set it on Low underneath what was supposed to be their supper. After another glance at the clock, she wondered how long she should wait. She sat down at the small table and recalled her conversation with John. At first, he had looked visibly hurt, until Eva said that he could check with her in a couple of days. Her feelings wouldn't have changed by then, unless Jake made it quite clear to her that she was his employee and friend—and nothing more.

---

Jake couldn't believe he'd dragged Yvonne to this place, a spot he hadn't been to in years but that was a permanent part of his youth, something he'd never forget. There was no way she was going to believe his story. As she trudged awkwardly in his rubber boots down the narrow path into the woods—also grown up like the canopy of trees on the road—he felt responsible for her well-being. He wouldn't have brought her here if he'd known how much the conditions had worsened. Obviously, kids today didn't take this path to what Jake and his friends had once considered a secret place.

"You okay?" He was ahead of her, pushing branches aside and holding them so she could get through the brush.

She actually had a hand clenched around one of his suspenders as they walked, which should have felt odd, but at least he knew he hadn't lost her somewhere behind him.

"Yes, I'm fine. I was thinking earlier, I'm in the middle of every teen flick where the seemingly nice man drags the heroine out into the woods to kill her."

She made the comment without any emotion, and Jake stopped dead in his tracks and turned around, snapping his suspender in place as her hand let go of it. "What?" His chest tightened.

Yvonne burst out laughing. "I'm kidding. But you know how it always goes in those slasher movies."

Jake stared at her, knowing his expression must show his confusion. "*Nee*, I don't know. We don't watch movies."

She blinked at him. "Oh. That's right. No electricity, no TV. Duh." She rolled her eyes.

"I promise I'm not going to kill you." He felt the weight of his words all the way to the pit of his stomach, but she just put a hand over her mouth after she smiled.

Then she cleared her throat. "I believe you." She waved an arm forward as she squeezed her lips together, an obvious effort not to smile. "Carry on." She raised her chin and her eyebrows.

Jake wanted to go back. Even though this place held a special significance for him—and others—Yvonne was going to laugh at what she would consider a tall tale. She was already comparing their trek to scary movies and joking around.

They'd taken about fifteen more steps when Jake finally saw the tree he'd been looking for. A virus had killed most of the ash trees over the past couple of years, and lots of them had toppled over since he'd been here, but the tree he'd been looking for stood exactly where it had always been, big enough that two grown men couldn't get their arms around its girth.

"Here we are." He sighed as he lay a hand against the tree, then pointed to his initials. There were at least two dozen more initials carved into the tree since he, Amos, and Lloyd had carved theirs all those years ago. Proof that, despite the overgrown path, there were some kids—or maybe curious adults—who had made the trip out here. But it had clearly been a while.

"Uh . . ." She leaned closer, and her eyes traveled from one set of markings to another. "You brought me to a tree with carved initials? I don't even see any cute little hearts around the initials." Her eyes darted nervously back and forth between Jake and the tree, ultimately locking on Jake as she raised an eyebrow.

Jake hung his head and sighed again. "This was a bad idea. I don't know why I thought you'd want to see this place. Maybe I just wanted to see it again." He shrugged. "I don't know."

He waited as her eyes narrowed suspiciously.

"Every person who carved their initials in this tree claims to have seen the same thing," he said. "Although, I'm not *claiming* I saw anything. I *did* see something."

She kept her eyes fused with his as she raised her palms to the sky. "Am I supposed to guess?"

Jake took a deep breath, never having felt more foolish in his life, and prepared for a roaring round of laughter. "I saw a Sasquatch, and the other people who carved their initials in the tree claimed to have seen it also."

Yvonne stared expressionless at him. "You mean, like Bigfoot?"

Jake stiffened, knowing it was going to make him angry when she laughed, even though the situation surely warranted it. Most people didn't believe in such things. And Yvonne was older, educated, and wasn't going to buy this at all. "*Ya*, I guess that's what some people call it." He twisted his mouth from side to side, willing himself not to get angry.

"What did it look like?" Her hazel eyes glistened with what appeared to be curiosity.

When he was sure she wasn't going to laugh, he said, "It was big, way taller and broader than I am. And . . ." He still wasn't sure if she was just playing along and boisterous laughter was getting ready to erupt. "And it had red eyes."

She bit her bottom lip, then lowered her brow at him. Somewhere along the trek, she'd pushed her sunglasses up on her head again. "How old were you?"

"Fourteen." He scratched his cheek and wondered if his face was red. "*Mei* two friends saw it too." Tapping the tree, he said, "And all these people saw something too."

She was quiet as she gingerly ran her hand over some of the carvings.

"This feels so dumb. I don't know why I thought you'd want to see this." Jake shook his head, frowning.

For the first time, she smiled. "Are you kidding me? This has been the best part of the day. How many people get to say they saw a Sasquatch? That's amazing. I was in Colorado once, in a small town called Bailey. They have an entire museum dedicated to the many sightings of Sasquatch in the area. I happened to be in there when a teenager told me that he'd seen one before, and he said it had red eyes. Then my friend I was visiting in the town told me that she had also seen one. She said the same thing—red eyes. I think it would be fabulous to see something so rare." She paused. "Although I'm aware most people probably don't believe in such things." Shrugging, she said, "But I do." She pointed a finger at him. "Now, if you said you'd seen a ghost, we would be having a different conversation."

Jake was still reeling and coming to grips with the fact that she hadn't laughed. "You believe in a Sasquatch but not in a ghost? I think there are probably more people who believe in ghosts."

"Well . . ." She folded her arms across her blue blouse, which was now speckled with leaves and bits of debris. She sighed. "If you believe in ghosts, then you have to believe in an afterlife, that the soul goes on. And I don't."

Jake shifted his weight and stared at her. "You don't believe in *Gott*?"

She shook her head. "I didn't say that. There probably is

a God, but He's not up there waiting for us. I think He lends a hand while we're here on earth, though."

"Have you always believed this way?" A sadness wrapped around Jake as his eyes studied her face, searching for something that wasn't there. Faith.

"Pretty much." She uncrossed her arms and waved one in the air. "I think God is probably real, but the rest is just . . ." She stared somewhere over Jake's shoulder. "Just not real."

Jake waited until she looked back at him. "Can I ask what made you decide this?" He was stepping into territory he had been taught to avoid. His people didn't believe in ministering to outsiders.

"It's basically the way I was raised." She took a deep breath and blew it out slowly. Jake was sure there was a story there, but he wasn't sure he wanted to hear it. "I'm thrilled that you brought me to a place where all these Sasquatch sightings have happened. Just amazing. I wish we would see one now."

Jake was relieved when she changed the subject. He took out his pocket watch, the one his grandfather had given him. "Wow. It's getting late. We've still got plenty of time before dark, but I guess we should get going."

Yvonne dropped her sunglasses down on her nose. "Yeah, you're probably right. It's been a full day. A great day." She waited for him to take the lead, although she didn't latch on to his suspender this time.

Jake had surprisingly had a good time also. The pushy

English woman had turned out to be a fun and lively companion, and she didn't even laugh about his Sasquatch sighting. But now, as their time was coming to an end, his thoughts returned to Eva and John. Jake was supposed to read with Eva this evening. She'd even brought supper. He wondered if plans had been changed now that John was in the picture.

"Thank you for a lovely day and for sharing your special place with me," Yvonne said once they got off the narrow path and back onto the main road. "It was unexpected, and I enjoyed it very much."

"It was a *gut* day." It saddened him that Yvonne felt the way she did about God, but that was not his burden to bear. He would pray for her to find her faith, though. "I'm glad you had a nice time."

They were nearing the bookstore when she pushed her shades up on her head and waited until he looked at her before she spoke. "Still nothing I can say to get you to change your mind about the book?"

Jake sighed. He should have known she wasn't going to let it go, but maybe this was her final attempt. "*Nee*." He needed to be firm. "There is zero chance that I will sell the book."

With that, the store came into view. Jake didn't see Yvonne's expression at his reply, and if she said anything, he didn't hear her. All he saw was a closed shop and an empty parking lot. Eva's buggy was gone. He looked at his pocket watch again. It was ten minutes after six. His heart sank as he wondered how long Eva had waited for him after closing the store at five.

"Can I use your restroom before I get on the road?" asked Yvonne as he turned into the lot. "It's not far to Gasthof Village, but . . ." She gritted her teeth.

"*Ya*, sure." Jake tethered his horse, found his keys, and opened the door for her. "I'll walk you back. It will be dark back there." He took the flashlight from the counter just inside the door and shone it on the floor in front of him, and Yvonne followed him to the back room. "Straight through there." He handed her the flashlight as he picked up one from the small kitchen counter. The aroma of chicken and dumplings hung in the air, and his stomach grumbled, but it wasn't just because he was hungry. "I'll be up front or out giving *mei* horse some water."

She took the flashlight. "Thanks."

Jake trudged back to the counter, to the spot on the left of the register where he and Eva left each other notes or phone messages, but there wasn't anything there. He chastised himself again for missing supper and their planned reading time. *But couldn't she have waited for me?* Her departure probably had something to do with John.

Every time Jake pictured the two of them together, it fueled a combination of emotions—regret, jealousy, and questions. How could he now look at Eva every day knowing she was seeing John? He'd never expected to react so strongly to this new scenario.

He popped the register open and was glad to see that

Eva had taken the money with her, which she'd done before when Jake wasn't there to close the store. That done, he went outside to wait. He was thankful he didn't live far. His old mare was surely worn out.

After he filled up the water bucket and gave the horse a long drink, Yvonne emerged and rushed straight to her car.

Jake locked up the store as she gave him a quick wave. "Thank you again!"

He waved back, hoping she was far enough away not to see the moisture in his eyes.

Yvonne sat down on the bed and pulled off her boots, wiggling her toes and reflecting on the day. She had stopped in the restaurant for dinner and now wished she'd found a place to buy a bottle of wine. Maybe tomorrow.

Yawning, she kicked her feet up on the bed and leaned against her pillow before calling Trevor.

"I guess I miss you a little," she said after he answered.

"So, I haven't been replaced by the Amish guy, then?"

Yvonne chuckled. She'd called him earlier to tell him that Jake would be showing her around. "I don't know. He's *really* nice looking." It was true, and Jake was a nice—and entertaining—man, but Trevor held the key to her heart. "But alas . . . I'm in love with this great guy named Trevor whom I'm going to marry in a few months."

"Well, I'm happy to hear that I haven't been upstaged.

I'd hate to start all over, looking for another woman to marry."

"Ha-ha," she said, smiling. "You know I get a little nervous about the whole marriage thing from time to time, but I love you with all my heart, and I really do believe that we will be happy for the rest of our lives."

"I know we will be, and I can't wait to start our lives as Mr. and Mrs. Adams."

Yvonne breathed in a sigh of contentment, deciding marriage probably did require some work, as Jake had mentioned. She'd maintain her independence, even if she had to fight for it a little. But Trevor wouldn't push her on that. He knew she wasn't cut out to sit home and play housewife. From now on, when her nerves tried to get the better of her, she was only going to picture their lives together as blissfully happy.

"So, tell me about your day," he said.

"It wasn't anything like I expected, but I actually had a really good time." She filled him in on the day's events.

"Sasquatch, huh? Not sure I believe in that stuff." He laughed, pretty much solidifying that he didn't.

"Jury's out for me. Too many people claim to have seen the big furry creature with red eyes. Remember, a while back I told you my friend Sherry swore she saw a Sasquatch up on the mountain where they live?" She paused. "I guess I'm open to the possibility."

"I guess I'd have to see to believe."

"Speaking of seeing to believe, I didn't earn any points

with the Amish guy when a conversation came up about religion. My fault. I sort of stepped into it, but when I said I didn't believe the soul goes anywhere after we die, I think Jake Lantz felt the need to save me. But he probably didn't know where to start. Besides, we don't know each other, and it seemed a heavy conversation to dive into, so I changed the subject."

Yvonne and Trevor didn't talk about religion much. Trevor didn't align with her beliefs. He believed in heaven and hell, and they had agreed to disagree a long time ago. Maybe that was why he was quiet now, unwilling to respond to what might end up as an argument.

"Anyway," she said through a yawn, "it was a nice day."

"Are you coming home tomorrow? I actually miss you too." She could feel him smiling back in Texas and appreciated his warm tone and the fact that he hadn't pushed her on anything religious.

"I've got one more thing up my sleeve. The Amish girl who works for Jake seems totally in love with him. I can tell by the way she looks at him, and I think he has feelings for her too. The woman is beautiful, and she seems super nice. I'm going to try to impart some of my worldly wisdom so she can get her hooks in Jake. She just needs to up her game."

He laughed a little. "I see where this is going. And in return, you're hoping for an ally to talk Jake into selling you the book."

"Bingo." Yvonne grinned. "And don't call it manipulative, because the outcome is good for all."

"Except Jake breaks his promise to his grandfather." Trevor's voice held a sense of regret.

"I don't like that part of it, but if the book is so important, it's meant to be shared, right?" She squeezed her eyes closed, knowing Trevor would counter.

"Shared? Maybe. Sold? Apparently not." He paused for a long while. "You said you liked this Amish guy, Jake. Why force him to break a promise? You don't need the money. And before you say anything, yes . . . I know you like the challenge. But this time, maybe George just doesn't get this particular rare book."

"You might be right. But at the least, I'd like to know what's so important about the book. Jake wouldn't even let me see it." She sighed. "I don't know. He knows me a little better now. Maybe he would have let me have a peek at it. I can't stand the thought of leaving here without knowing the contents."

"Why does it matter? You said you were told the book has healing powers for those who are spiritually lost. That doesn't sound like your kind of book."

Yvonne chewed on her bottom lip and tried to decide if there was a jab in his statement. Deciding there was, she stayed quiet.

"Honey, don't get mad. I probably shouldn't have said that."

She waited a few moments. "I'm not mad."

"I love you. I know you. And I can tell when you're upset or angry. I'm sorry."

"It's just . . ." She took in a deep breath and sighed. "I don't know. Curiosity, I guess. And I love you too. I'm going to get a shower, but I'll call you before I go to sleep."

"Yes, I've heard that before." His voice was light, but tonight she'd make a point to call him before he went to sleep.

"I promise I will."

After they'd ended the call, Yvonne stared at the foot of her bed—and at the book atop the red-and-white floral bedspread. If she hadn't gone into the bookstore to use the bathroom, she probably wouldn't have noticed the basement door was ajar. She'd just happened to shine the light around the area, then had had an overwhelming urge to rush down the stairs since she knew Jake was outside tending to his horse. And there, in plain sight, had sat the hundred-thousand-dollar book. All three hundred pages.

Luckily, when she'd stuffed it underneath her shirt, then practically run to her car, Jake was closing up the store. She'd locked her purse in her car before they'd taken off in the buggy that morning. All she had was her car keys in her pocket. But Jake hadn't even noticed the slight bulge in her shirt.

Yvonne had never stolen anything in her life—and she wasn't now. She was only borrowing it. Tomorrow she would carefully put the book in her purse, arrive at the bookstore early, and somehow sneak her way down to the basement. No one would be any the wiser.

She would read as much as she could tonight and at least know what all the fuss was about.

# CHAPTER 6

Eva walked into the bookstore with a knot in her throat, but she held her head high, determined not to cry in front of Jake. She'd practiced all morning, after being up way too late the night before, shuffling back and forth between anger and hurt. She had waited for him to return for almost an hour after closing the store. He could have called if he was going to be late. He also could have phoned her later in the evening when she was home and offered an explanation.

She did have to consider that perhaps he was bothered that John had been in the store, especially if Jake had heard the rumors that John wanted to date her. But most prevalent at the moment was Eva's jealousy that had eventually swum to the top of all her emotions. Jake had spent the day with an outsider and apparently hadn't thought enough about their plans to even call her.

He was sitting behind the counter with his hands folded, his hat lying on the wooden surface next to him. His face was redder than she'd ever seen it before, and based on the way his eyes blazed into hers, she could almost feel his anger searing her skin.

Eva was only a few steps past the door when she stopped and wondered how the tables could possibly be turned. "What? What's wrong?" she asked sheepishly, even though she was certain he should be the one apologizing.

"Did you forget something last night?" His jaw clenched as his eyes narrowed, and she could still feel the burn.

She shifted her weight indignantly as she brought a hand to her chest, her small black purse swinging at her elbow. "Did *I* forget something?" She huffed. "I believe I should be asking you the same thing." She fired back the same unforgiving expression he was holding on to. Surely, he'd apologize now.

"Why did you leave the basement door open when you left last night?" His voice was uncompromising, but at least his eyes had softened a little.

Eva thought back. There were the two young men who had frightened her. Could they have gotten into the basement? *No*. They'd been there early, and she would've noticed if the door was open as she worked throughout the day. Later she'd heated the chicken and dumplings. And then . . . Then she'd unlocked the door, gone into the basement, wondered where they might sit, taken the book from beneath the rolltop on the desk, then gone back to the chicken and dumplings. Could she have forgotten to lock the door? No. She recalled fumbling with the lock. But maybe she hadn't actually locked it like she thought. Either way, his anger wasn't justified.

"I-I had trouble with the lock on the basement door. I unlocked it because I assumed we would read down there, and I checked to see if we might need anything. When I locked it back up, maybe it didn't click into place, and—" She gasped before her throat seized like it might close up. "The book. I took the book from . . . Is it . . ."

"It's gone. The basement door was open, and the book is gone." He stood up and placed both his hands on the wooden surface in front of him, leaning forward. "Did you take the book home with you? Please tell me you did."

Eva hung her head as she blinked back tears. "*Nee*, I didn't take the book home."

Jake waved his arm around the bookstore. "No one broke in, Eva. The place was locked up tight when I got here about thirty minutes ago. So how did someone get in and take the book?"

"I-I don't know. There were these two men earlier in the day that made me nervous, but it wasn't them, because I saw the book when I went down there, and I can't imagine how someone might have gotten it, and . . ." She was rambling and crying at the same time, but she couldn't even look at Jake, knowing how important that book was to him. "I'm sorry," she said through her tears as she kept her head down.

Jake pounded his fist on the counter, a display of anger

that Eva had never witnessed from her boss. She startled, her eyes wide and moist. "I'm sorry!" she repeated, louder this time.

They began talking over each other, boisterously, with Eva apologizing and Jake saying he didn't understand how this had happened. And then the bell on the door chimed.

"Stop!" Yvonne took several long steps into the store until she stood beside Eva and faced off with Jake. "Stop all this yelling. I could hear you outside."

She glanced back and forth between Eva and Jake before she ran a hand through her hair and sighed. Her eyes were puffy, and she looked like she'd been crying. Then she reached into her purse, took out the missing book, and set it on the counter. She took a few steps backward until she was standing next to Eva. "I took your book. Last night when I went to the bathroom and I saw the basement door open. So quit yelling at Eva." She lowered her head, shaking it. "I shouldn't have done it. I've never taken anything in my life. I just . . . borrowed it."

Jake stood there, his nostrils flaring. Eva was speechless, unsure what surprised her more—Jake's outburst or that Yvonne had taken the book.

"I had no intention of stealing it. I just wanted to see . . . to read . . ." Yvonne pressed her lips together as tears formed in the corners of her eyes. "I only read about forty pages, but . . . I'm so confused." She dabbed at her eyes, and Eva glanced at Jake, who now looked just as stunned as Eva felt. "Never mind. I'm sorry I took it. Well, I'm not. I mean . . ."

She squeezed her eyes closed, brushed away a tear, and said, "I shouldn't have taken it. I shouldn't have read *any* of it."

Her gaze landed on Jake. "As soon as I can get a flight, I'll be heading back to Texas. You don't have to worry about me bothering y'all anymore. I won't be badgering you about selling that stupid book." With a shaky hand, she pointed to the book, opened her mouth to say something, then pressed her lips together and ran out the door.

Jake's mouth hung open. Eva was still reeling that Jake had spoken so harshly to her, and even more confounded at Yvonne's revelation. But Yvonne now stood in the parking lot with her hands over her face, crying. Eva shot Jake the meanest look she could before she rushed outside. She put a hand on Yvonne's back. The woman tried to blink back tears when she saw Eva, but instead she began to cry harder.

"Everything is all right." It wasn't, but Eva was at a loss for words. "Can I get you a drink of water, or is there anything else I can do?" Eva almost couldn't believe she was comforting the woman who had just earned her a verbal lashing from Jake. But even though she didn't know Yvonne at all—and was certainly upset that the woman had taken Jake's book—she hated to see her crying.

"Don't be nice to me," Yvonne said in a high-pitched voice. "So it was you who left the basement unlocked. Big deal. I'm the one who went down there and took the book." She pulled a tissue from her purse and blew her nose, beginning to regain a tiny bit of composure as she looked at Eva. "I just wanted to know about it, to read a little of it and see what makes it so important. I'm sorry Jake yelled at you that way. He doesn't seem like the type."

Eva lowered her hand from Yvonne's back and sighed. "He's not. I've never seen him like that."

"Well, his anger was misdirected." Yvonne sniffled. She was dressed in blue jeans and a yellow blouse today, much more casual than her other visits. "I thought I could sneak the book back into its place without anyone knowing it was ever gone. I had come to terms with the fact that Jake isn't going to sell it. We had such a fun day together that I considered just asking him to show it to me. But an opportunity presented itself, and I took it, in case he refused again to let me see the book. It was just a weird hunch to go down there, and I'm not usually that impulsive."

Eva sighed. "Jake is a forgiving person, and since you and he hit it off prior to this, I'm sure he won't hold a grudge."

Yvonne dabbed at her eyes with her fingers. "When you say it like that—'hit it off'—you make it sound like something romantic." She locked eyes with Eva. "Your boss is a very handsome man."

Eva felt her heart dropping into her stomach. She couldn't compete with a fancy English woman as pretty as Yvonne. Apparently, Eva had been wrong about Jake not getting involved with an outsider.

Yvonne held up her left hand and wiggled her finger, the one with a large diamond ring on it. "I have a handsome fiancé back home whom I am madly in love with. You have nothing to worry about as far as Jake and I are concerned." Sniffling, she gave her head a quick shake. "I don't remember the last time I cried, but that book . . ."

Eva clung to Yvonne's statement about Jake, even though she was angry at him for his harsh words. But the book was also taking on a mysterious edge. "What was it about the book that upset you so much?"

Yvonne took a deep breath and bit her bottom lip. "All of it. Like I said, I only read about forty pages, but something spoke to me in a way that I wasn't expecting." She shook her head. "It just confused me. Then, when I walked in and heard Jake yelling at you, I guess I just lost it. I'm sorry he took out my misdeed on you."

Eva wondered if maybe Jake had reconsidered about selling the book. Maybe he'd thought it over and decided to break his promise to his grandfather, and then when it went missing, he went all crazy.

They both turned to Jake when the bell on the door chimed as he stepped onto the porch. He raised both his shoulders, held them there, then let them fall. "I'm sorry. I shouldn't have yelled at you that way, Eva. And, Yvonne, obviously you are upset, and I'm sorry for my part in that. But you shouldn't have taken the book."

"She knows that." Eva spat the words at him before she turned back to Yvonne. "Are you going to be okay?"

"Yeah. I guess. I'm probably better off that I won't be finishing that book. I'm going to forget I ever read any of it." Yvonne swiped at her eyes.

"Do you want to go get a cup of *kaffi* at the little café not far from here?" Eva touched Yvonne on the shoulder.

"I'd like that a lot. I'm happy to drive. Or . . . I love riding in the buggies." She smiled a little for the first time since she'd arrived.

"Then the buggy it is. Do you want to drive? Bonnie is a dear, sweet horse. She won't give you any trouble at all."

Yvonne pressed her palms together, the hint of a smile on her face. "Really? I would love that, if you're sure it's okay. Will she get spooked in traffic?"

Eva giggled. "There's not really any traffic where we are. We can go to the same café you and Jake went to for breakfast, or there is another place not much farther up the road."

Yvonne cut her eyes at Jake before she looked back at Eva. "I think I'd like to try the *other* place, if that's okay with you." She glared at Jake before they started walking toward Eva's buggy.

Perhaps neither of them should be judging Jake right now. But he could have conveyed his feelings without yelling. Eva didn't even turn around.

---

Jake stood in front of the bookstore with his mouth open, wondering what had just happened. Both women had just sliced and diced him with their eyes, but he was pretty sure his actions had been justified. Although he hadn't expected either of them to cry.

By the time he was back in the store and sitting on the stool, he realized he had been way too hard on Eva. Now he wondered if she was even coming back. At the least, she would have to bring Yvonne back to her car. He was disappointed in Yvonne, but she could have easily taken off with the book and gone home with it. But she'd chosen to return it. Regardless, Jake hadn't gotten a word in where she was concerned. Her hysteria had walked in the door with her, and she hadn't let up until Eva got her calmed down.

What could she have possibly read in the book that upset her so much? Now Jake wanted to read it more than ever, but he wasn't sure Eva would even be speaking to him when she returned. Sighing, he put his head in his hands. He didn't notice a buggy pull in, and he startled when the bell on the door chimed. It was the elderly sisters who ran The Peony Inn, a bed-and-breakfast up the road. Usually, Jake welcomed the eccentric ways of the two widows—Lizzie being the queen of quirkiness—but he wished he could just be alone with his thoughts right now.

They walked in side by side. Esther was the older, heavier sister who stood almost a foot taller than Lizzie, who might not weigh a hundred pounds. But Lizzie had enough spunk to make up for what she didn't have in size.

"*Wie bischt*, Esther and Lizzie. How can I help you today?" Jake did his best to smile, but Lizzie shuffled up to the counter and set her little brown purse down with a thud, scowling at him.

"What's wrong with you?" Lizzie raised her chin,

cocking her head slightly to one side. "And where is Eva? She's usually the one behind the counter."

"She's, uh . . . out having *kaffi* with a friend." Jake wasn't sure Eva and Yvonne were friends, but they'd certainly left as allies.

"And this is why you look like you've lost your best friend?" Lizzie folded her arms across her chest.

"Lizzie, don't badger the boy." Esther joined her sister at the counter, but despite her comment, she also seemed to be waiting for an answer, one eyebrow raised.

Jake sighed. Esther might give up, but Lizzie wouldn't rest until she got an answer that satisfied her. "I got upset with Eva about something, and I think I was probably much too hard on her."

Lizzie's eyes widened. "Please tell me you didn't make that sweet *maedel* cry."

Jake lowered his head in shame. "*Ya*. I did."

"What are you going to do to fix it?" Lizzie unintentionally spit when she talked sometimes. A problem with her dentures, Jake thought. He did his best to ignore it.

"I'm sure Jake will make things right." Esther nudged her sister just as Jake lifted his head. "Right, dear?"

"I hope I can." Jake could still picture Eva's tear-streaked face, but it was quickly replaced by another image—those beautiful brown eyes that had thrown daggers his way before she'd left. And there was Yvonne's little breakdown as well. He hated for her to leave in such an emotional mess. Maybe both women would return feeling better. He hoped.

Lizzie shook her head and rolled her eyes. "Men."

Esther cleared her throat. "Lizzie is here to look for some new novels to read. I am here to pick up some new pens and writing tablets. I like to leave some in each guest's room. We know where everything is, of course. We'll let you be and pray that things are resolved between you and Eva." She tugged on her sister's sleeve. "Come on, Lizzie."

After Lizzie grunted, they shuffled away, leaving Jake with only his thoughts, like he'd thought he wanted. But a pit of despair hung in his gut. He wasn't going to feel right until he made things right with Eva. What Yvonne had done was awful, but he didn't want her going home feeling so sad. He'd actually had a nice time with her the day before. He liked her, which made it that much more upsetting that she'd borrowed the book without permission.

He wondered what Eva and Yvonne were talking about. The only thing they had in common was him. He flinched.

Yvonne ran her finger around the rim of her coffee cup. "Thank you for letting me drive the buggy. It was a fun reprieve that took me out of my head for a little while." She stared at the beautiful young woman across the table from her whom she didn't even know but who had quickly stepped up to the plate to offer her comfort. "I rarely get hysterical like that. I'm so sorry Jake directed his anger at you the way he did."

"I've never seen him that mad." Eva blew on her coffee before she took a hesitant sip. "We had planned to read the book together. Since you arrived and were so interested in it, we were curious how any piece of literature could demand such a large amount of money." She paused, a knot in her stomach. "I don't know if that will still happen."

"I'm sure the experience would be different for you, but the book challenged the way I've always believed about the world, myself, and death." Yvonne shivered even though it was almost too warm in the small café they were in. The place was similar to the eatery she had visited with Jake, but smaller. And she and Eva were the only ones there. Yvonne wondered how some of these places stayed in business.

"Do you mind me asking why that is? Only if you're comfortable talking about it." Eva had dimples when she smiled even a little, which made her appear younger than when she wasn't smiling.

Yvonne wasn't comfortable talking about it, but she didn't want to be rude, especially after what she'd put Eva through. "My parents were killed in a car accident when I was young, and I was raised by my aunt and uncle. They were great people, but they didn't believe in an afterlife, and I never have either. I wanted to so badly after my parents died. I needed to know that they weren't gone forever, just part of the ground . . . My aunt and uncle, sympathetically and with total compassion, explained to me that I must accept the loss and not hold out any hope of ever seeing them again."

Eva's eyes brimmed with tenderness and compassion as she cupped both hands around her coffee cup and stared at Yvonne. "I am so sorry for your loss."

Yvonne swallowed hard. She had expected Eva to challenge her beliefs. She'd read that the Amish were Christians. "As a young adult, I read up on the subject, but I could never find enough hard evidence to change the way I was taught to believe. But that book gave me pause and touched on a few sensitive areas that did nothing but confuse me. It was the first time I'd ever felt real doubt about my beliefs."

Eva cleared her throat. "I don't believe there is a replacement for the Bible, but sometimes I think the Holy Spirit works in mysterious ways."

"A book, no matter how powerful, can't change the way you have believed for your entire life." Yvonne paused, recalling some of the testimonials she'd read in the first forty pages. "But I felt like God was testing me somehow, and it brought forth a bunch of emotions I couldn't process."

"*Ach*, so you do believe in *Gott*?" Eva raised a hopeful eyebrow.

"Yes, I do. I think He keeps us all on an even keel and helps when He can. But I don't believe the same way y'all do." Yvonne could have never predicted she would be having a religious conversation with an Amish woman, but she wouldn't have thought any book could have such an effect on her. She wasn't sure how she felt about revealing so much information, but Eva didn't seem to be judging her.

Eva smiled. "I like the way you talk. It's very . . ." She tapped a finger to her chin.

"Southern," Yvonne said, also smiling. "I was thinking the same thing about the way you talk. Kind of . . ." She tipped her head to one side.

"German?" Eva brushed back a strand of hair that had fallen from beneath her prayer covering. "We learn Pennsylvania *Deitsch* before we are taught *Englisch* when we start school."

Yvonne's phone buzzed in her purse. She pulled it out and looked at the number. For the second time, she'd failed to call Trevor before she went to bed the night before. "I'm sorry. I need to take this."

"Please, go ahead."

Yvonne didn't see a need to step outside since it was only Eva and her in the café. Even their waitress was out of sight at the moment.

"I'm sorry," she apologized to Trevor. "I forgot to call you before I fell asleep." She glanced at Eva. "I was reading a book, and I lost track of time." In truth, she'd been bawling her head off for reasons she didn't know how to explain to Trevor. "I'll make it up to you when I get home. I'm going to try to get a flight out this afternoon."

"I'll hold you to that," he said with an exaggerated sexiness in his voice.

Then she listened as Trevor told her that he needed to go to New York. The investors he had met with wanted him to fly back on their private jet to discuss another project in Manhattan.

"Wow. That sounds like a huge opportunity." Yvonne wasn't crazy about New York. She thought of herself as a city girl, but with a whole lot of country thrown in since her aunt and uncle had raised her in a rural area. New York was a bit busy, even for her, but Trevor loved his trips to the Big Apple. "How long will you be gone?"

"I'm not sure. Maybe a few days."

Yvonne glanced at Eva, who was patiently sipping on her coffee. "Listen, I think I might stay here awhile longer, since you aren't going to be home." She raised her eyes to see Eva staring at her curiously. "I got a bit sideways with the bookstore owner, Jake Lantz. I'll probably never see the guy again, but I'd like to leave on a good note."

Yvonne listened to a few more details about Trevor's trip. She would eventually tell him about taking the book. But not yet. She wasn't proud of her actions, but it had left her in a weird state of mind. If she told him about her experience last night, he would probably want to talk about it in depth. Yvonne wasn't up for that right now, and that conversation probably needed to happen in person.

"I will miss you terribly," she said, and she meant it. Sometimes it took a couple of days before she truly missed him, but she was emotionally whipped, and nothing sounded better than crawling into the comfort of his arms. She was still angry with herself for allowing words on a page to rip at her emotions so much. For now she just wanted to bask in the steadfast truth that Trevor loved her.

"I love you too," she said after he did. He told her he had another call coming in, so they quickly said their goodbyes.

She clicked the phone off and dropped it back into her purse. When she looked at Eva, the woman was so misty-eyed that Yvonne wondered if her verbal display of affection had embarrassed Eva. "What?" she asked tentatively. "Why are you looking at me like that?"

"That just sounded so nice." Eva put her elbows on the table and rested her chin in her hands. The woman's eyes transformed from misty to dreamy. "You really love him, don't you?"

"With all my heart," Yvonne replied without hesitation. "I'm super lucky to have him."

Eva sighed, then straightened and took a sip of her coffee. "I bet you are so excited about getting married."

Yvonne thought about all the arrangements that had been made. "I was a little nervous at first . . . I still am at times. But my nervousness is slowly becoming sheer excitement. Yes, I am thrilled about becoming his wife in the fall." She paused. "I know that y'all do things a little simpler here than we do." *Understatement.* "I'm guessing you don't make a big thing about weddings."

Eva laughed so hard, Yvonne thought she was going to spit coffee when she covered her mouth with her napkin. "*Ach*, you'd be surprised," Eva said.

Yvonne was intrigued, especially since she'd only

recently wrapped up months of wedding plans. "So, it *is* a big affair, then?"

The waitress, an older woman who walked with a limp, brought them a basket of muffins. "As you can see, we aren't really busy, and I thought you girls might like a snack."

"*Danki,* Lanora. That's very kind of you." Eva selected a banana-nut muffin, and so did Yvonne.

"So, do tell. What is an Amish wedding like?" Yvonne was genuinely interested.

Her dimples in full view, Eva took a deep breath. "We usually have around four hundred guests, and—"

"What?" Yvonne said around a mouthful of muffin. She quickly chewed and swallowed. "That's over twice as many as are invited to mine and Trevor's wedding. I'm guessing around a hundred and twenty-five will show up. A bunch are from out of town or out of state."

Eva was still grinning. "The marriage of two people is a sacred vow, and it is celebrated as such. The event starts early in the morning, and the last of the guests don't leave until late afternoon or early evening. We have a large meal, and it is a full day filled with festivities." Her expression fell as she shrugged. "Although, I'll be twenty next month, and I'm wondering if I'll end up an old maid."

Yvonne put a hand over her mouth to keep from smiling, but she finally couldn't stifle her amusement. "I'm thirty-two. It took me this long to find the perfect man for me." She recalled the little research she had done about the Amish, remembering that they often marry young. "Sweetie, I assure you, you aren't—and won't be—an old maid." Pausing, she thought about her alternative motives—to get Eva to help her with Jake, to convince him to sell the book. But with everything that had happened, maybe she could make up for some of her misdeeds by offering Eva some words of wisdom. She recalled telling Trevor how Eva needed to up her game when it came to Jake. "It seems obvious to me how you feel about Jake. I see the way you look at him, and I've caught him looking at you in the same dreamy way. But you're going to need to be a little more outspoken to get his attention, a little more . . . flirty. Unless there is something going on with you and a guy named John Yoder."

Eva's brown doe eyes widened as a blush filled her face. "What? And how do you know I, uh . . ."

"I mentioned something to Jake about how gorgeous you are." She grinned when Eva's face reddened even more. "It's true—and he agreed—but he also said something about a man named John Yoder who wanted to date you. The guy in the bookstore."

Eva shook her head. "John is not the one who holds *mei* heart." She almost swooned in her seat, and Yvonne smiled. "It's always been Jake, but it would be unladylike for me to . . . um . . ."

"Seduce him?" Yvonne chuckled. "Maybe something a little more subtle. But . . ." She pointed a finger at her new friend. "You make him apologize for the way he yelled at you today. That wasn't justified."

"He's not normally like that. Like I said earlier, he is

very forgiving, but also quick to apologize if he's wrong." She smiled. "Jake's the best man I've ever known."

Even his name seemed to dreamily slide off Eva's tongue.

"I think he was just deeply upset about the book." Eva sighed.

"Well, it's a very upsetting book." Yvonne shivered again just thinking about all the confusion it had caused her.

"I'm wondering if we will actually still read it together like we'd planned." Eva glanced around the room, as if to make sure no one had slipped in. "The basement is dark, and I thought we would read down there only by the light of lanterns, and that we would experience whatever was in the book together. It hadn't been important to Jake until you showed such an interest, and I think it rekindled fond feelings about his grandfather."

Yvonne threw caution to the wind and slathered butter all over the second half of her muffin. "Well, that is certainly setting a romantic scene, reading by lantern together. But the content might put a big fat hole in that scenario." She paused, thinking. "Or maybe not since your people believe in heaven and . . ." She wasn't sure whether or not to say the word. "And the other place."

"Maybe if you had finished the book, you might feel differently?" Eva asked, her eyes glowing beacons of hope.

"No, I think I had enough of that piece of literature to last me a lifetime." It seemed like a strange choice of words, and it must have to Eva since the woman raised both eyebrows. "Anyway, let Jake apologize, and I'm sure he will.

Then resume your plans to read together in the basement. But you probably need to let him know that you aren't interested in that John Yoder fellow."

"Maybe I should just grab him and kiss him!" Eva straightened in her chair with an ear-to-ear smile.

Yvonne's mouth fell open. "Well, I guess that's one way to go."

They both laughed, which felt good. Yvonne was going to root for Eva, maybe even pray about it. It wasn't something she did all the time, but she had reached out to God before. She'd also pray to get some sort of peace about what she'd read. Maybe God could clear all that up for her—one way or the other.

# CHAPTER 7

Jake sat at the counter sulking. He wasn't proud of his behavior with Eva and Yvonne. He was anxious for them to return so he could hopefully make amends. Business was slow for a Saturday, and no other customers had come since Esther and Lizzie left. Plenty of time for Jake to think.

A wave of apprehension swept over him when Yvonne guided Eva's buggy into the parking lot. She pulled the reins back and eased the horse to a stop as if she'd been doing it her entire life. Jake stood from where he was sitting behind the counter and waited for the women to get out of the buggy, hoping Eva didn't slip into the driver's side and dash away.

Both women headed toward the store, arm in arm and laughing. Jake felt outnumbered before they even walked in. He reminded himself that both of them had done wrong, but making them cry was worse.

Their expressions sobered as soon as they entered the store, and they walked to the counter and faced off with Jake. First Yvonne folded her arms across her chest, then Eva did. Neither said a word.

"Once again, I'm sorry." Jake glanced back and forth between the two women. "I was angry, but I should not have yelled at either of you." He didn't think he'd hollered at Yvonne, but overkill on the apologies might be in order just the same. "And, Eva, I'm also sorry I was late and missed chicken and dumplings and reading."

Eva lowered her head and sighed. After a couple of seconds, she lifted her eyes to his. "It's okay." She said the words, but the hurt lingered in her expression.

He turned to Yvonne.

"You don't really owe me an apology," she said. "I took something that belonged to you without asking, and I'm the one who is sorry." She lifted her arms and pressed her fingers to her temples. "Sorrier than you know. I wish I hadn't read those pages."

Jake was anxious to start reading and hoped Eva would still want to. Or would she have plans with John? He was also wondering what could have upset Yvonne so much.

"Anyway"—Yvonne tucked her hair behind her ears—"if it's okay with you, I'm going to give Eva a hand going through some boxes in the back room. She said she needs to take inventory of shipments that have recently arrived. A way to make up for my error in judgment."

Jake grinned. "As long as you don't steal anything."

"Ha-ha." She closed her eyes for a moment before she looked back at him. "I really am sorry. Believe it or not, I've never stolen anything in my life."

Eva cleared her throat, glancing at Jake then back at Yvonne. "He believes you." She waved an arm. "This way. Follow me. And I want to hear more about your wedding plans. It all sounds so exciting."

Yvonne smiled. "Absolutely."

They walked off and left Jake at the counter, not sure what he was supposed to do today. Tend to the customers, he supposed.

Eva listened in awe as Yvonne shared the details of her upcoming wedding in October. "Your dress sounds beautiful, and I love orchids. Those will make a beautiful bouquet."

"Thanks. Planning a wedding is a lot of work, so it's good to have confirmation I'm making the right choices." Yvonne picked up a stack of books nearby and started checking them off a list Eva had given her. They were sitting on the floor cross-legged, facing each other. "I think the hardest part was deciding on a menu for our reception." She laughed. "If there is one thing Trevor and I don't agree on, it's food. He has a long list of things he doesn't like to eat, and I have an equally long list of food I don't like." She rolled her eyes. "And there are not many crossovers between the two lists."

Eva shook her head. "*Ach*, that must make it hard to prepare meals."

"Yes, it does." Yvonne set the books aside and reached for another pile. "We eat a lot of chicken. It's one thing we both like. And, speaking of . . . I heard Jake say you made chicken and dumplings. I'd love to have your recipe, unless it's a family secret or something."

"*Nee*, no secret. I'm happy to give it to you."

They both turned when they heard footsteps. "Eva, I put Bonnie under the lean-to out back, along with my horse. It's pouring rain, which makes it doubtful most people will venture out. It's been slow for a Saturday anyway." Jake eyed the dozen or so boxes spread out on the floor. "Need some help?"

"You're the boss." Eva heard the curtness in her voice that was perhaps unwarranted. Jake had apologized, and that should be that.

He frowned. "I don't feel like it at the moment."

Eva and Yvonne exchanged glances and grinned. "We're talking about wedding plans, a subject all men just *love*." Yvonne batted her eyes at Jake, which didn't make Eva feel at all uncomfortable now that she knew Yvonne a little better. And it was obvious how much she loved her fiancé.

"Uh . . ." Jake pointed over his shoulder. "I actually just remembered some paperwork I should do up front. It looks like you have a system going anyway."

Yvonne chuckled. "Yeah, okay. I figured that would scare you off."

"I don't scare that easily." He rolled his eyes.

Eva wished she had some of Yvonne's confidence. The older woman had a playful personality, like Jake, so it was no wonder they'd connected as friends so easily. But Eva wasn't looking for friendship with Jake. She had that.

"Eva, I'm almost scared to ask, but are we still going to read together tonight?" Jake closed one eye, flinching a little.

"*Ya*, if you'd like to. The chicken and dumplings are in the refrigerator also. Which reminds me, we are almost out of propane."

"I'll get propane on Monday. And I'm quite sure I don't deserve the chicken and dumplings, but I'm glad to hear you didn't take them home." He smiled, and Eva thought he looked relieved. "Maybe we can just close up around three instead of five. It's supposed to rain like this until early evening.

"*Ya*, okay," she said.

Jake pointed over his shoulder, grinning. "So, I'll just be doing that paperwork and let you two get back to wedding talk."

Eva nodded and waited for Yvonne to make a comeback, but she kept her head down and focused on the list in front of her. She waited until Jake was gone before she lifted her head. "Why are you two reading the book aloud together?"

"Um, well . . ." Eva felt herself blushing. "Jake said he read about ten pages, but some of the words were difficult for him. We only go to school through the eighth grade, so . . ." Shrugging, she didn't finish.

"Don't be embarrassed." Yvonne shook her head. "I wasn't familiar with some of the words in what I read either. I had to look them up on my phone." Her shoulders slumped. "When I wasn't bawling my head off."

Eva wasn't sure what to say, but she was going to try to understand why the book had had such an effect on Yvonne. "You said the book confused you and made you question what you have always believed. Was it a specific part that upset you so much?"

Yvonne tapped the pen she was holding against her knee. "Well, I guess it was the man's testimonial—the author. He builds a pretty good case about why there is no afterlife, based on science, astronomy, and a bunch of other things I've researched. So I was with him on that. But then he started to break down all of those theories—and not based on scientific evidence, but strictly based on his own personal faith and how it changed throughout the course of his life. He gave explicit examples, and he wrote with such honesty and genuine belief that our soul goes on." She blinked her eyes a few times, and Eva could almost feel the unspoken pain in her expression. "It's like . . . I wanted to believe him, but I just can't. I don't think I ever will. So, for me, the book just upset me." She shrugged before she took a deep breath. "I think it's a lovely idea—that we all get to be together forever after we die—but I don't buy it."

Eva was out of her comfort zone, but she had to ask.

"Do you think you might have felt differently if you had read the entire book?"

Yvonne offered up a weak smile. "I guess we'll never know."

After a lengthy silence, Eva said, "Would you like to read it with me and Jake? Maybe we could help you to understand or feel better about it." She wasn't overjoyed about sharing her time with Jake, but this felt more important.

Yvonne grunted as she grinned. "Oh, no. I'm not getting in the way of that little basement read-along you two have planned. Besides, I don't think it would make a difference."

Eva chewed a fingernail. "I think I am about to step out of line, but have you ever read the Bible?"

"Of course." Yvonne didn't hesitate. "When I became an adult, I researched and questioned the way my aunt and uncle brought me up. And there were stories in the Bible that certainly challenged those beliefs. This book was different. It was a normal guy, in present-day times—Well, not exactly present-day. Maybe over a hundred years ago, but certainly more current than the Bible. And there was something about his writing that just stung when I read it."

There was a deep and curious longing in Yvonne's eyes that tugged at Eva's heart, saddened her that such a nice person didn't believe in anything beyond their short time on earth. She was thinking about what to say when Yvonne cleared her throat.

"So, I've got a few years of experience on you." She grinned, obviously veering from the subject at hand. "What is your plan this afternoon and this evening? Are you going to cozy up to Jake?"

Eva quickly put a finger to her lips, hoping Jake hadn't heard the comment from around the corner. She cast her eyes down at the inventory sheet she had in her lap, feeling a blush coming on. "*Ach*, I don't know," she said barely above a whisper.

Yvonne grimaced playfully. "Is this the same woman who said she might grab him and kiss him?" she asked in a quieter voice.

Eva covered her face with her hands and couldn't stifle the giggle that escaped. "I did say that, didn't I?"

"Yep." Yvonne grinned. "You might not have to be that overt, but you've got to get that handsome fellow to see you as the beautiful grown woman you are. And you might need to slip in something about John, somehow let Jake know that he's not the guy for you." She stretched out to her left until she could reach her purse draped over the back of a chair. She pulled out a small aerosol bottle, popped the top off, and handed the bottle to Yvonne. "Trevor loves this stuff."

Eva stared at the bottle, bit her bottom lip, then handed it back to Yvonne. "We aren't supposed to wear perfume."

Yvonne puckered her lips. "Hmm. Well, it's not exactly perfume. It's a body spray. Does that make a difference?" She wiggled it in her hand.

Eva was fairly sure the fragrance would be frowned upon, but she took it, sprayed a little in the air, then breathed in the lavender aroma. "*Ach,* this smells so *gut.*"

"I don't want to be a bad influence, so if you aren't comfortable—"

Eva spritzed her neck before she quickly handed it back to Yvonne. She shrugged. "I don't break the rules very often, so . . ."

"Well, okay, then." Yvonne stuffed the body spray back into her purse and started digging around. "I know makeup is out of the question, but I have some clear lip gloss that's shiny. It's supposed to make your lips look fuller. I'm not sure it does, but shiny lips are always a good look." After a few attempts digging around in her purse, she pulled out a small tube. "Only if you think it would be okay."

"I'm sure it keeps your lips moist. Like Chapstick, and that's allowed." Eva reached out her hand. After she'd applied it, she gave it back to Yvonne before she ran her tongue along her lower lip. "It tingles."

"Aw, and now you smell good and have full lips." Yvonne paused, smiling softly. "Although, you have such natural beauty, you really don't need anything to enhance that. We just want Jake to take notice of things maybe he hasn't before. Especially if you plan to plant a big kiss on him."

"I was joking." Eva shook her head. "That would be much too forward."

"You're probably right." Yvonne still had her legs crossed beneath her as she stretched her arms back and leaned on her hands. "I'm sure you have girlfriends that you confide in, but I'd love to take you to lunch tomorrow and hear all the details."

Eva lowered her head. "I-I really don't talk to *mei* friends about these types of things. And tomorrow is Sunday. We don't have worship service, but I usually spend that time with *mei* family."

Yvonne straightened. "And you absolutely don't have to tell me a single thing either." She rolled her eyes. "I'll be painfully curious, but I'll live. And we can still have lunch, but on Monday, if you'd like."

Eva nodded. She'd never had an English friend before, only acquaintances. Yvonne would be gone in a couple of days, but for now she was enjoying the woman's company and kindnesses—despite the way things had started out.

Yvonne lifted herself to her feet. "I'm going to go, but I'll come by around noon on Monday if that's a good time for lunch."

"*Ya*, that would be *gut*."

Yvonne draped her purse over her shoulder as she winked at her. "Good luck."

Eva smiled at her new friend. "*Danki*."

Yvonne ate a late lunch at the inn restaurant before going to her room to call Trevor. She'd made up her mind not to tell him about the book yet. As much as she wanted to discuss certain aspects of it, there was a part of her that wanted to forget she'd ever read it. She'd been comfortable with her beliefs her entire life and had had multiple conversations with

Trevor about everything. However, this was something she wanted to do in person. There would be discussion, and as much as she dreaded the conversation, she didn't want to keep things from him. She would shamefully tell him about taking the book without permission and how things went downhill after that. Then she'd tell him why the content upset her so much, and he would try to offer her an explanation that might make her feel better without trying to shift her beliefs. At least that's the direction she was hoping he would go. Trevor had accepted the fact that he couldn't change her mind about heaven and hell. Even though he'd given it his best try.

Her thoughts were so scrambled that there was a trickle of relief when she phoned him and the call went straight to voice mail. She'd worried she'd start babbling when she really did want to talk to him in person. She left a message for him to call her back and hung up, knowing she had one more call to make. One she dreaded. She hadn't called George since before she left home, and she was surprised he hadn't phoned her.

"Hi, George. Sorry I haven't called before now." She took a deep breath. George Meyers was an older man, mid-seventies, and he'd only recently insisted Yvonne call him by his first name. It still felt weird since he was generally a very formal person. "Mr. Lantz is refusing to sell the book. I'm not sure how much you are willing to pay." She'd decided to hold off telling him that she'd already offered more than he had approved.

There was silence on the other end of the line. Yvonne waited. There was rarely chitchat where George was concerned, but the man never acted hastily. "I'll go up to a hundred and twenty for the book."

Yvonne squeezed her eyes closed as her stomach roiled. "Um . . . I already offered him up to a hundred and thirty. If he had accepted, I would have, of course, called you immediately. My apologies for not getting that approved, but at the time I thought I could get him to commit." She paused, and when George didn't say anything, she went on. "He said he isn't selling for any amount."

A longer silence this time. "One fifty. Final offer."

Even though Yvonne's commission would get a big boost, she dreaded having to ask Jake to consider a higher offer. She sighed as quietly as she could. "All right. But George, can I ask you something?"

He waited in silence.

"What is it about this book that makes it so important?" He didn't answer for a few seconds. "I mean, is it the fact that only a hundred copies were printed? Or . . . another reason?"

"I collect rare books. It's a rare book." His voice sounded strained, almost irritated, at the question.

Yvonne chewed a fingernail as her pulse picked up. "Does it have anything to do with the content?" Whether or not he was becoming irritated, Yvonne wanted to know.

"No."

She wondered for the first time since she'd worked for

George if he was being honest. "Well, Mr. Lantz said he made a promise to his grandfather not to sell the book. That no amount would get him to sell."

"Ms. Wilson, do I need to handle this deal myself?" He hadn't called her by her last name in a long time. His voice was normally deep, but right now it was also forceful and laced with a mixture of disappointment and anger.

"I don't think it will matter. He isn't selling."

She thought about how much she needed this sale. George was her biggest client. Trevor would take care of her and had paid for most of the wedding, but Yvonne had insisted on paying for her wedding dress, which was still in layaway. She was also still paying on an emergency appendectomy she'd had two years ago. An event that had turned out okay, but not without complications. She had her own insurance policy, but she had a six-thousand-dollar deductible. Yvonne had hoped to have her medical bills paid off before the wedding.

Another big expense had been paying for her uncle's funeral. Yvonne had put the entire thing on her credit card when her aunt didn't have the money. Her aunt and uncle had raised her, and she didn't begrudge the cost. But it had seemed ironic at the time that her aunt wanted an expensive casket and full send-off when none of them believed he was being "sent" anywhere. In any case, another thing she was working to pay off before the wedding.

She was lost in thought when she realized George hadn't responded to what she'd just said. "Are you still there?"

"Is the book signed by the author?" George's voice sounded more leveled out but stern just the same.

"Yes, the dedication reads, 'To MAC with love.' Then the author's name is handwritten beneath it." Yvonne always checked to see if a book was autographed. Most that were worth any money tended to be signed. "It was also typed on a manual typewriter, although I can't tell if that is the original manuscript or if it was photocopied at some point."

"It's the original." George spoke with authority. "A lucky break that out of the hundred copies, you found the original."

It almost sounded like a compliment, but Yvonne was skeptical. "With all due respect, how do you know that?"

"Because it is signed."

Yvonne waited for further explanation, but George only sighed.

"I feel like I have done the best I can with Mr. Lantz. These people are Amish and live simple lives. The money doesn't seem important to him, but keeping his promise to his grandfather does." She paused. "But I will present your offer of a hundred fifty thousand to him." Her stomach twisted into knots. She could already see the look on Jake's face.

"Ms. Wilson, you have been successful at acquiring every book I've sought. I don't want this to be the exception." There was a long pause. "Are we clear?"

He had addressed her as Ms. Wilson again, and without

him saying so, it was clear their working relationship was on the line, and she didn't want to lose him as a client. "Yes, sir."

After they'd ended the call, Yvonne swallowed back the lump in her throat. *Of all the books in the world, why this one?* It was as if she'd stumbled into a pit of bad karma and was slowly sinking in it. She was sure Jake wouldn't sell, and she was ready to be done with that book.

She lay back on her bed and closed her eyes, deciding to focus on happier thoughts, like envisioning herself walking down the aisle toward Trevor, whose father would be giving her away. They were Christians—her fiancé's entire family. Yvonne didn't know if they were aware of her beliefs. She suspected not. They'd asked if she had a religious preference as to where the wedding should be held, and she'd said she didn't. Yvonne had attended services with Trevor a few times at the church he'd grown up in and the one his parents still attended. Yvonne's future mother-in-law lit up every time Yvonne and Trevor walked through the sanctuary doors. Yvonne wasn't close to Trevor's parents, mostly because they lived over an hour away. But they also tended to be a bit stuffy. Yvonne hoped they would get to know each other better after she and Trevor were married.

After she'd played out the entire scenario in her head—even selling her house—she thought again about how lucky she was.

Her thoughts shifted to Eva. She hoped her new and unexpected friend would make some headway with Jake. The guy was honorable if he was truly planning to step aside so John Yoder could date Eva. But her new friend had made it clear that Jake was the one she cared about. And it was obvious to Yvonne that Jake cared for Eva too. Even if it was awkward, Eva needed to let Jake know her feelings, that he was "the one" and she wasn't interested in dating John.

She smiled to herself as she recalled the dating phase with Trevor, the way they'd fallen in love quickly and deeply. There wasn't a better feeling in the world—the newness, the discovery, the passion.

She dozed off thinking about their wedding day. It would be perfect.

# CHAPTER 8

Jake sat at the small table in the back room, having lit two lanterns, his mouth watering as Eva heated up the chicken and dumplings. They'd decided to eat and then read the book at the table. Actually, Jake had decided. The basement would be cozier, but he wondered if it would be too intimate, or inappropriate, to be alone with Eva in that type of environment. He wanted to know what—if anything—was going on with her and John. More than once recently he'd thought about kissing Eva, but he had forced the thoughts away in consideration of John's feelings for her. He was well aware that Eva had blossomed into a beautiful young woman, and he probably should have more seriously considered and acknowledged his feelings for her. But until now, he hadn't been exactly sure what those feelings were. He'd fought so hard to keep romantically detached that friendship and romance were tangled up in a web of confusion, and he didn't feel right pursuing her under the circumstances.

"Jake, did you hear what I said?" Eva stood on the other side of the table, holding a bowl of chicken and dumplings.

"Uh, what?" His thoughts were still rolling around in his mind like tumbleweed in a storm, while outside rain noisily pelted the roof. "Sorry."

"I said you might want to add more pepper." She set the bowl in front of him, then walked back to the small counter and retrieved a loaf of bread, along with a tub of butter. She finally sat down across from him with her own bowl, and they bowed their heads in prayer.

Jake stared across the table at her and wondered again if she had been on a date that he was unaware of. He was confident she hadn't dated John—yet. But had she had any other suitors?

When she caught him ogling her, he hurriedly dunked his spoon in the bowl, blew on it, and savored the flavor. "This is great," he said, glancing at her.

"*Danki.*" She smiled, but it was fleeting.

He suspected he knew why. "Eva, I need to tell you again how sorry I am that I yelled at you about leaving the basement door open. I was just upset that the book was gone."

She locked eyes with him, her lips pressed tightly together as she held her spoon over the bowl. "Don't ever yell at me like that again."

"Never." Shame was a sin, but it had a hold on him just the same.

She kept her eyes on his. "You really hurt me. I made a mistake, and you should know me well enough to know that I felt terrible about it. If I didn't know better"—she took a deep breath—"I would think you were mad at me about something else besides just making a careless mistake." Her eyes now bored into his in search of the truth.

Jake gulped back his shame and had to admit she was right. Part of his outburst was anger about John. It was unwarranted, and now was his chance to tell her that he was jealous—another sin he'd need to pray about. But he'd vowed to himself to let things play out with John one way or the other.

"I was upset about the book. I promise to never yell at you again." He waited until she smiled a little and nodded before he took another bite of the soup. "So *gut*," he said through a mouthful.

She reached for a slice of bread, and after a few seconds, she said, "I really like Yvonne. I know she's really sorry about taking the book without asking. But . . ."

Jake waited, since the comment seemed to come out of nowhere. He felt badly about the way he had treated Yvonne, too, although his anger in that regard had felt more justified. He wondered where Eva was going with this shift in the conversation.

"Everything is *Gott*'s will, and everything happens on His time frame. But Yvonne doesn't believe in an afterlife. I think that by reading those first forty pages, it has her thinking, possibly considering otherwise. Maybe everything happened exactly as it should have." She tilted her head back a little as she peered at him. "Except for you yelling."

Jake lowered his head and twisted his mouth back and forth.

"But you're forgiven, and I'll try not to be careless again." Her cheeks dimpled, which always warmed Jake's heart. But there was something a little different today. He wanted to ask her why her lips were so shiny, but then she'd know he was looking at her mouth.

"She mentioned something to me about that too. About her beliefs." Jake paused, thinking back. "She didn't really elaborate. I tried to get her to open up a little, but she didn't. I don't know her well, so I didn't push. Anyway, I took her to the tree where everyone carves their initials—those who believe they saw a Sasquatch . . ." He wasn't sure if Eva knew what he was talking about.

"I've been there," Eva said as she buttered a slice of bread.

"She seems to believe in the Sasquatch more than believing in ghosts. That's what I got out of it."

"Yvonne was raised by her aunt and uncle, and they aren't Christians." Eva stopped moving, held the knife with butter on it, and her gaze drifted somewhere over Jake's shoulder. "It's sad. She's such a caring person. But I think that's why the book upset her so much. It challenged her beliefs and got her confused."

"Maybe that's *gut*. Maybe she will read the Bible and seek out answers."

Eva shrugged. "She said she'd already read it."

There was sadness in her voice, mirroring Jake's feelings. "Maybe we will understand more after we read a little of the book."

After they ate, Eva washed the dishes in the small sink and Jake dried. He envisioned himself and Eva in their own kitchen doing the same thing. Why, all of a sudden, were these images invading his mind?

*John Yoder.*

He breathed in an unfamiliar and pleasant aroma as he stood next to Eva. Something . . . lavender.

When they were done with the few dishes, Eva stashed the remainder of the chicken and dumplings back in the small refrigerator.

"Ready?" Jake rubbed his hands together, and after she nodded, he went to get the book from the basement. The door was locked, and he suspected it always would be now. After he came back up the steps and secured the door, he rounded the corner until he could see out the windows that spanned the front of the store. The rain had stopped, but two men—around Jake's age, it appeared—were casually hanging around in the parking lot. English fellows with no car in sight. Jake had already flipped the sign on the door to *Closed*, but he was tempted to step outside and ask if they needed help. There was something shifty about them, though, even though he tried not to judge.

They hadn't seen him, and he decided to ignore them. The front door was locked, so he took the book and shuffled to the back room, looking over his shoulder once to see that the men had slowly moved on and were heading toward the street.

"There were two *Englisch* men loitering around in the parking lot. I'm not sure if they're up to something or not," Jake said when he reached the back room, scratching his cheek.

"Uh-oh." Eva breezed by him, leaving a trace of lavender in her wake. Jake followed her, but she stopped short and didn't turn the corner, which caused Jake to lightly bump into her, his hands landing on her waist.

"Sorry," he said as he inched backward and dropped his arms.

She peeked her head around the corner, then slowly walked to the counter and peered out the window. "They were in here before. I recognize them, even from the back. They bought a small angel—one of the ones we get from Barrington's Wholesale that are normally sold as a group, but they only wanted one. The taller man asked to use the restroom. I felt very unsettled when they were in here. It was when you spent the day with Yvonne."

Jake still had the feel of Eva's waist beneath his hands. She was tinier than he would have thought. "Uh, what?" He sidled closer to her since he heard concern in her voice. "Why didn't you tell me about this?" He twisted to face her as he caught another whiff of lavender.

"I did. You were busy yelling at me." She scowled before turning her attention back to the two men. "I wonder why they were back and just hanging around?" Her eyes back on Jake, she twisted her hands in front of her, searching his eyes for reassurance that everything was all right.

Warning bells rang in Jake's head, but he didn't want to alarm Eva any more than she seemed to be. "We're all locked in tight. Nothing to worry about." Although one brick through the window would put an end to that semi-safe feeling he was trying to send in Eva's direction. "And they are almost out of sight."

Eva kept her eyes on the men.

"Ready to read the hundred-thousand-dollar book?" He nudged her slightly with his shoulder, something he'd playfully done for as long as he'd known her.

She swiveled to face him, her dimples in full form. "I believe that would be the hundred-and-thirty-thousand-dollar book at the last offering."

He shrugged, well aware what that much money could do. It wouldn't just cover the repairs needed to the store but also repairs needed on the farm, things he'd put off far too long because he wasn't home all that much. His lack of time had caused the repairs needed only to get worse.

"I wonder if we'll ever see Yvonne again once she leaves?" Eva fell into step with him as they walked to the back room. Before he could answer, she slowed at the basement door and touched his arm. "I know you said we could read up here to be closer to the coffee or if we wanted a snack, but I think I'd feel safer in the basement."

Jake swallowed hard. "Okay." He should have argued

otherwise since he didn't feel like they were in danger. But he didn't want Eva feeling uncomfortable. Now he would be the only one feeling awkward in such an intimate setting. As they continued walking, he snuck peeks at her, trying to decide if she was setting the scene for a romantic encounter. Or was his mind working overtime?

While she filled a thermos with coffee, Jake grabbed two cups and took the keys from his pocket. Together they went to the basement, Jake clinging to the cups as he shone the flashlight on the steps, the book tucked under his arm. Eva had the thermos and one finger hooked beneath his suspenders, similar to the way Yvonne had done in the woods. It felt different with Eva, and he was acutely aware of her touching him.

Jake placed the book on the desk, lit two lanterns, and pulled two chairs close together. After Eva had poured them each a cup of coffee, they sat side by side. Jake leaned forward and pulled a small chest closer to them to use as a makeshift coffee table. They both set down their coffee, and Eva gazed into Jake's eyes. His stomach flipped and roiled in a way it never had.

"Ready?" she asked as she nodded at the book.

He took it from the desk, put it in his lap, and slid it her way so it was across both their laps. Then he opened it up.

---

Eva cleared her throat. "'To MAC with love,'" she said softly as she gingerly ran her finger across the dedication. The author had signed his name on the same page. "Look how different the type looks from regular books." She pointed to the dedication. Glancing his way, she noticed his jaw tensed. He was nervous, although she wasn't sure why. Was he that curious about what could make this book worth so much money? Or did she make him nervous in this cozy setting? She'd caught him looking at her mouth more than once. Did he have any thoughts about kissing her?

"*Ya*. It was probably typed on something like that," he said as he picked up a flashlight from the desk beside him and shone it across the room. "*Mei grossdaadi* used to use that Remington typewriter. I remember him pounding away on it when I was a *kind* and even when I was older."

Eva had a thought and flipped back two pages to the copyright notice. "It's too old for him to have written it. It was published in 1875."

Jake shook his head. "*Nee*, I don't see *mei grossdaadi* writing a book. I think he used the typewriter mostly to send letters to friends and relatives. He thought his handwriting was terrible." Jake grinned. "And it was."

Eva turned the page, and there was a foreword. "Do you want me to read aloud first?"

He nodded. "*Ya*, sure."

She felt Jake's leg gently brush against hers as she took a breath and glanced his way. "Okay. Ready?"

Nodding again, he said, "*Ya*, ready."

Eva leaned her face closer to the book about the same

time Jake leaned forward to turn up the flame on the lantern. Then she read aloud.

Let me preface by saying I do not believe there is a replacement for the Holy Bible. Thus, if you are reading this book, you have possibly or notably slipped from your faith, given up on our Lord, or doubt His supreme existence. This book shall serve as purposeful in that regard. It is not a work of literature to debate the events in the world at this time, but only to mark my own experiences as a Christian man who was not always so. In a fact of reference, I shall only be relaying my experiences as seen through my own eyes in a nontheological attempt to bear witness and truths as I see them.

Take from it what you will, but there is no greater understanding than the relationship between God and His servants, the promise of what is to come, and the sacrifices expected of us to fulfill the commandments laid out before us. Scholars, the weak, those inflicted with disease and deformities, as well as the brave and the humble, will all walk equally side by side, with no weighty standing relevant to our stature within a community here on earth. We are as one, yet often divided by war, opulence, and our willful ability to self-torment as we go against the covenant set in place to protect and keep us.

Forthwith is my story.

Eva stared at the page before she turned to Jake, her face

so close to his they almost bumped noses. After straightening and putting a little distance between them, she pointed to the word *opulence*. "Do you know what that means?"

He shook his head, then carefully slid the book to his right until it was only in her lap. Standing and taking a couple of steps, he opened a drawer of the desk and returned with a dictionary.

"It means of great wealth or luxuriousness," he said after finding the word. Grinning, he said, "I was wondering if you knew what it meant."

She shook her head. "*Nee*, I didn't. And all of this sounds funny, different than the way the *Englisch* talk. I suppose because it was written so long ago." She paused, turned to face him, careful not to almost bump noses again before she looked back at the book and turned the page. "Look. No chapter headings. He calls them sections. Do you want to read Section One?"

"Uh, only if you don't want to." He rubbed his forehead. Eva wondered if he had a headache or just wasn't comfortable reading aloud.

"I'm fine to continue." She turned the page but kept her eyes on him until he nodded. Then she began.

## Section One

There is no heaven, a place where the soul rises and finds peace within the loving arms of an all-knowing God. It is a myth, a waste of a man's time to entertain such frivolous thoughts. We are born from the womb of our mothers following the planting of a life by the mate of our choice, and this seed of life grows into a human form. As our bodies weaken and deteriorate over time, we ultimately lose the ability to sustain life. We are buried or burned, in accordance with our beliefs and wishes, and we are ultimately given to the earth as a form of rejuvenation for future generations.

The existence of hell, a place where demons roam and destruct in a pit of fire and misery run by a fallen angel commonly referred to as Satan is also a falsehood put in the minds of those gullible enough to believe in such foolishness.

Such are the ways that I believed. Until I no longer did.

Walk with me on my soul journey, whereas I will prove to you that not only are heaven and hell real, but they are closer in proximity than the average man might choose to believe. We are caught in a realm of choices that establish our final resting place outside of our body when it can no longer function as a physical being.

Where are you going? Heaven or hell? You have a choice, and it would behoove you to choose wisely.

Eva snuck a glance at Jake, his expression as strained as the knot that twisted in her stomach.

"I'm not sure we should be reading this." Eva cast her eyes down on the yellowed pages. "I don't think the bishop would approve."

"We can stop," Jake said without looking up. "But it sounds like the author has a testimony and that it turns him into a believer."

"I hope so." She sighed as she turned the page titled *Section Two*.

Jake slid the book slightly his direction. "Here. I'll read this next part, and then we can decide if we want to go on."

Eva nodded before Jake turned the page and began to read aloud, running his hand along each line of print.

> At a time when civil unrest is barely behind us and still haunts our memories, death is still on the mind of many a man. Mortality is never far from our thoughts as disease and poverty strike those who cannot fight either destructive force. Such be it with my father and mother, both of whom succumbed to cholera within the eleventh hour of each other. It was at this time I entered hell, a place of my own making, not really believing it existed, except in the dark recesses of my mind, tormented by my grief to a point that sharp talons ripped at me until I bled from the inside out.

Eva lay a hand on top of Jake's, halting him, as her heart thumped against her chest. "I-I can see why this book upset Yvonne, since both of her parents died."

Jake slipped his hand from underneath Eva's. She hadn't even consciously put it there, but she was acutely aware when he made a point to sever contact.

"But it sounds like the author is going to try to convince the reader that his beliefs changed," he said again as he locked eyes with her.

"Apparently he didn't change Yvonne's mind." Eva lowered her eyes to her lap. The evening wasn't playing out the way she'd hoped. They were cozy, but Jake kept a level of distance between them. And Eva feared the book would upset her.

"Maybe she didn't give it a chance. It sounds like she quit reading it after forty pages, and maybe that wasn't enough."

Eva opened her mouth to say something, but a noise upstairs startled her. "Was that breaking glass?" she asked in a whisper, too afraid to move.

Jake was up instantly, flashlight in hand, as he tiptoed up the stairs and quickly lowered a narrow board that slid down and clicked into place, locking them in. He scurried back down the stairs, his finger to his lips. Then he extinguished the lanterns and pulled her to him—one arm around her back and the other around the other side cupping the back of her neck. She knew better than to say a word, especially when she heard male voices coming from upstairs.

# CHAPTER 9

Yvonne lay back on the bed with her phone on speaker and wiggled her freshly painted toenails. "Yes, I did my own toenails," she said to Trevor. "And I'm even going to do my own fingernails."

"Well, look how well you are adapting to the Amish way of life."

Yvonne laughed. "The Amish don't do their fingernails or toenails, at a salon or otherwise. And I suspect that if it were allowed, they'd all have to paint their nails the same color, and what's the fun in that?"

She was happy to keep the conversation light, keeping to her plan that she would discuss the book with Trevor in person.

"Well, I've almost wrapped up my business, and things are going really well. So well, I'll wait and tell you all about it when I get home, which will be Monday midday."

"Oh, that's great. I can try to get a flight out tomorrow afternoon. Oh, wait, I promised Eva I would have lunch with her on Monday. I gave her a little coaching on how to snag the Amish guy she's interested in, which happens to be the same guy who won't sell me the book. I'd like to hear how it went and then say goodbye to both of them."

"Sounds like you made some new friends, so it wasn't a totally wasted trip."

"Well, the beginning of a friendship, I guess. I haven't been here long. Even though Jake Lantz might be ruining my career by not selling the book." She paused, tapped a finger to her chin. "Although, I gotta tell you, I'm quite the buggy driver. You'd be impressed."

"Maybe we can take a trip there the first of the year. We've got Hawaii coming up as our honeymoon."

She closed her eyes as visions of margaritas by the pool danced in her head. Then she was assaulted by an unpleasant thought. She leaned up on her elbows and scowled. "I talked to George."

"Hmm . . . How did that go?"

"Not good." Yvonne sighed. "You know, I have found him every book he's asked me to track down and managed to close the deal. But he almost acted like I was going to lose him as a client if I couldn't secure this sale." She recalled the harsh tone George had used while they were on the phone. "It's uncharacteristic for him to be like that."

"The book must be really important to him."

"Apparently." She recalled those first forty pages and

shivered. She'd felt violated. By a book. It was silly, but it was as if the author had wormed his way into her most private thoughts and tried to infuse his own, which left her with a mushy place in her mind. "George approved more money, but I already know Jake won't sell. So I might be in a jam soon unless more offers from prior clients pop up. Although none of them pay as much as George."

"I told you that you don't need that job. After we're married, I'm putting you on all my accounts, and you can still do whatever you want. We can take care of it when we get home. We don't have to wait until after we're married. You can just sign a new signature card when you become Mrs. Trevor Adams."

Her independence might need to take a short hike if she lost George's business. She had bills to pay. "You are overly generous, Mr. Adams, but you know I would like to take care of my own debts if at all possible."

"I know that, and I respect that. But I don't want you worrying about anything. We can talk about it when I get home."

*Among other things*. "Okay. I'll eat lunch with Eva, tell her and Jake bye on Monday, then drive to Indianapolis to catch a flight, assuming I can get a flight. I'll work on that when we hang up."

"Do your best because I miss you terribly, beautiful."

"I miss you, and I love you with all my heart."

"I love you, too, Mrs. Adams."

Yvonne pressed End and kept her word. She hopped on

her iPad and was able to get a flight back to Houston at four on Monday. All she needed was the security code on the back of her credit card since her other information had autosaved. She reached for her purse, which was bulging and filled with too much stuff, things she carried when traveling. After she rummaged through loose receipts, she tossed a small tote bag filled with a portable battery and extra charging cords on the bed. She dug her hand inside all the way to the bottom.

Her heart flipped in her chest until she recalled the rummaging she'd done to find the lavender spray and lip gloss for Eva. Her wallet had to be in the back room at the bookstore. As much as she hated to interrupt Eva and Jake's reading session, she needed her credit card. The airlines only showed three seats for the flight home on Monday.

It wasn't quite dark yet, so she carefully slipped her freshly painted toenails into a pair of flip-flops, even though it was probably too chilly for sandals. She'd be in and out of the store in a flash unless her wallet had fallen out in the rental car. She grabbed her purse and room key, then headed out. *Please be in the car so I don't have to interrupt Eva and Jake.*

Jake released his hold on Eva when she groaned a little. He didn't realize he was holding her so tightly as he strained to hear what was going on upstairs. The musty smell of the basement hung in the air amid the total darkness.

"They know we're here," Eva whispered as she stayed in his arms. "The horses are tethered outside with our buggies."

"The horses are under the lean-to out back, so maybe they didn't notice them. Either way, that's a big bar across the door. I don't think they can push it open." Jake wondered if they had guns. "What could they want from *mei* small bookstore?"

"Money. Is it still in the cash register?"

Jake sighed. Most folks paid with credit cards today. "*Ya*, it is. Not much. Maybe a couple hundred dollars."

"Maybe they'll just take the cash and be on their way," she said in a trembling whisper.

Jake eased his left arm from around her but kept his right arm draped over her shoulders, his hand cupping her arm. "We're going to be all right." He spoke with as much conviction as he could muster. It wasn't their way to be violent. They'd been taught passiveness their entire lives. But as he pulled Eva closer, Jake wasn't sure he could abide by those teachings if anyone tried to hurt her.

He squeezed her arm and held his breath when someone wiggled the doorknob to the basement, then began pushing against the door. Eva covered her face with her hands. "*Ach, nee*," she whispered before she buried her face against his shirt.

Jake sat perfectly still as he held tightly to Eva, once again cupping her neck with his free hand. "Don't make a sound," he whispered, but they both jumped when the doorknob jiggled again.

"We know you're down there," one of the men said. "And if you stay down there, maybe no one will get hurt."

Jake's shirt was wet from Eva's tears as his pulse picked up. He'd never been in a position like this, and he was more scared than he wanted to admit, but as time ticked slowly by, he was sure he would fight to keep Eva safe, right or wrong.

He clicked the flashlight on and shone it on the wood floor. "Take this, keep it pointed down, and tiptoe to that corner." He pointed. "And hide behind those boxes."

She shook her head and pressed her trembling body closer to his.

"Eva, please." They both jumped again when one of the men pounded on the door. "Just go. And turn the flashlight off when you get there."

She finally did as he asked. Jake felt around the desk for the other flashlight he knew was there. He gripped it with clammy hands and held his breath as he kept it turned off. Heavy footsteps pounded against the wood floors for another couple of minutes, then all was quiet. Jake wasn't sure how long to stay down there. How would he know when the men were gone?

After another long ten minutes, he could barely hear Eva crying, mostly sniffling. "Eva," he whispered.

The flashlight clicked on as she shone it toward the floor. Even in the darkness he could see her tear-streaked cheeks. He put a finger to his lips and motioned for her to join him. She kept the light pointed toward the floor as she shuffled back his way, then sat shoulder to shoulder with him in silence.

After another few minutes, he said, "I think they're gone." He clicked his flashlight on and laid it in his lap before he twisted to face her and gently held her cheeks in his hands. "You're okay." With his thumbs, he cleared the tears from her face and instinctively leaned in to kiss her on the mouth, but at that last second, he pressed his mouth to her cheek. She was trembling. "You're okay," he said again, and she nodded.

"I should go see if they're gone." He started to lift himself from the chair, but she latched onto the sleeve of his blue shirt.

"*Nee*. Don't go up there." Her voice shook as her eyes, barely visible in the dim light of the flashlight, begged him not to leave her.

"We'll wait a few more minutes."

They sat in silence, side by side, not moving or talking. Then Eva actually squealed when someone pounded on the basement door. Jake froze. If the intruders weren't sure they were down there before, they were now.

"Jake! Eva! Are you down there?"

"It's Yvonne." Jake clicked on the flashlight, bolted from the chair, and took the basement stairs two at a time, tripping once before he reached the top and lifted the arm that kept anyone from entering.

He bumped shoulders with Yvonne as he rushed past her and toward the front of the store. He stared at the broken glass for a few seconds, then eyed the opened drawer of the cash register, which was empty.

After he checked the rest of the store, he met Yvonne and Eva, who had come upstairs, just outside the entrance to the basement.

"I called the police." Yvonne put a hand to her chest. "I totally freaked out when I saw that the glass in the window was broken. I knew right away that someone must have broken in when I saw the cash-register drawer open."

In the distance, Jake heard sirens. "What are you doing here?" he asked her, his heart still pounding against his chest as Eva stood nearby, sniffling.

"As much as I hated to bother you two, I think I left my wallet here somewhere." She turned to Eva. "Remember, when we were sitting on the floor and I was digging around in my purse? I think I must have taken out my wallet, and it didn't make it back into my purse. And there were all those boxes around us . . ."

Jake headed toward the back, and after he'd moved a few boxes around, he said, "I don't see it."

"Great," she said. "There wasn't much cash, but my credit cards were in there." She groaned as she slammed her hand to her forehead. "And it's going to be hard to get on a plane without my driver's license."

"Police!"

Jake did an about-face and rushed to the front of the store, glad to see a familiar face.

"I heard the call come in, so I took it." Abraham Byler

had left the Amish faith to become a police officer when he was nineteen. He hadn't been baptized yet, so he wasn't shunned by the community. He tended to respond to anything criminal in their area. "You all okay?"

Eva and Yvonne had joined them up front.

"*Ya,* Eva and I were in the basement, and I had the door bolted." Jake took a deep breath as his pulse started to return to normal.

Abraham raised an eyebrow.

"We were reading a book," Eva interjected. "We had both seen the men loitering around outside. I saw them a couple of days ago. Jake saw them today. We thought we'd feel safer in the basement."

"Looks like you were right." Abraham had pulled out a small pad from his pocket like he was going to take notes, but his eyes were on Yvonne. "Did you make the 911 call?"

"Yes. I saw the broken glass." Her bottom lip trembled. "I knew Jake and Eva were here reading, and I was scared to death for them."

Abraham took a pen from his pocket, but he still hadn't written anything down. He couldn't seem to take his eyes from Yvonne.

"The horses! I've got to go check on them." It wasn't even dark yet, so Jake didn't argue when Eva scurried toward the front door, but he was glad when Yvonne followed her, just to be safe.

"Who's the *Englisch* woman?" Abraham had held on to some of the Pennsylvania Dutch he'd grown up with.

"Her name is Yvonne. She's in town on business, and she and Eva have become friends." Jake didn't feel the need to say what kind of business Yvonne was here for. He silently thanked God that he'd had the book with him in the basement. Although he doubted the crooks would have known its value.

"The horses are fine." Eva was winded as she walked back into the store, frowning as she eyed the broken glass. "I gave them some extra water, but their pails were mostly full from the heavy rain earlier."

Abraham—or Officer Byler as he was officially known—nodded at the register. "Anything gone besides money?"

"I haven't checked, but there's not really much to steal." Jake shrugged, but Eva was already going around the corner, so he followed. Yvonne hung back and told Abraham that her wallet was missing.

"I can't tell for sure if any of the gift items are missing. I'd have to check everything against the inventory, but at first glance, I don't see anything, do you?" Eva's eyes scanned each shelf, before she moved to the next aisle.

"I don't see anything missing." He took off his straw hat and ran a hand through his hair, then locked eyes with Eva when she was back in front of him. "Are you okay?"

She didn't hesitate to throw her arms around him and bury her face against his chest. "*Ya*, but I was so scared."

Jake thought about how close he'd come to kissing her on the mouth. But now that they were out of harm's way, he gently eased her away. "I wouldn't have let anything happen to you."

"I know." She smiled meekly but also spoke the words rather dreamily.

In those moments when he'd feared for their lives, he hadn't given much thought to his body language during the ordeal. He only knew that he would probably have broken the rules to save Eva if it had come to that.

Abraham was questioning Yvonne when they returned to the front of the store.

"So, you didn't see a car when you pulled up?" he asked.

Yvonne shook her head. "Nope. And I didn't see anyone. They must have fled on foot."

"We don't have much crime around here." Abraham wrote on his small pad before glancing at Yvonne. "The occasional domestic situation, car accident . . . things like that. I'm guessing whoever did this were drifters." He glanced back and forth between Eva and Jake. "Did either of you see the men?"

"I-I think I know who might have done it, but I can't be sure." Eva described the two men who had come into the store.

"Jake, you got any plywood that we can put over this broken glass until you can get someone out here to replace the pane?" Abraham stashed his small pad and pen back in his pocket.

"*Nee*, not here. I'll have to go home and find something."

He glanced at Eva then Yvonne. "Could you maybe follow Eva home, just to make sure she gets home safely?"

"Of course." Yvonne tucked her hair behind her ears. "Officer Byler, do you need me for anything else?"

Abraham had stared at Yvonne a lot, but he shook his head. "*Nee,* but be sure to get your credit cards canceled."

"Ugh." Yvonne stuffed her hands into the pockets of her blue jeans. "I've also got to find an alternate means of identification so I can get on a plane Monday." She winked at Eva. "My man is coming home Monday, so I shall be"—turning to Jake, she grinned—" out of your hair. But Jake, can I talk to you privately for a minute?"

"I'm done here." Abraham tipped his hat, mostly at Yvonne, before he walked out. Jake thought Abraham might have asked her for coffee or something if Yvonne hadn't made the comment about her fiancé coming home. Officer Byler had been eyeing her ever since he saw her.

"I can wait outside," Eva said after Abraham had left.

Yvonne shook her head. "No, it's okay. I just didn't want to say anything in front of him." She nodded to Abraham, who was getting into his patrol car. Then she cringed before she looked at Jake. "As much as I hate to bring this up, I talked to my client last night, and he is willing to go a hundred fifty thousand for the book. I told him you wouldn't sell, but I'm obligated to mention it."

Jake stared at the broken glass, and again he thought about what that kind of money could do. He just offered up a weak smile.

"Yeah, I didn't think so." She lowered her eyes for a few moments before she met eyes with Eva. "What did you think about the book?"

"We didn't get to read much of it, but I can see why it upset you." She paused. "The author also lost both of his parents."

"Well, yeah, that was a jab in the heart from the beginning, but it's his story that . . ." Shrugging, she looked away. "I don't know. Confusing."

Jake cleared his throat. "You two should get on the road before it gets dark. *Danki* for following Eva home, Yvonne."

"No problem. I'm sorry this happened. I hope you didn't lose too much in the register." She nodded to the open drawer, and Jake shook his head. "I guess I'll go back to my room and start canceling credit cards. And Google alternate forms of ID so I can get on a flight back home on Monday. Eva, if I can't get a flight out Monday afternoon, I might have to bail on our lunch and leave Monday morning."

"You do whatever you need to do." Eva smiled before she went to Jake and hugged him, kissing him on the cheek. "*Danki* for not letting anything happen to me."

Jake forced a smile, but the feel of Eva so close to him brought forth more feelings he didn't know he had. In the face of danger, he'd reacted spontaneously. Right now, he was sure he was blushing. He wasn't sure what to do with these new feelings cropping up in all directions. He supposed he had to take a wait-and-see attitude and give John a chance. It had a been a long and stressful day. Right now, he just needed sleep.

# CHAPTER 10

Eva arrived at work Monday morning with all of Jake's favorites—cinnamon rolls with extra icing, fried apple pies, and two slices of shoofly pie. He was sitting behind the counter when she arrived.

"The window looks *gut*. I'm glad you were able to get it repaired so quickly." She stopped in front of Jake, set the basket down, then detailed the contents.

"It smells great." Jake half smiled as he glanced up at her briefly before returning to *The Budget*.

"Anything interesting?" Eva always tried to skim the pages of the weekly newspaper to see if anyone in their community had published a wedding or birth announcement, and it was nice to keep up with events going on in other Amish communities too.

"*Nee*, not really. I see that a cousin in Ohio is expecting her first child, but that's about it. *Ach*, and the weather is going to warm up next week."

Eva picked up the basket. "I think it's warm enough." She grinned, waited a moment for Jake to look up. When he didn't, she said, "I guess I'll take these to the back, then finish working on the inventory unless you need me to do something else."

"*Nee*, I'll cover the front for a while." Jake kept his head down.

Something felt amiss. "*Danki* again for the way you handled things Saturday."

"I didn't really do anything except hide." Frowning, he turned the page of the newspaper.

"You kept me safe." She smiled broader, but when he didn't look up or say anything, she walked to the back with the spring in her step falling flat. She could still recall Jake's arms around her, the way he had cupped the back of her head and held her to him. Even though the circumstances were undesirable, she had hoped maybe that little bit of physical contact would have helped him to feel her attraction to him.

Jake had always been playful around her. Now he seemed aloof. Or was she imagining it? Maybe Yvonne could help her sort things out at lunch. Hopefully, Yvonne had gotten her credit card situation and flight handled to leave in the afternoon. If she hadn't and had to leave this morning, Eva was sure Yvonne wouldn't go without saying goodbye. She felt badly that her new friend would be going home without making the purchase she had longed for. But in Jake's defense, he had told her before she arrived that he wouldn't sell the book. Eva wondered if she and Yvonne would write and keep in touch. They really didn't have anything in common.

Eva sat down on the floor near the boxes and inventory sheets. As she began making notes, she speculated on whether she and Jake would read any more of the book this evening. He hadn't brought it up, and neither had she. There was leftover chicken and dumplings. Perhaps she could lure him in with that.

*I shouldn't have to lure him in.*

She was also concerned if the book was going to upset her. She wondered if the author would truly find redemption, which he seemed to imply from the beginning. But the language and presentation were harsh. Maybe she would ask Yvonne what to expect in the pages to follow. She'd see how it went. Yvonne had reacted so badly to the book, she didn't want to unnecessarily upset her.

When she finished the inventory, she pushed the boxes up against the wall. Jake would carry each one to the aisle where it belonged, and then Eva would unpack and shelf each book.

She walked to the front of the store. "Want me to take over?" She nodded outside where a vanload of women tourists were piling out. "They'll be buyers."

"*Ya*, sure." He walked past her without looking in her direction. Later she'd ask him if they were going to read.

Or ask him what was wrong. She was pretty sure she knew. He'd let down his guard, allowed himself to get a little more physical with her at a time when they were both afraid. Now he was trying to reestablish that they were only friends. Several times lately she'd caught him looking at her as if he'd like for them to be more, but perhaps she had misread his expressions. Short of throwing herself at him, she wasn't sure what to do. She'd made it apparent that she enjoyed spending time with him.

Eva had been right about the ladies who had climbed out of the van. They spent several hundred dollars between them, and Yvonne showed up not long after Eva had tended to the last customer.

"Perfect timing," she said as she smiled at Yvonne then glanced at the clock on the wall.

"I know it's early for lunch. But I have a four o'clock flight, so I'll need to leave for the airport around twelve thirty. Can you go in a few minutes? By the time we get there, it will be close to eleven, when most places open."

"I'm sure that will be fine." She stood from her stool behind the counter. "Did you get your credit cards taken care of?"

"Yeah, which was a total pain. Trevor had to give me his credit card number over the phone so I could book my flight." She sighed. "I'll have to go through an extra security drill at the airport since I don't have my driver's license, but when I called, they said any form of ID would be helpful." Chuckling, she said, "My expired Costco card was stuffed in a side pocket of my purse, along with an old press pass from when I worked for a newspaper for a few months. The airlines said that should do the trick in addition to the extra pat downs and luggage search. Ugh. Not to mention, I'm driving around without a driver's license." She glanced at the clock on the wall behind the counter again. "But Trevor is already in the air, so he'll be home by the time I get there." She smiled. "I've really enjoyed my time here. It would have been better if Jake had wanted to sell the book, but . . ." Shrugging, she continued to smile. "It's been great getting to know both of you."

"Let me tell Jake we're leaving." Eva walked around the corner and found Jake sitting at the small table eating a cinnamon roll.

"Yvonne needs for us to have an early lunch so she can drive to the airport and catch her plane on time. Is that okay with you?" She waited for him to look at her.

"*Ya*, that's fine." He took another bite of the cinnamon roll without lifting his eyes to hers.

"Um . . . there are chicken and dumplings left over in the refrigerator if you're hungry, or I can bring you back something and we can save those for supper again before we read."

His face clouded with an emotion Eva couldn't quite read, but she could tell what he was about to say before he even began. "I-I need to get home tonight. And maybe we should wait awhile, until this is behind us, before we stay late to read again."

She wanted to tell him that it hadn't been late when the burglary took place. It was still daylight. She also wanted to tell him that the two men were probably long gone. But the undertones of his meaning were clear. He didn't want to spend any extra time with her.

"Well, feel free to eat the chicken and dumplings. Or I don't mind bringing you back something for lunch?" she asked again.

"*Nee*, but *danki*. I can fill up on these pastries." Even her chicken and dumplings were getting shunned.

He finally lifted his eyes to hers. "Have fun with Yvonne."

Eva tried to smile but could only manage a nod.

Yvonne listened as Eva detailed the events of the night before. "You must have been terrified," she said after they'd each filled a plate from the buffet. Normally, Yvonne wasn't thrilled about buffets, but the one where she had stayed at Gasthof Village had been great. The food at Stoll's Lakeview Restaurant, where they were dining now, was also good. Best part, the view of the lake, and she and Eva had chosen a table that overlooked the water.

"*Ya*, I was scared. But Jake kept his arms wrapped around me almost the entire time, constantly comforting me." Eva barely smiled as she mostly moved food around on her plate instead of eating it.

"Um, I would think that felt good, to have him show his concern in a physical way." Yvonne took a bite from her second slice of bread. She was going to need to seriously diet to fit into her dress.

"I-I know he was just reacting to the situation, but *ya*, it did feel *gut*. But now"—she began to blush—"he's standoffish, even more so than before."

"Maybe he's more shaken about what happened than he is letting on. Maybe just give him some time." Yvonne took a sip of iced tea.

"I don't know how much more time I can give him. I've been courted by several men in our district, and I've said no to all of them, hoping Jake would step forward. But he hasn't."

"Did you mention to him that you weren't interested in dating that guy that came into the bookstore? John Yoder?"

"I don't feel like I should have to tell him that unless he asks. If he wanted to know if John asked me out—cared enough to know—he could have questioned me about it after he saw John in the store." She paused, sighing. "John pinned a note to the fence post yesterday, asking me out." Shaking her head, she added, "I haven't answered him yet. But maybe I should consider it." She groaned under her breath. "I'll be twenty in a couple of months."

Yvonne thought for a few moments. "Like I told you before, twenty isn't that old. It may seem old to you because I know young marriages are more acceptable here, but for what it's worth . . . I'm glad I waited. And if John Yoder hasn't captured your heart the way Jake has, you'd be wasting both your time. There is no grander feeling than falling in love. I thought I had been in love before, but it wasn't the real thing, the way it is with Trevor. Sometimes I get nervous about spending my life with the same person, and wonder if people hold on to that kind of love, but I've been pushing away any fear. I just don't have room for it in my life, and I choose to believe in me and Trevor, forever."

Eva got that dreamy, faraway look in her eyes that Yvonne had come to recognize. "I just know you are going to look beautiful in your wedding dress. We don't have fancy dresses like that when we get married. They're actually the same kind of dresses we always wear, but the garment is new and finely pressed." More dreaminess as she batted her eyes. "I'm sure your wedding will be heavenly." Her eyes widened as her cheeks flushed.

"It's okay to say 'heaven' or 'heavenly,' Eva." She stared at her across the table. "You really believe, don't you? I mean, that if we live a good life, that we'll all meet up again?" She scratched her neck, sighing.

"*Ya*, I believe it with all of my heart. All you have to do is believe that Jesus is the Son of *Gott*, that he died on the cross for us, then also do your best to live a *gut* life here on earth." After a long pause, she said, "I'm not sure if Jake wants to read any more of the book. I think he's nervous about spending time with me. I'm not sure I want to read any more of the book, for different reasons, because the author's tone is so harsh. I'm also not sure the bishop would approve of us reading it." She set down her fork. "You made it through forty pages? Does the author's storytelling soften any?"

Yvonne took a deep breath. "I guess you could say the overall tone changes. The author has a bit of an epiphany."

Eva raised both eyebrows as she tipped her head to one side.

"*Epiphany.* It's like a big discovery or a realization that something is true." Yvonne shivered. "He actually claims to have seen Jesus with his own eyes. He was so convincing that . . ." She shook her head.

"That you were tempted to believe?" Eva's cheeks dimpled a little.

"I don't know if 'tempted to believe' is the right phrase, but he was slowly peeling away layers of emotion I didn't even know were there. And everything became confusing, and it upset me."

"I still think maybe you should read the entire book." Eva looked so hopeful that Yvonne almost agreed but then remembered something important.

"Uh, your boss is never letting go of that book, even for me to borrow." She pointed her fork at Eva. "And I think that is probably for the best."

Eva lowered her eyes. Her friend clearly didn't agree, but Yvonne wanted them to part on a happy note. "Did I tell you that my bridesmaids are all wearing turquoise dresses? Trevor's sister is my maid of honor, and three friends from college are my bridesmaids. I'm not really close to any of them, which is sad to say, but I was in my three friends' weddings, so it seemed I should ask them to be in mine. And Trevor's sister is super sensitive. I think her feelings would have been hurt if I hadn't asked her to be my maid of honor." She sighed. "I guess I'm kind of like you as far as not sharing personal details about my relationship with other girlfriends. I thought it was an age thing, that I'd gotten too old for that." She smiled at Eva. "But you seem to have discovered early that such details can be cherished and not necessarily shared with the world. Having said that, it's been fun talking with you about our men, weddings, and how to get Jake to warm up to you. You're going to have to write to me and let me know how it goes."

Eva nodded. "I will. And I'll be daydreaming about the glorious wedding you'll be having."

Yvonne smiled. "You know, you don't have to daydream about it. Why don't you just come?" She winked at Eva. "You and Jake. I'm going to mail you an invitation when I get home."

Eva actually gasped. "You mean travel all that way to see you get married?"

"Is that allowed?" Yvonne chuckled.

"We would probably have to take a bus or hire someone to drive us. Plane rides are reserved for funerals or other emergencies. Is it a long drive?" Eva's face glowed. "How wonderful that would be." She paused and then scowled. "Although I don't have any idea where things will stand with me and Jake."

"It's a long drive, but by the time I get married, I'm going to guess you and Jake will be well on your way to being a couple, if not already committed to each other. It would be a fun trip for you, and I'd love for you both to be there."

"I hope you're right about Jake. And I've never been to Texas or an *Englisch* wedding."

Yvonne dabbed her mouth with her napkin. "I hate to cut our conversation short, but if you're through eating, I probably need to get you back to the bookstore so I can get on the road to the airport. And I'll want to tell Jake bye too. Even though he ruined my career." She rolled her eyes. "I honestly think I might lose my biggest client for my failure to get him to sell the book."

Eva brought a hand to her chest. "*Nee*, that's not right. Please tell me you're teasing."

"No, I'm actually not. But don't look so mortified. Trevor will take care of me. Don't get me wrong, I like to take care of myself financially, but if I lose my client, I won't starve. Trevor won't let that happen."

"It still seems unfair."

Yvonne shrugged before she stood and laid her napkin on her plate. Then she burst out laughing. "Not only am I driving illegally, I don't have any money to pay the bill. No cash or credit cards. Wow. I have a checkbook. Do you think they'll take an out-of-state check?"

"Let me pay for this." Eva smiled. "I had already planned to anyway."

"*Danki*," Yvonne said as she walked alongside Eva, nudging her slightly. "See, I've learned a little while I've been here. And Trevor said we might even come back and visit."

"I'll be hoping so. And I'll be hoping to see you get married too."

"I can't wait." Yvonne stood nearby while Eva paid for lunch, then thanked her before they walked to Yvonne's rental.

She seriously doubted Eva would make an attempt to attend her wedding. It would be a long trip to see a woman she didn't know very well get married. But it was strange how life worked out. She'd come here to make the sale of a lifetime and failed, but somewhere along the line she'd made a new friend, possibly two if Jake considered her a friend at this point. A part of her wished she could stay to learn more about this culture she knew very little about, but she missed Trevor.

By the time they got back to the bookstore, it was twelve fifteen, and Yvonne was going to need to say quick goodbyes so she could get on the road to the airport. She hated goodbyes, but she felt like she'd see Eva and Jake again. If not at her wedding, then maybe she and Trevor really would come for a visit. Trevor would like the peacefulness of the community. It was a far cry from his beloved New York, but he had mentioned often how he also enjoyed quiet downtime. The bungalow he'd rented for their honeymoon in Maui was off the beaten path—peaceful, he had said.

When Yvonne and Eva walked into the store, Jake was sitting behind the counter, his head buried in a newspaper, but he looked up right away and smiled. "How was lunch?"

"*Gut.*" Eva folded her hands in front of her. "Yvonne has to hurry, though, if she's going to catch her plane home."

Jake stood and rounded the corner. Yvonne extended her hand. "Can I just say that I've had a lovely time, even though my electricity will probably get turned off since I didn't close this deal." She shrugged. "But who needs electricity, right? You guys seem to do just fine."

The poor guy's expression fell so fast as he shook Yvonne's hand, she regretted teasing him right away. "Lighten up, Jake. I'm kidding. I would have loved to have bought the book for my client, but"—she glanced at Eva and smiled—"I feel like I've made a new friend." She raised an eyebrow at Jake. "Maybe two?"

"Two." He dropped his arm to his side. "Wishing you safe travels back to Texas."

"*Danki.*" Yvonne giggled. "Okay, so it's probably the only word I'll ever use, but maybe Trevor will be impressed when he hears it."

She hugged Eva. "Write to me." As she pulled back, she felt her phone buzzing in her purse. She eased away and dug around. "I'd better get this in case it's Trevor. He worries."

Finally, she found her phone. "Oh, it's Trevor's father. This will be something about the wedding," she said when she saw his name pop up on the screen. "I'll say goodbye to you guys, for now!" She blew a kiss toward Eva and Jake, then waved and went out the door.

"Hi, Fred. What's up?" Her father-in-law-to-be was less formal than Trevor's mother. She might not have addressed his mother as casually. "Is everything okay?"

There was an eerie silence before he spoke. "There has been an accident, and . . ."

Yvonne stopped walking as she felt herself going icy cold inside. Her heart pounded.

"It's Trevor," Fred said in a shaky voice, no mistaking his anguish. "He's gone."

*Gone?* Yvonne tried to keep her knees from buckling. "What does that mean, '*gone*'?"

"Yvonne, our son has died."

Fred was crying hard now, but in between his sobs, Yvonne heard his garbled words echoing in her mind like she stood alone in a dark cave. *Plane . . . No survivors . . . Crash . . .* She didn't hear much more, only Fred speaking unintelligible words as he wept.

Yvonne dropped her phone and fell to the ground, the gravel in the parking lot digging into her knees through her black slacks. The stinging pain was nothing compared to the knife that had just sliced her insides open and changed her life forever. If she'd known pain before, it didn't compare to what she felt now—the burning in her chest, a heaviness she'd never felt before, a chokehold around her neck. She couldn't breathe. Even though she gasped for air, taking in quick gulps, it was as if there wasn't any oxygen, only nothingness.

The bell on the door rang. She heard footsteps, then felt a hand on her shoulder and heard voices, but she couldn't speak. There still wasn't any air in the space around her. Clutching her blue blouse with fisted hands, she opened her mouth and looked straight into the sun, her retinas burning. Then she screamed and yielded to the compulsive sobs that controlled her.

# CHAPTER 11

Eva gently closed her bedroom door. "She's sleeping now," she whispered to her mother, who was standing in the hallway. Then she covered her face with her hands and cried. "I've never seen such pain."

Her mother put an arm around Eva and coaxed her toward the stairs. Sniffling, Eva took Yvonne's phone out of her apron pocket. "She asked me to make some calls for her, starting with her aunt, but . . ." Her eyes were wide as she sought guidance from her mother, who held out her hand.

"I will make the calls, *mei maedel.* Did she give you a list?" Her mother blinked back tears. "So tragic."

Eva reached into her pocket again and took out the scribbled notes she'd taken. "It was hard to understand her part of the time, but I know she wanted her bridesmaids called too." She hung her head as they walked downstairs. "It hurts me to see anyone in such agony."

Her mother rubbed her shoulder. "I know."

Eva's father was sitting on the couch when they walked into the den. He stood. "How is the girl?"

"As would be expected," her mother said.

"She's sleeping right now." Eva dabbed at her eyes. "My heart hurts for her. I don't know her well, but I know she was so excited about her wedding that was coming up." She started to cry again.

Eva's father was a tall, stocky man whose resting expression consisted of an almost permanent scowl that intimidated most people—those who didn't know him. Inside, he was soft as pudding and cared deeply about people and their feelings. He looped his thumbs beneath his suspenders and stared at the floor. "It will take much time for the *maedel* to begin to feel normal." He sighed. "Jake is on the front porch."

Eva nodded, blotted her eyes with a tissue, then hugged her mother before she went out.

"How is she?" Jake paced as he asked the question.

"She's sleeping," Eva said through more tears that threatened to spill. "*Mei mamm* is going to make phone calls for her. Yvonne wasn't sure if her fiancé's parents had phone numbers for her bridesmaids and aunt—the one who raised her."

"I know it's *Gott*'s will when something like this happens . . ." Jake looked at Eva, his face a mask of despair. "But it's hard to make sense of it. She had her entire life ahead of her with this man."

"Life truly is short." She stood still, waiting to see if Jake would offer her a hug. He'd carried Yvonne to her SUV and laid her in the back seat, then drove them all to Eva's house. Until then, she'd had no idea Jake knew how to drive a car. He said he'd learned with some other boys in a parking lot when they were young and in their *rumschpringe*.

"Josh, David, and Amos went to get both of our buggies. I didn't want to leave until I knew Yvonne was all right." He began pacing again. "I didn't think we should leave both our buggies and the horses at the store for too long. I'll head home when they get here."

Eva's brothers hadn't hesitated about asking what they could do. Sometimes they got on her last nerve, but in a crisis or time of need, they could always be counted on.

"So, what now?" Jake stopped walking and folded his arms across his chest.

"I don't know." Eva started to cry again. "I guess we will know after *Mamm* talks to Yvonne's aunt. I just couldn't make the call." She shook her head. "It's just so awful. And like you said, I know we should accept this as *Gott*'s will, but six men died in that plane crash. Six families will grieve for a long time. It's so sad."

A few minutes later, Josh came around the corner in his buggy, followed by David in Jake's buggy and Amos in Eva's buggy. Josh stayed behind, tethered the horses, and began filling pails with water. David and Amos crossed through the yard and came up the steps. They both shook Jake's hand before turning to Eva.

"How is your friend?" Eva's youngest brother, David, asked.

"Devastated." Eva sniffled. "*Danki* for taking care of the horses."

David didn't say anything, but he hugged her before he walked into the house, followed by Amos, who stopped to give her a quick hug before they disappeared inside.

"I guess I should go. Can I call you later to find out how she's doing?" Jake had dark circles underneath his eyes.

Eva nodded. "I'll turn on my mobile phone." Her father was strict about use of phones, but she knew he wouldn't balk at a time like this. She waited for Jake to offer her a hug goodbye, but he just nodded before he turned and walked down the porch steps.

After he was out of sight, Eva walked back into the house. Her mother was sitting at the kitchen table with Yvonne's phone to her ear. She was consoling someone and fighting her own tears. "Yes, it is very tragic," *Mamm* said as she looked up at Eva, who sat down at the table across from her.

When she ended the call, her mother placed the phone on the table and put her face in her hands. "Two of the bridesmaids saw the plane wreck on television. They didn't know one of the victims was Trevor. The girl's aunt is getting on a plane to come here and take Yvonne home. She will be here tomorrow." Her mother lowered her hands, revealing a red face with lines down the sides of her cheeks where tears had fallen.

"*Danki* for making those calls, *Mamm*. I just . . ." Eva stared at her mother, beyond grateful that she had handled the task. "I just . . . couldn't."

"I'll make us some hot tea." Her mother stood and went to the kettle.

Eva sat there, her senses dulled, her body exhausted. She couldn't even imagine how Yvonne would feel when she woke up.

Yvonne opened her eyes to late-afternoon sunlight streaming into an unfamiliar room. It was warm, but like a day at the beach in early summer, with a nice breeze that brought calm and a longing for a hammock as you listened to the waves crash against the ground, rolling in rhythm. As she blinked and wondered briefly where she was again, her memories from only a few hours earlier fell onto her like a hundred-pound barbell, suffocating her until she almost couldn't breathe.

Trevor was gone. Killed in a plane crash. And she would never see him again.

She curled into a fetal position atop the twin bed she lay on and buried her face against the pastel cover beneath her. Curling her hands into fists beneath her chin, she squeezed her eyes closed again, willing it all to be a bad dream. Her head throbbed so badly, she thought she might throw up.

"Yvonne."

She heard the voice, recognized it. But she didn't move. She couldn't. Instead, she kept her eyes tightly closed and prayed she would wake up and none of this would be real.

Eva placed something on the nightstand in between the twin beds, then sat down on the mattress and put a hand on Yvonne's back. "I brought your phone back to you. *Mei mamm* made the phone calls for you, and I've brought you some herbal tea. Your aunt will be here tomorrow."

Yvonne didn't move. To open her eyes and acknowledge Eva's efforts would mean acceptance that she wasn't going to wake up from this nightmare. Her brown hair fell across her face in matted strands, moist from tears that wouldn't stop. Eva brushed it away, then returned her hand to Yvonne's back, rubbing gently.

"There is nothing I can say to make you feel better." Eva's voice trembled as she spoke. "But I am here, and I will be sitting on the other bed if you need to talk or if there is anything I can get you."

Slowly, Eva rose, and Yvonne was by herself on the bed again. She opened her eyes and gazed at her Amish friend sitting across from her, her hands folded in her lap atop her black apron that covered a maroon dress. Then she covered her face and cried.

"Please don't tell me anything to make me feel better, because I will never feel better." She heard the misdirected anger in her voice. Eva didn't deserve that, but Yvonne was beyond caring what anyone thought. Her life had just ended. She cried for another few minutes before she opened her eyes again. Eva was dabbing at tears with a tissue.

"Why did this happen?" Yvonne's chest ached as new waves of anguish seared her heart.

"I don't know," Eva said softly, her voice shaky.

Yvonne slowly sat up, but her head began to spin, and her throat was trying to close up. "I need to call Trevor." She gulped hard as hot tears slipped down her cheeks. "I need to tell him that I love him. I need . . . him. Call him, Eva. Call him for me."

Eva had never seen anyone in such agony, but although she would do anything within her power to ease Yvonne's grief, she couldn't give her the one thing she longed for so badly: her life. The one she had just lost.

"I can't call him," Eva said softly as she fought her own tears. "He's with *Gott* now."

Yvonne glared at her for so long it caused Eva to shiver, but then her expression went solemn. "I wish I could believe that."

"You can." Eva didn't know where to take the conversation. She silently prayed for God to guide her, but when nothing came, she wondered if it was because she wasn't the person to be ministering to Yvonne. She wasn't qualified.

"If I believed that Trevor was in heaven, then I would want to die, too, so that I could be with him." Yvonne's returning glare felt like it might burn a hole in Eva, but the woman was allowed her grief. "I could take a razor blade and slit my wrist right now, and then I'd go to heaven too." Her bottom lip trembled, but there was fire in Yvonne's eyes.

"*Gott* has things for you to do here on earth. It's not your time. And I know that's hard to understand right now, but—"

"What will I do, Eva? What will I do? Will I go back to my house and pretend I wasn't in love, that I wasn't going to get married in a couple of months? Maybe I can try on my wedding dress, the one I haven't even paid off." Tears of grief spilled down Yvonne's cheeks like raging rivers of anger. "Granted, George probably won't fire me now. He'll feel sorry for me. 'Poor Yvonne, her fiancé died in a plane crash!'" She was almost yelling now, but Eva sat still, her lips pressed together. "What are the odds of that even happening? But it happened to Trevor. It happened to the man I love, and I want you to tell me why!" She began to pound her fists on her legs, harder and harder.

"Stop! Yvonne, please stop!" Eva rushed to her and grabbed her wrists. "You're hurting yourself. Don't!"

"I hate everything." Her eyes blazed with misdirected anger. "I hate God." She turned her eyes to the ceiling and screamed, "Do you hear me, God? I despise You!"

"Stop it, Yvonne. Please stop!" Eva tried again to grab her wrists, but a firm hand took hold of Eva's arm and tugged her backward.

"Eva, *move*."

She turned to see her mother pulling her away, and Eva stumbled back. Her mom sat down on the bed beside Yvonne, forcefully pulled her into her arms, and held her tightly. Yvonne still had her fists clenched, lightly pounding on her legs, but she eventually slowed to barely a tap before she leaned into the embrace. Then she sobbed harder than Eva had seen her so far, wailing as if she was in terrible physical pain. Eva's mother never let go of her, and when Yvonne began to calm down, Eva's mother rubbed her head. She never said a word.

Eva left the room in tears, glad her brothers had obviously gone to work and her father wasn't around. She sat on one of the rocking chairs on the porch and sobbed into her hands, selfishly wishing her mother was holding her instead of Yvonne. So much pain. It was hard to process, especially since Eva had never had a loss comparable to Yvonne's. Her grandparents had passed, but they had both been sick, and it was expected. She wondered when Yvonne would get over the shock of losing Trevor. Or *if.* And hearing her talk about cutting her wrists and joining Trevor, not believing, hating God . . . It was all too much.

She turned toward the front door when the screen slammed closed and her mother walked onto the porch.

Eva threw her hands up. "I didn't know what to do! I obviously didn't handle things the right way. I've never seen someone suffering so badly, and it made me hurt too."

Her mother sat down in the other rocking chair, reached over, and took Eva's hand. "Of course it made you hurt to see someone you care about in pain." She squeezed her hand. "*Mei maedel*, when a person is called home to *Gott*, there is still grief, even when we believe it was His will to take that person when we weren't ready yet. There are phases. Sadness, anger, and eventually acceptance. But it doesn't happen quickly."

Eva gnawed on her bottom lip as she wiped tears from her eyes. "You don't think she would do anything to harm herself, do you?"

Her mother let go of her hand, leaned back against the back of the rocking chair, and sighed. "I hope not, but I don't know her. You don't know her very well, either, but I suspect she is just going through the phases I mentioned."

"I know her well enough to know she doesn't believe in heaven." Eva quickly found her mother's eyes, not wanting to miss her reaction.

"I see." Her mother paused as she crossed one leg over the other, her blank expression not giving much away. "So, in her mind, she'll never see this man again."

"Right," Eva flinched. "Her pain must be magnified because of that."

"I'm sure it is, but *mei maedel*, Yvonne will be going home tomorrow. There is nothing you can do to sway her way of thinking. You can only pray for her. And since her aunt is flying here to accompany her back home, I assume she and Yvonne must be close."

"She raised Yvonne." Eva felt unjustifiably angry at Yvonne's aunt—a woman she'd never met and knew nothing about except that she had stripped Yvonne of any hope for an afterlife. There was no point in telling her mother that part, she supposed.

Her mother stood, groaned a little, then held out her arms.

Eva fell into the hug, sniffling.

"You've been a *gut* friend to Yvonne. Someday she will look back and remember you fondly for taking care of her during this difficult time."

"I just want her to be okay." Eva eased out of the embrace. "Is a person ever okay when something like this happens? I wouldn't want the bishop to overhear me asking such a question, but the pain seems like it wouldn't ever go away."

"We lean on our faith during such times. I admit, it is different for Yvonne because she feels no hope of seeing her fiancé again." Her mother brushed back strands of hair from Eva's face. "But, again, all you can do is pray for her."

"I know."

Eva walked back upstairs and found Yvonne asleep again. Eva sat on the bed and began praying for her friend.

Jake didn't call Eva until almost nine. "How's she doing?" he asked after she answered.

"Wait a minute. I'm going to go outside," she whispered. She crept down the stairs and out the screen door. "Okay.

Sorry. She was sleeping, so I didn't want to wake her up." She sat in one of the rocking chairs. "I admit that I don't understand the grief she's going through. *Mamm* said there are phases a person goes through after the death of a loved one. Yvonne seems to be bouncing back and forth between despair and anger." She paused to take in the clear sky full of twinkling stars, to appreciate the glory of it amid such an awful day. "Her aunt is picking her up tomorrow and will fly home with her."

"Do you know what time?" There was a sense of urgency in Jake's voice.

"I think the aunt's flight comes in around ten tomorrow morning, then the drive from the airport, only to turn around and drive back for another flight. Seems like maybe they should have planned to spend the night, but I'm sure there is a lot to do, and . . ." She shrugged. "I don't know. I just feel so sorry for Yvonne. She was so excited about her wedding."

Jake was quiet.

"Are you still there?" Eva yawned as she stared at the stars, twinkling as if Yvonne's world hadn't stopped spinning today. But millions of people had lost loved ones today, just like every second of every day. And new lives came into the world every second. If she thought too much about it, it seemed overwhelming.

"*Ya*, I'm still here." After a short pause, he said, "*Mei mamm* said she'd open the bookstore tomorrow. I'd like to come say goodbye again to Yvonne. But . . ." He was quiet. "There's also something I'd like to talk to you about."

Eva straightened as her pulse picked up. "What?" she asked.

"I'd rather talk to you about it in person if that's okay."

It wasn't. Eva was sure she would lose some much-needed sleep, but she said, "*Ya*, okay."

"I'll try to get there around eight thirty, after your *bruders* have left for work. Can you meet me in the barn when you see me pull up so we can have some privacy?"

Eva's heartrate picked up even more. "Okay."

After they hung up, she stayed outside for a while. Had today's events caused Jake to realize that time was precious? Was he ready to give them a chance at something more than friendship? Had he begun to realize her feelings for him? Did he share those sentiments?

He had sounded so serious on the phone, as if perhaps his eyes had been opened to new possibilities. Under different circumstances, she would have rushed upstairs and analyzed their upcoming meeting with Yvonne. But for now all she could do was speculate. Even though her heart still hurt terribly for Yvonne, she felt hopeful about her own future.

# CHAPTER 12

Eva met Jake in the barn a little before eight thirty after she heard his buggy pulling into the driveway. He was leaning against her father's workbench, his ankles crossed, and with a brown paper bag in his hand. Eva eyed the bag, then lifted her tired eyes to his.

"I want to give Yvonne the book." He raised the bag a little before lowering it. "*Mei grossdaadi* said I was never to sell it. He didn't say anything about giving it away."

Eva studied his sober expression, the dark circles from the day before still evident. "Why would you do that?"

Sighing, Jake's gaze traveled somewhere past Eva as if lost in thought. "She's said things, and I've overheard things—that she might need money."

Eva thought back to when Yvonne said she might lose her client, how she had to pay off her wedding dress, but that Trevor would take care of her. The last part no longer an option. "Money won't cure Yvonne," she said.

Jake placed the bag on the workbench before he folded his arms across his chest. "It's not just about money." He reached up and scratched his forehead. "Last night, before I called you, I lay on the bed and dozed off. I had the weirdest dream."

Eva waited as Jake's eyes, glassy and dazed, drifted back over her shoulder.

"*Mei grossdaadi* was standing in *mei* bedroom, and he was holding the book. He gently pushed it toward me, to where I was sitting on the bed, and it floated into *mei* hands. Smiling, he said, 'All is not lost.' And then he was gone." He paused as he glanced at the paper bag. "I had the strongest feeling that I should give the book to Yvonne."

"Jake, you were tired. It was a dream. I don't think that meant that you were supposed to give Yvonne the book." Eva was sure Yvonne's reaction in the parking lot had hit Jake hard, too, but this didn't feel like a rational thing to do.

"Have you ever dreamed about anyone who has passed?" Jake peered at her, his eyes probing hers for answers.

Eva thought about his question. "*Ya*, I have. I dreamed about *mei grossmammi* several times after she died, but I never remembered much about the conversation. I just had a sense that she was trying to comfort me somehow."

"I've had dreams about people who have passed too,"

Jake said, sighing. "But this felt different. I don't know how to explain it."

Eva took a few steps closer to him and nodded toward the bag. "That book is worth a lot of money, apparently. More money than Yvonne would need, I would think, to solve any financial problems she might have. I didn't sense from her that she was in a perilous situation with regard to money." She pulled the black shawl she'd grabbed tighter around her shoulders. "If you're having some kind of guilty feelings about her being here when her fiancé died, that doesn't make sense. The plane would have gone down whether she was here trying to purchase the book or at home."

"I know."

They were quiet for a minute.

"You are hoping she will read the book, aren't you, that maybe it will change her way of thinking?" She put a hand to her forehead and shook her head. "Jake, don't you remember how upset she was after just reading the first pages?"

"I just feel like I should give it to her." He reached into the bag, took out the book, then stared at it before he looked at Eva. "She can sell it, read it, or whatever she wants."

Eva's mind traveled to a place less generous as she thought about all the repairs Jake would be able to take care of if he sold the book. Not to mention that without the book, there would be no reading sessions together at night. She cringed at the selfish thought.

"I can't sell it," he said firmly. "I can *give* it to her, but I can't sell it."

She shrugged. "It is yours to do with as you please, but this is a huge decision."

"It doesn't feel like it. I guess that's how I know it's the right thing to do."

Eva looked over her shoulder when she heard her name. When she didn't respond, Josh yelled again. "I'll be back," she said to Jake before she turned and walked out of the barn to see what her brother wanted.

"Yvonne came downstairs looking for you," Josh said, his hand to his forehead, blocking the sun. "She went back upstairs, but I thought I'd let you know since she didn't come down for breakfast and no one has seen her."

"*Ya*, okay." Her brother walked back into the house, and Eva turned around to see that Jake had followed her into the yard, carrying the bag with the book inside. "I'll go visit with Yvonne, then let her know that you want to talk to her." She bit her bottom lip. "As for the book, follow your heart."

She didn't look back as she walked toward the house, but she did reflect on how wrong she'd been. Jake hadn't come about anything to do with them, as a possible couple or otherwise. Again, it felt selfish, but Eva was having thoughts about how short life was, that you should tell people how you felt about them and not let time slip by until your dreams were out of reach. Maybe Jake would come to that realization soon. She hoped so.

Yvonne sat on the bed in fresh clothes, even though she hadn't showered. One of Eva's brothers had brought her red suitcase from the car and set it outside the door. She'd found it there when she'd gone to the bathroom. Now it lay on the bed beside her as she waited for her aunt to arrive.

The weight of her loss didn't feel any lighter this morning, but she had charged her cell phone and checked to see if Trevor had left a voice mail or sent her a text. He hadn't. As much as she wished she had any final words from him, she prayed the whole thing had happened instantly, that he hadn't been afraid or felt pain. As a grown adult, she knew she had to try in some way to keep herself together—even if she felt like she was five years old and needed someone to hold her, to carry her both physically and emotionally. The knot in her stomach and the hole in her heart felt permanent.

Eva walked silently into the room, sat down on the other twin bed, and faced Yvonne. The young woman's face was flushed, and it was obvious she was emotional.

"I-I'm sorry . . ." Yvonne inhaled a big breath and blew it out slowly in an attempt not to cry. "I'm sorry that this happened here, that you've had to deal with me during this . . ." Despite her best efforts, a tear rolled down her cheek.

Eva quickly rushed to her side and put an arm around her. "Please don't worry about that. Don't give it another thought. I only wish there was something I could do to ease your pain. I've been praying for you."

Yvonne dabbed at her swollen eyes with the wadded-up tissue in her hand. "This doesn't feel real to me, you know?"

She twisted to face Eva. "People will come over and call and tell me how sorry they are. They'll bring meals, offer to do anything I need. I'll suffer through a funeral, and good-intentioned people will tell me that Trevor is in a better place. It was like that when my uncle died." Eva's arm fell from around her, and Yvonne waited for words of comfort. But Eva stayed quiet, which was what Yvonne needed. "This feels different, though. I've been on the other side of this—the one bringing the food, offering my condolences, saying the things you are supposed to say at funerals. And now . . ." She sighed. "I realize that all of those grief-stricken people probably just wanted to be left alone, to not have to pretend that everything will be okay." She reached for Eva's hand and held it. "I wish I could just stay here."

"You can." Her new friend didn't hesitate. Yvonne wondered if Eva had lost anyone close to her, but she didn't want to ask. Yvonne was thirteen years older than Eva and had likely seen more death than she had. But nothing felt like this, not even the death of her parents. She had been young when that happened and didn't have a solid handle on the finality.

Yvonne forced a small smile for her friend. "I can't," she said softly as she released her hand to catch another tear with her tissue. "I will be expected to go through all the motions. I've experienced pain. But nothing like this."

They were quiet, and Yvonne appreciated that more than Eva would understand.

"I know what you're thinking." Yvonne avoided Eva's

eyes. "That Trevor is in a better place, in heaven, reuniting with people he has lost." She finally looked up. "I have never wanted to believe that more than I do at this moment." Shaking her head, she said, "But I don't."

She waited for Eva to try to convince her otherwise, but her friend remained quiet. Yvonne hoped she didn't tackle the first person who told her that Trevor was in a better place. It wouldn't be her aunt. Yvonne recalled her uncle's funeral and the many people who had those sorts of sentiments. Yvonne had followed her Aunt Emma's lead and merely nodded politely. It felt awful for Yvonne at the time, but looking back, she thought it must have been much worse for her aunt.

"Thank you and your family for taking me in last night." She pointed to the nightstand. "I've left you my address, and I'd like to keep in touch."

"I'd like that too." Eva stood up. "Jake is in the barn. He has something he wants to talk to you about, and he'd like to say goodbye."

Yvonne stood up and wrapped her arms around her new friend. "I'm happy to have met you, and I'll be back in my home state rooting for you and Jake," she said through her tears.

"*Danki.*"

Eva carried Yvonne's suitcase and led the way downstairs. Only her parents were in the den. After Yvonne thanked Mr. and Mrs. Graber—who had insisted she call them Mary and Lloyd—for their hospitality, she hugged

Mary for a long while and whispered, "Thank you for everything."

"You will be in our prayers, dear." Mary blinked back tears as she gave a final wave to her.

Following one last hug from Eva, Yvonne picked up her suitcase, set it on the bottom step of the porch stairs, and went to the barn. Jake was sitting on top of the workbench. She recalled how she'd thought she could charm the book away from this handsome Amish fellow. Now the sight of him caused her to burst into tears. Jake and Eva had shown Yvonne kindnesses that would be with her for a long time.

Jake jumped from the bench and quickly embraced her. "It doesn't seem like it, but some day you'll be all right."

Yvonne knew that wasn't true, but she stayed in his arms and nodded.

He backed out of the hug and pointed to a brown paper bag on the workbench. "I have something for you."

Yvonne sniffled as she eyed him. She tried to say "What?" but she wasn't able to choke out the word around the knot in her throat. Her stomach flipped when he pulled *Walk with Me* out of the bag.

"I want you to have this." He pushed it her way.

Yvonne shook her head as a whole new round of tears poured down her cheeks. "Absolutely not." She swiped at her eyes. "If I've learned anything while I've been here, it's that money doesn't buy happiness."

Jake stared at her long and hard. "But it can take care

of financial burdens that you may or may not have. And I want you to have it."

Yvonne continued to shake her head, even after Jake told her about a dream he'd had. "I really think you should have it," he said in a desperate voice.

She walked closer to him, reached up, and cupped his cheek. "You are a good man, Jake Lantz." After she lowered her hand, she forced a small smile. "I appreciate the fact that you are worried about my finances, but I assure you that I will be fine." She wasn't sure about that, but she wasn't going to take the book. "You promised your grandfather that you wouldn't sell the book, and I'm not going to let you break that promise."

"I'm not selling the book, so there are no promises broken. I am giving it to you, to do with as you please." He pushed back the rim of his straw hat and stared into her eyes with the book still outstretched. "Please take it."

"No." She didn't even have to think about it. She'd changed as a person during her short time here. And her life had changed forever. "The book would sit in a closet on the top shelf, untouched, unread, and collecting dust. I couldn't bear to read it or sell it. And such a cherished possession shouldn't be shelved that way. It's yours, Jake. But your offer only enforces what I already said. You're a good guy."

Yvonne was proud she'd managed to say all of that before she started crying again.

"A car just pulled into the driveway." Jake put the book in the bag, then offered it to her again.

Yvonne shook her head before they left the barn and walked together to the porch. Jake picked up her suitcase and stowed it inside the vehicle. Yvonne followed.

"Goodbye, Jake." She gave a quick wave, still crying, then ran into her aunt's outstretched arms.

---

Jake stayed in the barn until all was quiet and everyone had gone inside. Maybe he should have gone into the house to meet Yvonne's aunt, but he wasn't up for another goodbye. He arrived at the bookstore just as his mother was pulling in.

"Sorry you had to make the trip, *Mamm*. I thought I'd be tied up at Eva's house longer than I was." Jake tethered his horse to the hitching post.

His mother stayed in her buggy. "Did everything go all right?" she asked.

As far as his mother knew, Jake had just gone to tell Yvonne bye. "*Ya*, I guess. As *gut* as could have been expected." *Not exactly true*.

"That *maedel* is in for a rough time." His mother shook her head. "Hopefully, she is a woman of faith and will lean on that."

Jake scratched his cheek but didn't say anything. It was hard to understand how a person could believe in God but not the existence of an afterlife. He thought again about his dream about his grandfather and wondered if God sent loved ones to do His bidding from time to time.

"I'd better get the shop opened up." He gave his horse a quick rub on the snout.

"Is Eva coming in today?"

Jake couldn't think of a reason why she wouldn't, except maybe lack of sleep. It had surely been an emotional time for her. "I think so."

His mother began to back up her buggy. "Okay. I'm making chicken and dumplings for supper. I'll leave some in your refrigerator at the house."

"*Danki.*" Jake loved chicken and dumplings, and he could probably eat them every day. He thought about the batch Eva had brought that was probably still in the refrigerator. He didn't know how long food lasted, but Eva was bound to ask about reading together again, something he had to get out of.

He'd only been at the shop about an hour when Eva walked in. No basket with muffins, which wasn't surprising. His mother had to be right that it had been an emotional time for Eva. And she didn't have any other type of dish, like for casseroles or anything, so either she wasn't planning to read tonight or she figured they would read and not eat. Or maybe the leftover chicken and dumplings were still good after all. Maybe she assumed he didn't want to read any more since he'd turned her down before. All of this speculation was giving him a headache.

"How did it go with Yvonne's aunt?" Jake asked from behind the counter.

Eva's eyebrows furrowed as her expression grew tight

with strain. "I feel badly about what I'm going to say, but I resented her aunt, which I know is wrong, especially in *Gott*'s eyes. It's just that . . ." She set her purse on the counter, scowling. "I feel like if her aunt and uncle hadn't steered her away from Christianity, that she would find some level of comfort knowing she would see Trevor again. It's wrong of me to judge the woman in that way, though."

"*Ya*, maybe. But I feel that way too." Jake shifted his weight on the stool, deciding he might as well have the talk with Eva about the book. She picked up her purse and was about to walk away but turned around.

"What did Yvonne say when you gave her the book? I didn't want to ask her in front of everyone." Eva raised an eyebrow.

"She wouldn't take it. She said she wouldn't read it or sell it." Jake recalled their conversation. "She was firm about it."

Eva chewed her bottom lip. "I'm not surprised," she finally said.

Jake waited for her to elaborate, but when she didn't, he knew he had to have a conversation with her about the book. "Eva, I don't think it's a *gut* idea for us to read the book."

Her mouth spread into a thin-lipped smile, which was never good. He'd seen his mother give his father that smile. It wasn't real. "You don't think it's a *gut* idea for us to read the book? Or you don't think it's a *gut* idea for us to read it together?"

*Yikes*. She wasn't beating around the bush.

"Uh . . . both." When she squinted her eyes, lifting her chin in a challenge, he searched for a way out. Or maybe he should just tell her a partial version of the truth. "You're the one who said you didn't think the bishop would approve of us reading it."

"I said he *might* not approve." She held her countenance as she tapped a foot. "We're grown adults. I've changed my mind. With the exception of steamy romances, or books with bad language or subject matter, I think we are free to choose what we read. I vote we read it."

"I vote we don't." Jake could feel his jaw tense. There wasn't a good way out of this.

"You're the boss." She stormed off before Jake could even tell her the truth, which apparently wasn't necessary now.

Eva didn't think she had any emotional strength left to deal with one more thing, and that included the fact that Jake didn't want to spend time alone with her. It took everything she had not to burst into tears, but when the temptation almost overtook her, she thought about Yvonne.

After she said another prayer for Yvonne, she decided to dust the gift area of the store. She'd take her place behind the counter if and when Jake relocated. He had made it perfectly clear how he felt, and Eva was done pushing for anything outside of friendship with her boss. She'd thought that after he'd held her in the basement, things might be moving in a different direction. But they were being burglarized at the moment, so she supposed that shouldn't count.

She set her feather duster on the shelf and reached into her pocket for the note John Yoder had pinned on the fence in front of their house on Sunday. She'd been embarrassed that her brother Josh had been the one to find it, and he'd teased her about it but promised not to say anything to anyone. She hadn't given it much thought until now. She took out the note and reread it.

Dear Eva,

If you would like to have supper with me one night this week, please leave a return note here. I'll be hopping to hear from you.

John Yoder

She smiled at his spelling of *hoping* and grinned as she briefly pictured John Yoder hopping. He was a likable man, nice looking, and her age. He wasn't Jake. But apparently Jake was never going to be hers, and time was getting away from her. Eva longed to be married and start a family. She'd turned down plenty of offers to go out on a date. But maybe it was time.

She went to the back room and found a pen, then leaned over the note on the counter.

Dear John,

I would be happy to go to supper with you tomorrow night (Wednesday). *Danki* for asking me.

Eva

She was done waiting around for Jake Lantz.

# CHAPTER 13

Yvonne stared straight ahead as her aunt drove them to the airport. "Thank you for coming to get me."

Aunt Emma glanced at her. "Honey, I would have never let you make the trip home alone. And I took the liberty of calling the rental company. I explained the situation, and they will send someone to pick up the SUV you rented."

Yvonne nodded. "I'm dreading having to face Trevor's parents." The nausea she'd had all morning was getting worse. She wasn't sure if it was because she hadn't eaten anything or if all of her emotions had gotten together and landed in her stomach. She didn't think she had any more tears to shed.

"They aren't the warmest people, but I'm sure they are devastated." Her aunt paused. "I can't even imagine if something happened to you."

Yvonne's aunt and uncle had never had any children of

their own, and Yvonne knew they'd always thought of her as their daughter.

"The Amish people seemed nice. I've never met anyone Amish before." Her aunt stopped when the light turned red, and she turned to Yvonne. "The young woman, Eva? It appeared you two might have become close."

"I guess. As close as you can be to someone in such a short time. She's a sweet girl." Yvonne was already starting to miss the smell of homemade bread baking at the Gasthof Restaurant and at Eva's house this morning. But it was a passing thought that only led her back to Trevor, the way everything did. "I think we will probably write to each other."

Her aunt accelerated when the light turned green. There was a long stretch of highway back to the airport, then a two-hour plane ride, then an hour's drive home. She was exhausted thinking about it, and it was surely worse for her aunt, who had just made the trip here from Houston.

"So, no deal on the book?"

Yvonne had told her aunt during one of their phone conversations that Jake wouldn't sell. "No. But . . ." She recalled how serious Jake had been in the barn. "He actually tried to *give* me the book before I left."

"What?" Aunt Emma sounded as stunned as Yvonne had felt when Jake made the offer.

"I know. It was crazy. I think maybe he thought I had financial problems now, but he also said he had a dream about his deceased grandfather and felt he was supposed to give me the book."

"I'm guessing you didn't take it?"

"No. I couldn't accept a gift worth that much money from most people, much less a good-hearted Amish man who made a promise to his grandfather never to sell the book."

"Hmm . . . a slightly different attitude than when you arrived there, determined to get Mr. Lantz to sell." Her aunt brushed at a gray strand of hair that had come loose from the clip-on messy bun she wore. Aunt Emma had gorgeous silver hair, but over the years it had begun to thin. Yvonne could only hope to look so good at her aunt's age. The woman still exercised and ate right, and Yvonne couldn't remember her ever missing an evening of slathering on night cream before bed. Her efforts had paid off. She was still a striking woman at sixty-five. And alone, despite several widowers who had pursued her.

"I guess my attitude did change a little. Money isn't everything." Yvonne could feel the tears welling in her eyes again.

"No, it's not. And speaking of . . . have you heard from George?"

Yvonne shook her head as she bit her bottom lip, blinking back tears.

"I'm sure he knows." The lines on her aunt's forehead deepened. "It's been on television. I've seen it on several news channels. Small jets don't go down often, but I think that one of the men was semifamous. He was a minister for a large church in Houston, one of those that does online services."

Yvonne knew better than to get into a conversation about religion with her aunt. Even though the woman had been supportive when Yvonne sought out answers on her own related to God, Yvonne was sure her aunt would say things that would unintentionally hurt her right now.

"What did it look like, what they showed on the news?" Yvonne squeezed her eyes closed, unsure if she wanted to know, but something deep inside of her needed to know.

"It's under investigation. They think it was an error on the pilot's part, but they didn't elaborate."

Her chest ached, but she pushed on. "I mean, what did it look like? The crash site."

After sighing, her aunt said, "Total devastation. I can't imagine that anyone suffered, if that's what you're wondering."

Yvonne wasn't sure when the tears had begun spilling down her cheeks. "I wonder if Trevor knew what was happening, if he was scared."

"Honey, try not to do that to yourself. I know you have unanswered questions, and maybe after the investigation you'll know more. But there are some things you might not ever know."

She was quiet as she wondered if she was the last person Trevor had thought about as the plane went down. If she didn't rid herself of these thoughts, they would continue to eat at her like torture, but she didn't know how to stop the questions from invading her mind.

"Do you want to stay with me for a few days, at least until after the funeral?"

Yvonne shook her head. "No. I just want to be home."

"Okay."

They rode the rest of the way mostly in silence. Yvonne replayed in her mind the day she'd met Trevor, the day he proposed, the conversations they'd had about the wedding, and everything in between. At the heart of it all was the reality that she would never see him again.

Somewhere along the drive she fell asleep and woke up when her aunt nudged her to say they were taking the exit to the airport. Yvonne went through the motions as they returned the rental car, then went through security—a longer than usual experience since Yvonne didn't have her driver's license. But they got through, and her aunt had booked them first-class tickets home.

The plane hadn't even taken off when Yvonne closed her eyes in an effort to go back to sleep. It was the only time she didn't have to think about the new reality she was facing. Life without Trevor. But as badly as she wanted to escape her grief, a whirlwind of thoughts assaulted her attempts to sleep. Again she wondered, had Trevor known what was coming? Had he watched in horror as the plane plummeted to the ground? Or had it happened too fast for anyone to fully embrace the panic that would cause? There were no final texts from Trevor, so she was going to believe the crash had been instantaneous.

Despite her effort to reconcile the ordeal and accept the possible outcome, she started to shake uncontrollably. Statistically, she knew her chances of dying in a car accident were greater than a plane crash. Even so, when the engine on the jet began firing to capacity, she covered her ears with her hands and cried. Her aunt quickly had an arm around her.

*Will it always be this way?*

Not just with plane rides. With everything?

---

Jake needed to talk to Eva about the book and why they couldn't read it together, but they'd had a steady flow of customers all afternoon. He'd turned over the counter to her after he'd checked out a group of English ladies who had bought a lot of books and gifts. Eva was much faster at checking people out.

Jake could recall a time, not all that long ago, when most of his customers were locals. Montgomery was drawing in more and more tourists. He had mixed feelings about that. It was good for the economy, but he didn't want to see their community become too touristy.

It was late afternoon by the time he was able to pin down Eva. He knew she was mad at him since he had smelled chicken and dumplings warming around lunchtime and she hadn't offered him any the way she normally would have. But he owed her the truth, and the sooner he talked to her, the better he would feel.

After he'd shelved the last of the books that had come in, he went to the counter where she was sitting.

"Can I talk to you?" He hesitantly approached her,

taking slow steps and avoiding her piercing glare. Jake wasn't sure how much of her anger was directed at him for not wanting to read the book together and how much because he didn't know how to take their relationship to the next level. Maybe if he was honest on all fronts, they could work through things together. Jake loved Eva, he now knew, but he didn't want to behave dishonorably since he knew how John felt about her.

"Actually, there is something I need to ask you." She stood up, her purse on the counter in front of her as if she was ready to walk out the door.

Jake glanced at the clock on the wall. He hadn't realized it was already five o'clock, the time they normally closed. He'd let her go first. "What do you need to ask me?"

"If it's not too much of an inconvenience, I would like to leave at four o'clock tomorrow." Her chin was raised higher than normal, and she wore an expression that dared Jake to deny the request.

"*Ya,* sure." Eva rarely took off work, and it was usually something important. "Is everything okay? I mean, doctor's appointment or something?"

"*Nee*, not a doctor's appointment." Her voice was curt but not disrespectful.

He waited for her to tell him the reason. When she didn't, he asked, "Can I ask what for?"

"It's only an hour early. If it's a problem, just tell me." She raised both eyebrows and gave him the thin-lipped smile again.

"*Nee*, it's not a problem. I just worry about you and wanted to make sure you aren't sick."

"I'm not sick. I have a date, and I would like to have time to get home and get ready." Her fake smile widened, and Jake felt like he'd been punched in the gut.

"Can I ask with who?" It wasn't any of his business, but he couldn't harness his curiosity.

She picked up her purse. "John Yoder." Then she wound around the counter. "The money is in the bag in the usual place." She was headed to the door but stopped in front of him. "*Ach*, I almost forgot. What did you want to talk to me about?"

It had finally happened. John had stepped up to the plate and asked Eva out. And she had accepted. Jake had done the honorable thing by waiting to see if John would make his move, and now his insides were twisting into knots. He was tempted to beg her not to go and to disregard any sense of nobility or honor.

"Uh . . ." Jake rubbed his forehead as he stared at Eva.

"You said you needed to talk to me?" She put a hand on her hip.

"It wasn't important. I'll see you tomorrow." It wasn't only unimportant. It had just become irrelevant.

"*Ya*, okay. Bye." She smiled, a bit more genuine this time, and left.

Jake stood as his chest tightened. He'd probably let the best woman in the world get away because he wanted to be honorable—a word and emotion he was beginning to loathe. Maybe he'd always thought Eva would turn down any advances from John. But she hadn't, and the thought of her finally dating the man stung more than he had expected it would.

Despite his despair, he said a prayer for Yvonne, that she'd arrive home safely and that the Lord would help her to heal. At least Eva was alive. Jake might have blown his chance to have her in his life as more than a friend, but when he thought about Yvonne and what she was going through, he tried to keep things in perspective.

He made the rounds to get the store closed up, but visions of Eva and John together took his emotions hostage.

---

Yvonne dropped her suitcase just inside the front door of her house. She'd said her goodbyes to her aunt outside, insisting she was okay when her aunt offered to stay with her awhile. She just wanted to bask in her misery by herself, to cry the way you did when you didn't want people to see.

As she stood in her entryway, she eyed her outdated pastel décor and thought about how nervous she'd been to sell her house. She'd burn it to the ground if she could have one more day with Trevor. Her things were just that—things.

She twisted her engagement ring around her finger as she shuffled through her house, stopping to pick up a framed photo of her and Trevor taking a selfie at Mustang Island. She pressed it to her chest as the tears came on again, clutching it as she continued to her bedroom. More framed photos on her dresser. Both of them dolled up for a night on the town in her favorite red dress that she would never wear again. A formal engagement picture they'd had taken in front of a fountain in downtown Houston. And a photo of Trevor down on one knee when he proposed. The waiter had done an exceptional job capturing the moment, the prelude to an event that would now never happen.

She tossed the picture onto her pillow and threw herself facedown on the bed and sobbed. *God, give me one more minute with him. Please. Just let me look at him again. I'll do anything. Let me hear his voice.*

She bolted upright, then scurried to her purse, which was on the floor by her suitcase. After she found her phone, she slogged back to her bed and pulled up her voice mails. She never deleted anything. Trevor might not have had any last words for her, but there were probably at least a hundred voice mails. She turned the phone on speaker and listened to the first one that came up.

*Hello, beautiful. Just letting you know that I'm leaving the office early today if you want to pay me a surprise visit.*

She went to the next one.

*There's a cat in my garage. A big orange cat.* Laughter. *I don't need a cat. But I gave it some tuna, and now she's rubbing up against my leg. I guess I have a cat. Come see when you get the message.* Laughter again.

It took her a minute to realize she was smiling.

She lay back on her bed with the phone next to her, and

for the next hour she listened to Trevor's messages. At some point, exhaustion won, and she fell asleep. When she woke up in total darkness, she reached for her phone and listened to another voice mail.

*Hello, beautiful, I love you, babe. You're my everything, and I can't wait until we're married.*

She pressed End, then saw that she had new voice mails and missed calls from Trevor's parents, her bridesmaids, George, the caterer—who might not even know yet—and two solicitors. The most recent call was from her aunt.

*Honey, please call me. I know it's late, but I'm worried about you.*

Yvonne looked at the clock. It wasn't that late, only eleven. Her aunt never went to bed before midnight, so she called and assured her that she was okay. *A lie.* Then she forced herself to get off the bed and go to the bathroom. From there she retrieved her suitcase and hauled it to her bed. She opened the side pocket where her toiletries were stowed, unpacked them, and mechanically took a shower. Even the water hitting her body felt different. The texture of her hair wasn't the same. And when she looked at herself in the mirror after she had towel dried, she didn't recognize herself. Maybe she was in shock. Perhaps nothing would ever look the same again.

Wrapped only in her towel with her damp, untamed hair lying on her shoulders, she sat on her bed. She thought about Jake Lantz. He'd said his grandfather had visited him in his dream. Why hadn't Trevor come to her in a dream?

Would he ever? Could that be the only way she'd ever see him again? She rarely remembered her dreams, but she would beg God to have a vision of Trevor. Maybe God would deny her that blessing since she didn't believe that Trevor was in heaven. Maybe only those who believed were allowed visions of deceased loved ones. Even though she had dreamed about her parents after they'd died so long ago. She briefly thought about how she could trick God into seeing her as a believer in an afterlife. But there was no tricking God.

As her mind rushed through a broad range of emotions, resentment found its way into her heart. She couldn't have loved her aunt and uncle more if they had been her parents. For all practical purposes, they had been. But what if she had been raised differently or by someone else who believed in an afterlife? She would have grown up that way, believing in the promise of eternal life, that she would see Trevor again. Her longing to believe was stronger than it had ever been, but there was no science to back up any of it, just as her aunt and uncle had taught her. It was too late to shift her way of thinking, wrong to force a belief because she wanted it to be true.

She dressed for bed, then opened the cabinet where she kept her blow dryer before remembering it was still in her suitcase. Most hotels had driers these days, but Yvonne preferred her own and always traveled with it.

After she walked to her bed, she just sat with her wet hair and cried. Why was it taking so long to do the simplest of tasks?

When her phone rang, she sniffled, peeked at the number, and knew she wasn't up for George right now. She was surprised he was calling so late. She hit End and lay down, uncaring that her pillow would be wet from her hair. It would be just as damp from tears by morning. After lying there awhile, unable to sleep—maybe because the light was on or her hair was wet—she sat up. And prayed.

*Dear God, I need You. I don't feel like I can get through this on my own. If there is any chance there is a heaven, can You please infuse that belief into my mind? Can You please let me see Trevor in my dreams? Can You please show me how to function like a normal person again? Amen.*

It sounded futile even in her mind. Maybe if she dried her hair, snuggled up in her covers, and turned off the light, sleep would find her. Perhaps Trevor would find her in her dreams.

She was getting ready to unzip her suitcase to find her blow dryer. But something else caught her attention. The side pocket of her suitcase was bulging, and she didn't remember putting anything in that compartment. She unzipped it, surprised she hadn't noticed until now. Then she gasped.

There it was. The book. *Walk with Me* by Jerry Lance.

# CHAPTER 14

Jake opened the store Wednesday morning, his head filled with speculations. What had Yvonne thought when she found the book in her suitcase? Would she sell it? Read it? Be angry at him and mail it back? Probably not, since it had an above-average price attached to it. Had he done the right thing, done right by his grandfather? He recalled slipping the book into her suitcase while carrying it to the car. It had been a bold move but had felt right.

Equally as distracting, if not more so, was the fact that Eva would be going out with John Yoder tonight. He wondered if Eva had ever been kissed. Would John try to kiss her on the first date? Surely Eva wouldn't allow that.

He was loading money into the cash register when she walked in the door. Jake had expected another day like yesterday, her sour expression and avoidance. But she wore a smile and carried a basket. Jake could smell the luscious aroma of baked items.

"*Wie bischt*," she said as she held up the basket. "Cinnamon rolls, two slices of apple pie, and three whoopie pies. Help yourself."

"Uh, *ya. Danki.*" Jake tried to smile. Whatever bitterness Eva had been harboring, she seemed cured. Was she that excited about her date with John tonight? Had she written Jake off that quickly when John asked her out?

He finished stowing the money in the register, then went to the back room. Eva was wiping down the counters, something she did every morning.

Jake didn't want things to be weird between them. He needed to tell her that the reason he didn't want to read with her was because there was no book to read. Up until now, that had been his excuse not to spend intimate time with her. Now, being close to her was all he could think about. The old saying "You never know what you've lost until its gone" reverberated in his mind.

"Remember yesterday when I said I needed to talk to you?" He leaned up against the counter, close enough to her that he caught a whiff of lavender that unraveled him for a few seconds.

She folded the dishrag, laid it across the faucet, then reached for a towel to dry her hands. "*Ya*. But you said it wasn't important."

"I guess it kind of is." He twisted to face her, and

she did the same, her eyes locked with his. Her beautiful brown eyes.

Her cheeks dimpled as she smiled. "What? Are you firing me?"

"Never," he said, probably much too quickly. Although if she became serious with John, she would likely quit. He couldn't picture running the bookstore without her.

"Then what is it?" Her expression stilled as she tipped her head slightly to one side. "You look a bit tormented."

Maybe she thought he looked that way because she was going out with John. That was partly true. "I gave the book to Yvonne. *Walk with Me*."

Her mouth fell open. "I thought you said she wouldn't take it."

"She wouldn't. I slipped it into the side pocket of her suitcase when she wasn't looking." Thinking back, it was probably a crazy thing to do.

Eva put a hand to her forehead. "Have you heard from her?"

"*Nee*. She can sell it, read it, whatever . . . but that's why I said I couldn't read with you. There was nothing to read." He watched her closely to see if there was any relief on her face that he hadn't been just pushing her aside—which, in a way, he had been. Thoughts of begging her not to go out with John resurfaced, but he took a deep breath and stowed them.

She walked to the kitchen table and sat on one of the chairs. Jake held his position against the counter. He couldn't identify anything resembling relief in her expression as she tapped a finger to her lips.

"What if her luggage had been lost?" She raised her eyes to his. It was the last thing he had expected her to say. "Then no one would have the book. And I doubt she will mail the book back since it's so expensive, for fear of it getting mishandled in the mail. She didn't want it. Why did you do that?"

"I don't know. I just had the strongest urge that I should." He shrugged. "We don't even know her well, but I felt called to give her the book."

"Do you regret it?" She leaned her back against the chair, slouching into it.

"*Nee*, I don't." He sat across from her, the baked goodies an enticement he couldn't resist.

"There's extra icing on the cinnamon rolls." Eva nodded, and he supposed she was trying to keep things as normal as possible, too, even though it felt like there was an elephant in the room. Or maybe he was the only one who thought that.

"*Danki*." He lifted the lid on the basket and helped himself to a roll. After a couple of bites, he tried to force himself back into the role of her friend and not the jealous man he now was. "Are you excited about your date with John?"

Jake wasn't even sure she heard him as she folded her arms across her chest and sighed. "Yvonne and I agreed to write to each other. Maybe she will tell me how she feels about the book in a letter."

She'd completely sidestepped his question about John. "Okay, let me know if you hear from her, and I'll do the same." He stood up to go bag up the trash so he could take it to the dump later.

"*Ach*, and *ya*, I am excited about *mei* date." Eva stood up, smiled, then reached for a roll before she left to head up front.

Luckily, she was gone and missed the scowl on his face. Who was he to interfere with Eva's happiness? He stomped off and slammed the back door on his way out.

Eva tried to rid herself of the smug feeling that caused her heart to sing. Although she hadn't agreed to go out with John in an effort to make her boss jealous, it was a bonus. Eva had done everything but throw herself at Jake lately, so now she'd ruled him out as a suitor. Maybe over time she'd get him out of her heart as well. This evening she was going to put forth her best effort with John Yoder.

As she scanned new catalogs from behind the counter, Officer Byler walked in the door.

"*Wie bischt*," he said, which would have sounded strange to anyone who didn't know he grew up Amish. A far cry from his job as a police officer. Eva couldn't imagine such a radical transition—from being a passive and subdued Amish man to carrying a gun and enforcing the law now.

"*Wie bischt*, Abraham." He'd told them a long time ago

to call him by his first name privately since they'd grown up doing so.

He held up two photocopied pictures. "Are these the men you saw in the store before it got robbed?"

Eva shivered before she put a hand to her chest. "*Ya*, that's them."

"They were drifters, but they drifted into the wrong Walmart. They got caught stealing on camera at the Walmart in Bedford. I just thought you and Jake might want to know. Jake can press charges if he wants to." Abraham's eyes scanned the room.

"I'm not sure what Jake will want to do. Let me go—" Eva stopped when Jake came around the corner. "Abraham knows who the men are who robbed the store. They also stole some things from Walmart. Do you want to press charges for the money they took from you?"

Jake took off his hat and scratched his head. "*Nee*. They were caught and will be punished for their crime. It wasn't all that much money, and I'm assuming I might have to go to court . . ." He shrugged. "I would prefer to just let it go."

Eva wasn't surprised. Their people tried to stay out of legal issues if at all possible.

Abraham nodded as his eyes roamed the room again. "Where's your *Englisch* friend?"

"Yvonne?" Jake asked.

"She was here the last time I was in here, the one who called 911." Abraham cleared his throat, but he blushed a little.

"Yvonne went back home to Texas." Eva's heart hurt just at the mention of her name. She wondered how she was doing.

"Too bad," Abraham said, grinning slightly but still a little red in the face. "I was going to see if she wanted to step out for lunch."

Abraham had dark hair and dreamy-looking blue eyes that were almost too pretty for a man. He was tall, and Eva thought he was very handsome. He was older than Jake, thirtysomething. She was surprised some woman hadn't snagged him yet. Maybe his job kept him too busy to court anyone properly. She didn't know. He was much too old for Eva even if Jake didn't own her heart. And he wasn't Amish.

"Did you see the plane crash on television? We haven't seen it, but we've heard it's been on the news." Jake shook his head. "Yvonne's fiancé was one of the people on the plane who was killed. Very tragic."

Abraham sighed as he rubbed the back of his neck. "I'm afraid I did see that on TV—the crash. Had no idea one of the passengers was her fiancé. Poor gal. That's gotta be rough."

Eva's mind traveled back to when Yvonne had received the news out in the parking lot. She was afraid that vision might stay with her forever. "It was incredibly difficult for her to lose the man she loved," Eva said.

"A terrible shame." Abraham was quiet but then raised an eyebrow as he finally looked at Eva. "Speaking of love, I ran into John Yoder this morning at the hardware store. He mentioned that he was taking you to supper tonight." He grinned. "First date, huh?"

Eva didn't like gossip, and she wished John wouldn't have told anyone. Even though she felt like her face was turning red, she glanced at Jake at exactly the same time he looked at her. She quickly looked away. "*Ya*, first date."

"I know where he's taking you, and I'll give you a hint: he had to hire a driver, and it's a top-notch place." Abraham beamed. "I've been there."

Eva rolled her eyes. "That's not a very big hint." She racked her brain to speculate where John might be taking her.

"I gotta get back to work." Jake's voice was flat and laced with irritation.

Abraham just waved and might not have noticed Jake's swift change in mood, but Eva did. A part of her wanted to scream at him, tell him he deserved to feel hurt or jealous. Another part of her wanted to run to him, tell him she loved him, that she wouldn't go out with John if Jake could just admit that he loved her too. But as sure as she was of that love sometimes, there was still doubt, and she refused to humiliate herself like that.

After Jake was out of sight, Eva said, "Tell me. Where is he taking me?"

Abraham laughed. "Nope. You'll have to wait and see." He winked at her. "I gotta go. Have fun tonight."

When the bell jingled on the door and Abraham was gone, Eva tapped her pencil against the counter, pondering where John could possibly be taking her. She tried to think of the nicest place she'd ever been and recalled a trip to Bloomington with her mother once for a doctor's appointment. On the way back, they'd stopped at Texas Roadhouse. Her mother even bought the driver lunch. It seemed fancy back then. She'd never been back, but she'd always wondered why there was a place called Texas Roadhouse in Indiana.

Thoughts of Texas took her back to Yvonne. Maybe she'd write to her tonight after her date. She hoped Yvonne was doing okay. As okay as a person in her position could be.

Yvonne sat in Trevor's parents' lavish living room as they told her the details of Trevor's funeral to be held on Friday. They'd gone that morning and made all the arrangements. Yvonne wasn't invited or given a chance for any input. She wondered if her name would even be mentioned in the obituary. She was Trevor's fiancée. Surely his parents wouldn't omit mention of her.

Fred and Grace Adams were visibly distraught, both with dark circles beneath bloodshot eyes. Grace had bedhead on one side, and her face was drawn and almost free of makeup. They rattled off the details of the funeral as if addressing employees in a boardroom, with formality and decisiveness. Even though Yvonne was the only one present.

"Do you have any questions?" Fred asked from his blue floral wingback chair that was definitely more for looks than comfort. Grace sat in the one next to him with an ornate cocktail table between them. Yvonne sat on the matching couch across from them, the first time she'd ever sat there without Trevor next to her.

"I don't think so," she said barely above a whisper.

"We've canceled the hall, the caterers, and the band. Is there anything else you can think of that should be handled?" Fred lifted a bushy gray eyebrow.

Yvonne shook her head as she eyed her engagement ring and wondered what she was going to do about her wedding dress in layaway and the bills on her counter. What was she going to do about the book that Jake had slipped into her luggage? And, most important, would the dagger in her heart ever work itself free and allow her to live a normal life? It didn't feel like it.

"Then I believe everything is settled." Fred stood up, a signal for Yvonne to leave, she assumed.

It had been only two days, and yet Trevor's death had been handled efficiently and promptly by his parents. Yvonne could still barely breathe and wondered how she would function from this day forward.

She hugged them both goodbye. Fred patted her back the way he always did, without much of an embrace, but Grace held her tighter than she ever had.

When she got home, she slithered into bed and stared at the book beside her, much the same way as she'd done the night before. Scared to touch it. Scared not to. She had avoided two more calls from George. Her client would offer his sympathies as best he could, but he would also want to know if Yvonne had been successful, if she had gotten the book.

*I certainly did.*

She snuggled under the covers and wished she could stay there forever. Sleepless nights were surely in her future, but Jake's intentions were only going to make that worse. She had to know why he'd done this, outside of a dream about his grandfather or speculating she might need money. The latter was definitely true, but a niggling feeling told her there might be more to it.

Jake and Eva didn't always keep their cell phones on. Yvonne had been told they were supposed to be for emergencies and business only. This felt like an emergency since Yvonne didn't think her stomach would ever settle until she talked to Jake. She tossed the covers back and reached for her phone on the nightstand.

When he didn't answer, she left a voice mail. "It's Yvonne." She paused and took a deep breath, struggling to keep her voice from shaking. "I don't know why you did this when I told you the book would sit on a shelf in my closet collecting dust. I know you had your reasons, crazy as they sounded, but the book belongs with you, Jake. Please call me back."

Sunlight streamed across her pastel blue-and-pink comforter as she stared at the book, recalling the man's in-depth story about how he'd come to find his faith, including the fact that he saw Jesus in person. Yvonne didn't believe that for one moment, but the telling of the story had caused her to weep—for the man, for herself, and for anyone else who might believe his story. He called it redemption. Yvonne called it rubbish. But why had she cried the entire time she was reading it?

She picked up the book, walked to her closet, and opened the door. She was on her tippy-toes and lifting it onto the top shelf when her phone rang. *That was quick.* Doing a quick about-face, she rushed back to her phone, but it wasn't Jake.

Yvonne stared at the name on the caller ID. *George.*

Another phone call she couldn't keep avoiding if she wanted some resemblance of peace. There would never be true peace in the literal sense of the word, but loose ends only made things worse.

With the book still in her hands, she brought it to her chest and held it there. Then she answered the call. "Hi, George." Tears followed.

# CHAPTER 15

"Yvonne, my deepest of condolences about Trevor. I was horrified when I saw the plane crash, and doubly so when your fiancé was identified as one of the victims. Do you know when the arrangements will be?" George sounded surprisingly more sympathetic than Yvonne would have envisioned.

"This Friday at eleven in the morning." She set the book on the bed and waited. George had followed politeness protocol and was going to ask about the book now. When he didn't, she gave him the address where the funeral would be held.

"Vivian and I will be there. Again, I am deeply sorry for this huge loss."

"Thank you." She'd almost said "*danki*," the one Pennsylvania Dutch word she'd learned while in Indiana.

The call ended, and Yvonne stood in her bedroom

holding the phone, gazing at the book on her bed. The one that still hadn't made it to the top shelf of her closet. She was torn about reading it. It had upset and confused her so much the last time that it didn't feel worth the risk. But what if the man who saw Jesus changed her mind about her beliefs, offering her some sort of comfort at a time when she needed it the most? Even though she didn't believe the author's story, the writer of the far-fetched tale seemed to.

When her phone buzzed in her hand, she jumped but quickly looked at the caller ID. She sat on her bed and answered. "Hi, Jake."

"How are you?" he asked, followed by a long pause. "Dumb question, I'm sure."

"Too many unanswered questions." She tucked her legs underneath her on the bed, stared at the book, then said, "I can't keep that book, Jake."

"Why? You were perfectly willing to buy it when you arrived. I think you should have it."

Yvonne tried to decide if she should be insulted. Ultimately, she decided that she shouldn't. They'd gotten to know each other a little, and he was being honest with her. "I feel differently now."

Jake was quiet. "I think you should read it, then sell it. I know the first part of the book upset you, but I believe there is a message within the pages, something that might give you comfort."

"Or torment me for the rest of my life." She spoke

without thinking. "Sorry. It's just that I'm not up for a religious debate challenging everything I've ever believed to be true."

"It is your choice to make."

She was tempted to lash out at him, tell him what a stupid thing it was for him to do, to give her a book worth over a hundred thousand dollars. She still didn't know what she was going to do about George, but she suspected the book would end up on that shelf in her closet, at least for a while. She would feel guilty if she sold it, even though she'd only keep her commission and send the rest to Jake, whether he liked it or not. But the alternative—reading it—was more frightening.

Jake asked her when and where the arrangements were going to be, also saying that he and Eva would not be able to make it to the funeral but that their thoughts and prayers would be with her. Yvonne had never expected her new Amish friends to travel all the way to Texas for a man they'd never met.

After a long pause, Yvonne said, "Jake, I'm going to change the subject, and I'm about to step into your business. The old cliché 'Life is short' has taken on a whole new meaning for me. It's no secret Eva cares about you, and I believe you have feelings for her too. Act on them. Don't wait."

Silence.

"Maybe you're right," he said after a while. "But it's probably too late. Eva is going on a date with someone in our district tonight. It's their first date, and the man is very nice. I've heard the ladies think he's quite handsome as well." He paused. "I've known his feelings for Eva for quite a while, so I've stayed in the background. That's the right thing to do."

Yvonne could hear the regret in his voice. "That doesn't mean things will ever go past a first date. A guy can't just stake his claim on a woman who may or may not care about him in a romantic way." She wondered if Eva might be trying to make Jake jealous. If so, she might have said too much already. "Two people have to love each other."

She glanced at the time on her phone. Indiana was an hour ahead of Texas, so Eva would already be on her date. "I'll be rooting for you and Eva." Her voice started to crack, and after Jake told her again that he'd be praying for her, they ended the call.

Even though every inch of her being told her to stuff that book away in the closet and lie to George that she didn't have it, a pull greater than her own resistance found her hand defying her mind and reaching for *Walk with Me*.

She made a pot of coffee—not that she needed it since sleep felt out of the question—then settled under her covers, which had been her hangout since she'd arrived home. With shaky hands she turned to page forty, where the author had just begun a conversation with Jesus.

*This is a mistake.* But she turned the page.

Eva opted not to spritz herself with lavender spray. Nor did she apply any of the clear lip gloss Yvonne had given her. John would appreciate her just the way she was or not at all. Still, even though that was her attitude, she didn't want to sabotage this date. She owed it to herself and John to see if there was anything there between them. Maybe she had focused too hard on what could have been with Jake.

"You look lovely," her mother said when she walked into Eva's room. "And I'm happy to see you going on a date. Do you know where he's taking you?" She walked to where Eva was standing and tucked a loose hair beneath her prayer covering. "Dark green is a good color for you." She smiled.

"Officer Byler—Abraham—stopped by the bookstore today. He had run into John, who told him he was taking me somewhere that required a driver. Somewhere fancy, apparently." She avoided her mother's eyes until her mother cupped her chin and forced her to meet her sympathetic gaze.

"*Mei maedel*, I know this is not the man you were holding out for, but John Yoder is a *gut* man. I hope you will give this a chance, because I suspect John has been holding out for you." Her mother winked at her as she patted her arm.

"I am. And I know he's a *gut* man." Eva was going to do her best and also hope she didn't constantly wish she was with Jake.

"Have you heard from the *Englisch* woman, Yvonne?" The lines across her mother's forehead deepened. "I've thought about her a lot since she left."

"*Nee*, I haven't heard from her, but I'm planning to

write her a letter." She hung her head and sighed. "I can't imagine what she's going through."

"I hope you never have to." Her mother pointed out the bedroom window. "Your date is pulling onto the driveway in a dark blue car. It looks nice."

Eva glanced out the window then back at her mother. "Please tell me that Josh, David, and Amos aren't in the living room. At least one of them will say something to embarrass me."

Her mother chuckled. "I told all your *bruders* to make themselves scarce, that they were not to come into the living room when John arrived. I'm sure he will come in to say hello to your father and me."

"*Danki, Mamm.*" She took a deep breath. "Here I go. I can't believe I've waited this long to go on a first date. I'm a little nervous."

"Just be yourself, *maedel*. You'll be fine."

Eva followed her mother downstairs and hit the landing just as John knocked on the door, which her father promptly opened. "*Wie bischt*, John." Her father shook his hand, and then John greeted her mother.

Eva tried to smile, but it turned out she was more nervous than she'd thought. They weren't even in the car yet, and Eva was already wondering if he would try to kiss her goodnight.

"What time would you like for me to have Eva home?" John asked her father.

Eva glanced at the clock on the mantel. Straight up 6:00 p.m.

"I believe ten is a reasonable time." Eva's father looped his thumbs beneath his suspenders, and John nodded before he turned to Eva.

"Are you ready?"

"*Ya.*" She walked ahead of him as he held the door open.

"You look nice," John said as he opened a door to the back seat of the waiting car.

"*Danki.*" Eva's stomach started to roil, and she wondered if she'd even be able to eat. She jumped when John slipped into the seat beside her.

He smiled. "Eva, please don't be nervous. We're going to have a wonderful time."

It was so heartfelt and honest that Eva started to relax right away. "Okay," she said before she smiled. "Where are we going?"

"You'll see." He winked at her. "I think you'll like it."

"I'm sure I will." Eva smiled back at him, her stomach settling and excitement building.

Jake spooned beef stew from a can into a pot on the stove, wishing he had some of his mother's cooking. She didn't know Eva was on a date with John Yoder or she surely would have left a meal in his refrigerator. Something more comforting than stew from a can.

As he turned up the burner and stirred his supper, his emotions bounced back and forth between jealousy and anger—neither right in the eyes of the Lord. Good doses of fear and regret were also mixed in. What if Jake's good intentions had cost him a future with Eva?

Life was out of sync. Normally, he went to work, spent the day with Eva, chatted with visitors, then went home, ate, and went to bed. If there was anything wrong with that schedule, it was the evenings when loneliness settled in. But he was usually so tired from working outside when he got home that he'd fall into a deep sleep.

Tonight he was restless, and after he ate his less than extraordinary stew, he found himself pacing his house, going room to room, wondering if anything was out of sync there too. But everything was as it should be. He considered visiting his parents, a short walk across the property, but why let his mood rub off on them? Instead, he showered, got into bed, and tried not to feel sorry for himself as he pictured Eva on her date with John.

After he'd tortured himself long enough about that, he moved on to Yvonne. Maybe he'd made a horrible mistake by giving her the book. If she didn't read it or sell it, would she really put it in her closet where it might rot until someone found it? His grandfather wouldn't want that.

He fluffed his pillow with his fist, much too hard, as if the pillow had done something wrong. Then he lay down and stared at the ceiling.

Eva was surprised how relaxed she'd managed to stay during the drive to Bloomington. John owned his own construction company, which explained the nice way he filled out his white shirt that he'd paired with black slacks. Instead of a straw hat, he wore a black felt one. Eva knew people would stare at them when they walked into the restaurant. The farther away they went from populated Amish areas, the more attention they drew. Eva suspected the ladies would home in on John's mesmerizing brown eyes and wavy dark hair. It was cut in the traditional style, but his cropped bangs hung like crimped ribbons above his dark eyebrows, and his hair curled slightly as it rested just above the collar of his shirt.

John had done most of the talking, telling her about his business and plans for the future. He was currently finishing renovations on an old farmhouse on property adjacent to his parents' homestead.

"It sounds lovely but like a big project," Eva said as she found herself hanging on his every word. He was soft spoken, which she already knew, but he conversed with a sense of calm that seemed to rub off on her. With Jake, she was always fighting for his attention, and her boss could go from calm to shook up in about a second. Moody. Jake was moody.

"*Mei bruders* have been lending a hand. Neither of them wanted the old place, but when I began the repairs, they jumped in to help." He smiled at Eva. "It's where I hope to raise a family someday. From the kitchen there is a beautiful sunrise, and in the bedroom the sun sets in full hues behind the trees that line the immediate two acres around the property."

Normally, Eva would have blushed, but John's smooth and silky words continued to keep her calm yet excited about their destination.

He pointed to their right. "We're here. Have you ever been there?"

Eva strained to see past John and into the lights that shone around the restaurant, then shook her head. It wasn't dark yet, the sun only starting to set, but the place was lit up like the fairgrounds they'd visited as children.

"*Gut*, it's not crowded," John said as the driver turned into the parking lot. "Probably because it's a Wednesday."

Eva smiled, eager to try a new restaurant. She didn't think anyone cooked better than her mother, but they had the same things all the time, mostly because her mother had to make large quantities to satisfy Eva's brothers' appetites.

After John exited the car, he offered Eva a hand and helped her out. Then he kept a hand on her back all the way to the front door of Samira's Restaurant. Once inside, all eyes homed in on them, as Eva had expected. The hostess led them to a small table for two toward the back of the restaurant, and she even pulled out Eva's chair for her before laying two menus in front of them. They each ordered iced tea even though the waitress had left a wine list on the table. Wine was reserved for weddings, though the ambience of the restaurant seemed to call for it.

"This is a beautiful place," Eva whispered from across

the small table. *Romantic* was the word that came to mind. She wondered where Jake would have chosen to take her on a first date. Would it have been somewhere this fancy? "Have you ever eaten here before?"

"*Nee*, I've only heard about it. I thought it would be fun to try something new together." He smiled, the dim lighting twinkling in his eyes, lending a golden glow that momentarily kept her fixated on him. *Romantic place and handsome man.*

Eva studied the menu, glancing over the top of hers to see that John was doing the same thing, a perplexed look on his face. His eyes met hers, and he cleared his throat. "I've never heard of most of this stuff." He chuckled, which instantly drew a giggle from Eva.

"Thank goodness. I was wondering if it was just me. I was thinking earlier how much I *lieb mei mamm*'s cooking but how nice it would be to have something different. But I have no idea what to order." She scanned the offerings that looked like they were in a different language.

"We can play it safe and order one of the pastas. Or we can get a little crazy and order Kurmo Tchallao, whatever that is, or Aamarok Lawang." He laughed again, and so did Eva. "I'm sure I'm not pronouncing either one of those correctly."

She sat a little taller and pressed her palms together, grinning. "I say we get a little crazy."

John smiled. "Crazy it is."

Eva basked in the glow of John's gaze for longer than

she had intended, but her mind drifted long before her eyes did. She wondered what Jake would have ordered.

---

By the time they arrived back at Eva's house, her chest had begun to tighten. It had been a lovely evening with good food and conversation. There had been laughter, and she'd been more relaxed than she would have imagined. John was a truly likable person, which she already knew since they'd grown up together. But he was even more personable in an intimate setting. Now she faced the biggest challenge of the evening. Would he want to kiss her goodnight, and should she let him?

He told the driver he wouldn't be long. Then he opened the door for Eva and ushered her to the front door.

"I had a really *gut* time." Eva's hands trembled, so she folded them together in front of her.

"So did I. *Danki* for going out with me. I-I hope I'm not being too forward by saying that I hope we can do it again soon."

The only light shone from the propane lamp in the yard, so Eva couldn't be sure, but John looked like he might be blushing. Maybe he was nervous too. And his comment seemed to warrant a response.

"I'd like that," she said, irritated that she thought about Jake. Again. At this very moment.

John gently took both of her arms in his hands and

leaned forward. It was coming. The kiss. She'd never had one. It would be inappropriate for a first date, but her feet were rooted to the porch. Her hands clenched in front of her. And her heart pounded like a base drum in her chest. As his lips came toward hers, Jake's face flashed in her mind's eye. She'd always dreamed he would be her first kiss.

When John's lips gently brushed against her cheek and not her mouth, she wasn't breathing.

"I'll be hoping to see you soon," he said before he eased away and turned to leave.

It was perfect. Everything. Even the simple kiss on the cheek completed the evening in perfect fashion—caring yet respectful.

John Yoder was everything a woman could want in a man.

But any euphoria Eva felt evaporated with each step she took. Into the house. Up the stairs. Across her room to sit on her bed.

*Why couldn't it have been Jake?*

# CHAPTER 16

Jake paced the store Thursday morning. Back and forth from the gift aisle to the back room, behind the counter, down the row of fiction books, then children's books. Then he did it all over again. He was coming around the corner from the gift section when Eva walked in. Jake stopped, didn't breathe, and said nothing as he studied her expression, as if it would tell him about her date. If she was bubbly and bouncy, it had gone well. If she was somber and didn't make eye contact, then perhaps it had gone badly.

As much as he didn't want Eva to be unhappy, he couldn't help but hope the date hadn't been more than barely satisfactory. "*Wie bischt*," he said tentatively, watching her closely. She didn't have a basket of goodies this morning. Was that because there were some left over from yesterday, or did she get home late last night and oversleep?

"*Wie bischt.*" She smiled, a little too much for Jake's

liking. Then she slid behind the counter, stowed her purse out of sight, and popped open the cash register, which Jake had already filled. "Looks like we're ready to go." She met his curious eyes. "Yesterday I noticed we are completely out of number 2 pencils. I don't know how that happened, but I'll get some ordered right away. It was too late to call yesterday when I noticed." She flipped the page on a spiral notebook that she kept nearby. "We also need more thank-you cards." She chuckled, which got under Jake's skin for no rational reason. "Guess folks have a lot to be thankful for, and that's *gut*."

She was writing, flipping pages, writing more. All Jake could think about was whether or not John Yoder had kissed her last night, but that wasn't something he could ask her. He plastered on the best fake smile he could.

"So how was your date last night?" He held his breath and secretly blamed her that he had gotten hardly any sleep last night. Gritting his teeth, he allowed some air to escape and reminded himself that he had no right to be angry or upset, no matter what her answer was.

"It was *gut*," she said without looking up.

They were friends. Was that all she had to say? "Where did you eat?" He shuffled her way and stopped a few feet from the counter.

"A place in Bloomington called Samira's." She grinned, her head still down. "They have food that was very different, so we went a little crazy and tried new things. It was surprisingly *gut*."

*Did he kiss you? Will you go out with him again?* He had to know. And why couldn't things just go back to the way they were? Now that she'd gone on a date, everything was different, and Jake didn't like it. He could feel an angry hurt bubbling to the surface.

"I hope John was a gentleman." He looped his thumbs beneath his suspenders and stared at her until she finally looked at him. Then she glared at him, enough that he took a step backward as she stood up from where she'd been sitting on the stool.

"Jake, I know that you feel a need to protect me." She flashed him that thin-lipped smile, the one that was never real when any woman delivered it. "But I am not your little sister. I am a grown woman. And we've both known John our entire lives. You know he is an honorable man."

He was tempted to tell her how *he* had been an honorable man, stepping aside since he knew John's feelings for her. "I know you're a grown woman." It was all he could think to say, except for the slippery words that threatened to slide off his tongue. *Did he kiss you?* Maybe in the deepest recesses of his mind, he'd always thought he would be Eva's first kiss, and that thought had bullied its way to the forefront of his every waking moment lately. The vision of her in another man's arms gave credence to the fact that Eva was, indeed, a grown woman.

"Can you think of anything else we need?" She sat down again and sighed as if she was totally exasperated with him, her head buried in the notebook again.

"*Nee*." He shifted his weight and folded his arms across his chest. Then he waited until she finally glanced his way.

"Jake, if you have something you want to ask me, just ask. Because you're not acting right." She blinked her eyes a few times, closed the notebook, and folded her hands atop it.

"'Acting right'? What does that even mean?" He gave his head a quick shake. "How am I supposed to be acting?"

She shrugged. "Never mind."

"*Nee*, if you have something you want to say, just say it." He realized after he'd spoken that his words almost mirrored hers.

"I don't have anything to say. I said never mind." She stood, picked up her little notebook, and came around the counter. "I'm going to walk each row and see if I've missed anything obvious. I keep a pretty *gut* inventory, but sometimes when a group of ladies come in and buy a lot, I forget to write everything down. I'm trying to be better about that." She eased around him and walked toward the children's book aisle. He was sure there was more of a swing in her hips as she walked. Or had he never noticed that before?

"Did he kiss you?" He almost hollered the question, which stopped her in her tracks before she spun around and faced him. Then she slowly edged toward him until she was close enough for him to breathe in that lavender smell again.

She got even closer and leaned her face up to his. Jake felt a shiver run the length of his spine as she batted her eyes at him. "Define 'kiss,'" she whispered softly, her breath on his face. Then she did an about-face and walked away.

Jake could feel the blood shooting up from his feet until it filled his face, and he was sure he was going to explode. He had absolutely no right to be angry, but he stormed out of the store anyway.

Eva's jaw dropped as Jake kept walking away. He was almost to the road when she finally closed her mouth. Maybe she'd gone a little overboard on the "Define 'kiss'" comment, but he didn't have any right to be questioning her.

After he hadn't come back for almost an hour, she started to feel bad about the way she had handled things. Maybe Jake did, too, and they would talk this through like adults. What would she say? *I've always loved you, but you never asked me out, so it was time to move on.* It was the truth but something she would never come out and admit to him.

Thirty minutes later, she began to get a little worried. She went to her purse and turned on her mobile phone in case he called. Not long after the phone powered up, it buzzed with a voice mail.

*Hi, Eva, it's Yvonne. Jake told me when we spoke that you had a date last night. I was just wondering how that went.* There was a long pause. *I wish I was there, away from all of this.* Yvonne's voice cracked a little. *Anyway, Trevor's funeral is tomorrow. I talked to Jake about sneaking that book into my luggage. I read it, by the way.* Full on tears. *Maybe, if you have time, you can call me.*

Eva had tears in her own eyes by the time she ended the voice mail. Yvonne was thirteen years older than Eva, but she sounded like a young child. Understandably. If Texas were closer, Eva would have tried to attend the funeral.

She walked to the window then onto the front porch. Lifting her hand to her forehead, she searched for Jake, but he was nowhere in sight.

Eva walked back inside to her stool behind the counter and called Yvonne.

"I'm sorry I sounded so pitiful, I just . . ."

Eva's heart hurt. "*Nee*, please don't apologize. And you know you are welcome to come back anytime you want." She bit her bottom lip when she heard Yvonne crying. "Is there anything I can do for you?"

"Yes." Yvonne sniffled. "Distract me. Tell me about your date last night. John Yoder, right?"

"*Ach*, Yvonne, this doesn't feel like the time to talk about such things when you are suffering so much."

"Trust me. It's the perfect time."

Eva swiped at her eyes, deciding maybe Yvonne really did need to talk about something outside of her own heartache. "I've known him all of my life. He's handsome, and the date was perfect. But . . ." She chewed on her fingernail as she squeezed her eyes closed.

"But he's not Jake." Yvonne sighed, still sniffling.

Eva told her what had just happened. "I know I shouldn't

have toyed with Jake that way, but he was in a terrible mood, questioning me, and even though a part of me was glad he was jealous, I still shouldn't have reacted the way I did. Jealousy is a sin, and I shouldn't have fueled his emotions that way."

"I'm guessing that Jake is facing his true feelings for you. Maybe it took a date with another man for him to realize that." Yvonne's voice was shaky, but she wasn't sniffling as much.

"It feels so wrong to be talking about this." Eva swallowed hard. "The book. Tell me about the book. I had no idea Jake slipped it into your suitcase until he told me."

"It-it . . ." Yvonne started to cry again.

"Please don't feel like you have to tell me about it." Eva brought a hand to her chest as her eyes filled with tears. "I'm just at such a loss. I wish there was something I could do to ease your suffering . . . about Trevor, about the book . . . I'm praying for you daily, and I'm sure Jake is too."

"Eva . . ."

She waited.

"Do you think Jesus can actually appear to a person? I mean, like sit down on the couch and talk to you?" Yvonne had stopped crying.

"I suppose when it comes to *Gott* and His *Sohn*, anything is possible." Eva paused. "That was in the book?"

"Yeah. It was. The author had lost his faith, something that had been instilled in him for as long as he could remember." She was sniffling again. "Both of his parents had died, and despite his upbringing, his grief consumed him, and he walked away from God. But he tells a story about Jesus visiting him. That happened in the first part of the book, one of the reasons I was so upset about reading those first forty pages. His retelling of the event was so real, so emotional, but . . . I just couldn't believe it. Then I kept reading. And now, everything I've ever believed seems up for grabs. I'd researched everything so thoroughly when I was younger, and there wasn't any science to back up any type of heaven or hell. I'd felt an entity stronger than me, close to me, lots of times. That felt solid enough to believe in a higher power. But I'm wondering if I was wrong about there being an afterlife. Or maybe I'm just grasping at straws because I need to believe that I'll see Trevor again." She started to cry in earnest.

A tear slipped down Eva's cheek. "I don't feel qualified to talk of these matters, but I'm going to do my best to tell you how I feel. What you do with the information is up to you, and please don't think I'm meddling."

"I won't, Eva. You're the only person I thought might understand. My friends, while well intended, aren't the ones I should be having this conversation with. They've brought food, bottles of wine, shoulders to cry on, and a complete lack of understanding when it comes to God and faith. They are all good women, and I'm sure they probably do have a spiritual side, but we've never discussed it, and this feels too important to open up a conversation with anyone who might confuse me more."

"I don't want to confuse you. All I can tell you is *mei* own personal feelings." *Please God, help me to get this right.* "I believe in miracles even though I have never personally witnessed one. Can Jesus show Himself to a person in His physical form? I believe He can do anything. And I do believe that you are having some of these feelings because you want to see Trevor again. There's nothing wrong with that. The Holy Spirit ministers to people in all kinds of ways. Maybe you haven't been ready to seek out *Gott* until now. But I also don't believe that a human being is capable of changing a person through words or otherwise. I believe that the Holy Spirit is always involved when a person goes through changes, for the better or worse. God doesn't push us down, but He is always there to pick us up. He doesn't cause bad things to happen, but He works to right things in our lives or guide us onto the right path." She paused. "I think there is only one book to rely on when it comes to *Gott* and His word."

"The Bible."

"*Ya*, in *mei* opinion."

Yvonne was quiet for a while, and Eva gave her time to think.

"Okay."

Eva was at a loss. What did that mean, *okay*?

"Now I'm going to tell you something, Eva. I told Jake the same thing. Life is short. If he is the one for you, don't wait. There are no guarantees of a tomorrow." Yvonne took a shuddering breath. "Somehow I have to get through this funeral tomorrow. I can't change my beliefs overnight. But somewhere in the midst of everything, I'm open to the possibility that maybe I've been wrong. And if it took an author named Jerry Lance to open my eyes to something different, even if I might not believe his story, then I guess I should be open to the possibility that there is a Holy Spirit that might guide us."

Eva smiled. "I think that is a *gut* start, and you will be in *mei* prayers tomorrow and always."

"*Danki*, Eva." A barely audible laugh. "See, I did take home a small part of Montgomery with me. Take care, my friend."

"May the Lord be with you today, tomorrow, and always."

"And with you."

After she ended the call with Yvonne, Eva covered her face with her hands. Then she sobbed so hard she thought her head might split open, along with her heart. She quickly dropped her hands, gasping for air, when the bell on the door rang.

Jake rushed in, rounded the corner, and grabbed her by the shoulders. "Eva, what's wrong? What is it? If it's me, I'm so sorry." He tenderly reached up and cupped her face, gently wiping away her tears with his thumbs. "Talk to me."

She buried her head against his chest, and he wrapped his arms tightly around her. "It's Yvonne. I just talked to her, and . . ."

"It's okay." He eased her away and kissed her on the forehead. "What did she say?"

"She's confused, she's grieving, and tomorrow is Trevor's funeral. It all just upset me." Eva put some distance between them. "I'm sorry for being such a mess." She took a tissue from a box on the counter and dabbed at her eyes.

"I'm sorry for Yvonne." Jake took off his hat and ran his sleeve along his forehead, bubbling with sweat. "And I'm sorry for what I said and for running out like that. It's not *mei* business whether or not John kissed you."

"I'm sorry too. I shouldn't have made such a snide remark." Eva needed her heart to stop racing, the way it always did when she was or had been in Jake's arms. "My heart hurts for Yvonne."

He stood close to her, but they were no longer touching. Eva's breathing began to level out. Now if she could only stop her tears.

"*Ya*, I feel badly for Yvonne too." Jake sighed but ignored her comment about making a snide remark. She wondered what he was thinking, aside from his feelings about Yvonne.

Jake knew he should say something about Eva's apology about the snide remark, but he had hoped she would follow up with an answer to his earlier question, even though it was none of his business if John kissed her, as he'd told her.

His heart sank to his stomach. "Define 'kiss'" sounded to him like John had kissed her. But he needed to stay true to what he'd said and not pressure her about it.

As she attempted to pull herself together, Jake couldn't stop looking at her lips. He'd never wanted to kiss her more than at this moment. Was it because another man had? Could he not stand to see her so upset? Did he love her? He did. Why hadn't he made his feelings known earlier? He knew why. He'd placed Eva in a category, one she'd grown out of. Somewhere along the line, friendship had turned into love.

"You're staring at my mouth." Eva sniffled as she raised an eyebrow.

It was a bold and truthful thing to say, and even though he was sure his face was red, he wasn't going to deny it. "*Ya*, I am." He swallowed back the knot in his throat and wondered if this was the time to show Eva how he felt about her. Being honorable was becoming harder and harder.

"And I know you're wondering about John and me, and . . . the kiss." She pressed her lips together. It wasn't that weird thin-lipped smile but more of a thoughtful expression, as if she was pondering something.

He nodded. "*Ya*, I am. But, as you said, it's not *mei* business, and I agree."

"Do you want me to show you how he kissed me?"

Jake's jaw dropped. "Uh . . ." He couldn't think of anything he wanted more than for her to kiss him, but doing so the way John had seemed a strange thing to attach to the question. "Okay."

She leaned up on her toes, her mouth so close to his they shared the same air. This was it. The kiss was going to happen. Then she veered left and gently kissed him on the cheek before she smiled and walked away.

Jake slowly reached up and touched the spot where her lips had been. Then he smiled too.

# CHAPTER 17

Yvonne hadn't stopped crying since she entered the church Friday morning. Even though tears were expected at a funeral, she couldn't seem to get a handle on her emotions, only nodding every time someone offered their condolences. She just wanted the entire day to be over.

Trevor's parents had chosen to have a closed-coffin celebration of Trevor's life, which had left Yvonne feeling sick to her stomach. They hadn't mentioned that in the few short conversations they'd had with Yvonne. Maybe it would have made things worse, but she'd thought she would be able to see him one last time. It could have been the condition of Trevor's remains that made a closed casket necessary. Yvonne hadn't asked, and she wasn't sure she wanted to know. At least Trevor's parents had chosen lovely photos to display, including those of her and Trevor, and they had written a beautiful obituary that also listed Yvonne as the love of Trevor's life and his fiancée.

She was flanked in the front row by each of Trevor's parents, which felt odd. Yvonne would have thought they'd want to sit side by side. Her aunt was on the other side of Trevor's mother, which also felt strange. Family filled the two rows behind them, and farther back sat her bridesmaids, groomsmen—who would also be serving as pallbearers—and a lot of other people Yvonne didn't know.

Following words and prayer from the minister, two of Trevor's friends spoke. Yvonne's wasn't sure when Trevor's mother grabbed her hand, but now they clung tightly to each other.

She listened, cried, and found herself constantly looking around, as if being in church would produce an image of Jesus, that he would tell her that she would see Trevor again and somehow fix the pain she feared she would carry for the rest of her life. And she thought about the Trinity—the Father, Son, and Holy Spirit. Even though it hadn't been a concept she had considered until recently, she prayed and begged God to flood her with some sort of relief.

Would Jesus look like a regular person? Was he disguised in a suit somewhere here in the church? It felt silly to think about it, but as her eyes scanned the few people she could see on either side of her, she didn't see anyone who would fit her description of God's Son. She twisted in her seat, peered at all the people behind her, until she felt

Trevor's mother's arm around her, guiding her to turn back around as if she were a small child misbehaving in church.

After the celebration of Trevor's life was over, there was a short service at the gravesite, but it was all a blur to Yvonne. By the time they got back to Trevor's house, a lavish meal had been laid out by caterers. Yvonne held up to her responsibilities and greeted everyone as best she could. She finally spotted George, and she knew she had to face him. His wife was on the other side of the room, and since she didn't know the woman well, she decided this would be the best time to talk to him privately.

"Thank you for coming." She held out her hand, but to her surprise, George hugged her and told her how sorry he was for her loss. Yvonne was sure he was saddened, but she knew him well enough to know that he would ask about the book, even at a funeral.

"I expect you to take some time off work," he said after he eased out of the embrace. "At least any projects that might come up from me. Hopefully, any other clients will give you the same courtesy."

Yvonne was happy to hear this. George was her biggest client. At present, he was the only one who mattered. She nodded. Her neck was going to ache later from the repetitive motion.

"I don't have anything new on the burner, no new book to track down, so take all the time you need." He was building up to the question searing his mind. "Um, were you able to get the Amish man to sell?"

There it was. Yvonne shook her head. "No. He wouldn't budge." She swallowed back more tears building, unable to offer up the complete truth—that she had the book at home. Then she had a horrible thought. What if George was meant to have the book? Would it have some sort of profound effect on him, the way it had with her? Maybe she was supposed to give him the book. Perhaps it was never meant to be sold, only shared.

"That's too bad." George frowned. "I actually had a buyer who was willing to pay even more than the amount offered to the Amish fellow."

Her thoughts calmed. George's interest in the book had nothing to do with spiritual matters, only money. Yvonne thanked him again for coming, then continued to walk the room, her feet as heavy as her heart.

After at least a dozen people told her she didn't need to be alone and offered to go home with her, she snuck out by herself. She needed the solace and privacy of her own house, in her bed, under the covers, where she feared she might live forever.

Once she was home and tucked in, she prayed. For Jesus to show himself. That she would see Trevor in her dreams. That the intense pain in the pit of her stomach would go away. And that she'd somehow find a way to go on each day.

And sleep finally came.

By the time Eva got home from work, her mind and body ached from the tension she'd felt all day. She and Jake had mostly avoided each other as each of them tried to go about work casually, as if a huge issue wasn't hanging in the air. Eva had to decide if she was going to go out with John. He had pinned another note to the fence post, asking her to join him for supper the following Tuesday. Luckily, Eva had found it before one of her brothers had.

After she'd bathed and gotten into bed, her head began to reel from all the emotional events of the day. She wished she could do something to ease Yvonne's suffering, and she wondered if things were going to stay awkward between herself and Jake. She wasn't going to allow Jake to cast her aside while also denying her a relationship with someone else. Did he not want her for himself but not want anyone else to have her? That wasn't love, which made her question whether she'd read him wrong. He had made no attempt to tell her how he really felt.

She picked up John's note and wrote underneath his request.

> *Danki*, John, for your kind invitation. I had a wonderful time on our supper date, and I would enjoy going out with you again on Tuesday.
>
> Gott's blessings to you,
>
> Eva

The next time, John might want to kiss her somewhere

else besides her cheek, and she just might let him. She owed it to herself—and to John—to open her heart, even if just a little, to the possibility of them as a couple. If Jake truly cared about her in a romantic way, it would have been the perfect time to tell her earlier in the day.

As she lay down, she thought about what Yvonne had said, how life is short. She knew her friend had made the comment as related to Jake. But the same sentiment could be applied to John. Should she disregard a handsome, kind suitor who seemed to really care for her, hoping Jake loved her the way she loved him? It felt risky. She wanted a family and children.

Despite her logical way of sorting things out in her mind, she couldn't stop thinking about the way she'd kissed Jake on the cheek, the way she'd lingered there long enough for him to possibly feel the emotion she was carrying. He had kissed her on the forehead. Was he comforting a friend or trying to tell her something?

What was he doing tonight?

Was he thinking about her?

Jake awoke feeling tired and grumpy the next morning. He had tossed and turned most of the night, and he couldn't get Eva out of his mind. Every time he thought about Yvonne and Trevor, his situation turned urgent. He had to find out if Eva planned to go out with John again. He was not going to step on another man's toes or deny Eva happiness if she was developing feelings for John. But would she have so tenderly kissed him on the cheek if that were the case?

For years he'd thought Eva had a crush on him, an English term he'd picked up when he was younger. Had her feelings for him changed? Again, he wondered if being honorable had been the right thing to do. Was he cheating himself—and Eva—out of a life together by letting John have his chance with her?

Things had been awkward between him and Eva the day before. Jake needed to clear the air, even if the conversation led him away from her.

Questions rattled around in his mind like loose marbles slamming together in chaos. He wasn't going to be able to focus on work or anything else until he talked to Eva, honestly and without holding anything back.

He didn't arrive at the bookstore until later than usual, only ten minutes before he was scheduled to open. The Peony Inn widows, Lizzie and Esther, were waiting on the front porch when he pulled his buggy into the parking lot.

"*Wie bischt*, Esther and Lizzie," he said as he tethered his horse to the fence post near their buggy. "I'm running a little behind this morning."

"We're early." Esther smiled. Lizzie didn't.

Jake cringed, wondering what was on the younger sister's mind. He was sure to hear about it any minute. Lizzie waited until after he'd unlocked the door and swung it open for them before she spoke.

"I heard a rumor that I think involves you." Lizzie shuffled her dentures around, as she was known to do sometimes.

Jake walked around the counter, popped open the cash register, and began loading the money. "A rumor?" He couldn't imagine what the sisters could have heard, especially that involved him.

Lizzie set her small purse on the counter and glowered at him. "I heard that Eva is being courted by John Yoder. Is this true?"

Jake had been trying to shrug off his bad mood all morning, and this wasn't helping. He looked down and took a deep breath before he said anything. "They went on a date, but I'm not sure how that involves me."

"*Ach*, dear boy." Lizzie lifted her chin and waited until she had his attention before she went on. "John Yoder is a fine young man, but anyone would be dense not to see that you and Eva belong together. I see the way you two look at each other." She pointed, then wagged a finger at him. "When you're not making her cry, of course."

Jake recalled the way he'd yelled at Eva a week ago. It seemed like a lot had happened since then. "Eva is free to choose whoever she wants to go out with." His chest tightened just saying the words. In truth, he'd never asked Eva out or given her an opportunity to choose.

"Lizzie, we have a lengthy list of things to get. Leave the poor boy alone." Esther stood by her sister's side, but after a few seconds she limped toward the office supplies. The limp seemed to come and go. Esther had told him before that it was arthritis.

Lizzie stayed put. "Luckily for you, I'm going to save the day." She shook her head. "If courtship between the right people was left up to men, no one would end up with the right person."

Jake finally lifted his eyes to her. "And how are you going to save the day, Lizzie?" His response was probably a bit more sarcastic than necessary, but Jake's day wasn't starting out with a bang. He was tired, and that always dragged him down.

If he'd offended Lizzie, she didn't seem to notice. "I've got just the thing for you." She dug around her purse and produced a small glass vial, similar to what he used to administer medicine to his horses, only smaller. "Two drops of this, and Eva won't be able to stay away from you."

Cringing, Jake could feel himself blushing, something he'd been doing a lot of lately, and it didn't make him feel all that manly. He glanced around and looked for Esther. The older—and wiser, Jake thought—of the sisters was shopping somewhere out of sight.

"What is this?" Jake took the vial and held it up closer to the skylight.

Lizzie leaned over the counter. "Love potion."

Jake lowered the bottle, then put a hand over his mouth to keep from bursting out laughing.

Lizzie lowered her brows at him and thrust her hands to her tiny hips. "Go ahead and laugh, but you'll thank me later." She waved a hand in his direction. "Just two drops. That's all it takes."

Jake decided the only way to get her to stop this silliness was to humor her, so he unscrewed the small cap, filled the dropper, then opened his mouth.

"What in the world are you doing? Have you gone *ab im kopp*?" Lizzie snatched the bottle from his hand while Jake closed his mouth, still holding the dropper. "Give me that." She took the dropper from his hand and screwed it back onto the vial. Then she shook her head. "It's for *her*. Not you. It's a special blend of herbs and spices." Lizzie set the vial on the counter and sighed in exasperation as she wagged her head again. "Two drops in her tea or coffee. That's all you need."

Jake nodded even though he didn't believe in such things. He could recall his grandmother going to a powwower when he was a young boy, and telling him the woman was able to give her a potion to make her allergies better. These days most powwowers were frowned upon, except by some of the elders. Jake had never heard of any residing in Montgomery. He was pretty sure the bishop wouldn't approve of Lizzie's tactics, but a blend of herbs and spices didn't exactly equate to a witch's brew. How harmful could it be? He stifled a smile, knowing he'd never stoop to such silliness.

Lizzie raised her chin. "I think that's worth ten percent off anything that Esther and I might purchase today."

"*Ya*, of course." He'd learned a long time ago just to agree with Lizzie.

He took the small bottle to the back room and stashed it in the cabinet where the spices were, unsure if it would ever be needed for anything. Certainly not as a magic love potion. He chuckled to himself before he walked back to the counter. Lizzie had apparently joined her sister.

A few minutes later, the ladies were done shopping, and Jake checked them out, giving them ten percent off of everything.

"Two drops," Lizzie whispered before she caught up with Esther moving toward the door.

Eva had just finished tethering her horse and started walking in the direction of the store. No picnic basket in hand and wearing a bland expression. Jake feared they were going to have another awkward day if he didn't have an honest conversation with her.

Eva was surprised to see Lizzie and Esther in the parking lot. They'd apparently done their shopping early. It was barely after ten. She waved, then continued to trudge toward the front door. She had tacked the note to John on the fence post, accepting his invitation to go out on Tuesday. Jake might have a jealous flare-up when she asked to leave early again, but he'd done nothing to indicate he had any intentions of moving their relationship past anything but friendship.

When she walked into the bookstore and Jake came

around the corner, she had to believe she had done the right thing in agreeing to go out with John.

"I think we need to talk." Jake scratched his normally clean-shaven face. This morning he already looked like he had an afternoon shadow. He also had dark circles underneath his eyes. He was still her handsome Jake, but he looked tormented.

"*Ya*, okay." Eva set her purse on the counter and stood facing him. "What about?" She was pretty sure she knew, but she had no idea which way the conversation would go.

He waved an arm for her to follow him. "Back room over some *kaffi*?"

She nodded and stashed her purse under the counter before she followed him.

Jake paced the kitchen, so Eva poured them each a cup of coffee and sat in one of the chairs around the small table. He eventually sat across from her.

He took a deep breath, and even though he had sweat beads across his forehead and a taut expression, he stared her right in the eyes. "I can't keep doing this, wondering and worrying about what's going with us." He paused. "I mean, we'll always be friends, but uh . . . if you are developing feelings for John, I guess I just need to know. I, uh . . . I'll have to plan ahead, I mean to replace you when you eventually get married and quit, and . . . I guess I just need to know what's going on."

Somewhere during his rambling, Eva's mouth had fallen open. "We only went on *one* date, Jake. Who said anything about me quitting or getting married?" She wondered if this was his way of telling her he cared about her more than as just a friend. Or did he just not want her to be with someone else but still wasn't ready to commit?

"Are you going to see John again?" Jake sat taller as he held her gaze.

She was tempted to tell him it was none of his business, but if he was trying to tell her something, he needed to spit it out. "*Ya*, we are going out again on Tuesday."

He stood up, the chair grinding against the wood floor as he pushed it backward. "*Ach*, well, then, I guess that's that."

"Jake, if you have something to say to me, just say it." *Please, just say it.*

He opened his mouth but only took a deep breath. "I just want you to be happy. If John makes you happy, then—"

He was interrupted when the bell on the front door rang. Eva looked over her shoulder, then back at Jake. She needed to tell him that she liked John but that *he* was the one who held her heart. If his feelings weren't the same, she'd be embarrassed, and then it would be hard to work with him. But it needed to be said.

"I'll go see who that is." She stood up and stared at him across the table. "Can we finish this conversation in a few minutes?"

"I think it's probably over." Jake scowled before he started toward the front of the store. Eva slowly followed, unsure of what his feelings were. Was he worried about losing her or eventually losing an employee? Or did he really care that much that she was going out with John for a second time?

Eva swallowed back a lump in her throat when she saw John standing just inside the store.

Jake stopped abruptly, so much so that Eva almost bumped into him. She sidestepped around him until she was in front of John.

"*Wie bischt*," she said as she tried to smile. *Bad timing.*

"Can I talk to you for a minute?" John took his eyes from hers and looked over her shoulder at Jake. "Sorry, Jake. We won't be long."

Eva glanced over her shoulder at her boss, who shrugged, plastering a smile on his face that she knew wasn't authentic.

"*Ya*, sure. Take all the time you need." He did an about-face and left Eva alone with John.

Eva had no idea what John wanted to talk about, but she was losing any doubt in her mind that Jake was anything but jealous. She just wasn't clear exactly where his emotions stood. But it felt like a bad idea for Jake to overhear whatever John had to say.

"Let's step outside." She motioned toward the door, and after John opened it for her, they stood just outside the entrance.

John gently touched her on the arm. "I'm sorry about this, Eva, but could we change our date to another night? Maybe Monday or Wednesday?" He lowered his arm and smiled. "I got a huge construction job from an *Englisch* family in Bedford. The only thing is, he needs all the work done on Tuesday, which means me and *mei* crew will need to work late." He pushed back the rim of his hat and smiled. "Any other day works for me. I'm looking forward to spending more time with you."

Eva looked over her shoulder. Jake had reentered the front of the store and was sitting behind the counter. They locked eyes, and Eva knew she had to make a decision, no matter the risk.

Jake wasn't sure what was going on outside. Eva and John had walked down the sidewalk and were out of sight. Were they stealing a kiss? His stomach muscles clenched as his chest tightened.

After what seemed like a long few minutes, Jake decided he was too jittery to sit behind the counter. He walked to the kitchen and paced, his thumbs looped beneath his suspenders. The thought of John kissing Eva caused angry butterflies to thrash around in his stomach, and his anxious heart felt like it was about to explode in his chest.

He glanced at the cabinet where he'd stashed Lizzie's supposed love potion. *No, don't do it. It's silly.*

After a dozen more steps back and forth across the small kitchen, he rushed to the cabinet, grabbed the small bottle, and quickly dropped two drops into Eva's coffee like Lizzie had said. His chest tightened even more. If there was even a one percent chance that there was any truth to Lizzie's ramblings, he couldn't take any chances. He squeezed several more drops into her coffee before he quickly put the bottle back where it had been. Just in time since he heard the bell on the front door chime.

Eva walked into the room, her cheeks flushed. He wasn't sure what that meant, but he took his thumbs from beneath his suspenders and leaned against the counter. "Everything okay?"

She nodded but avoided making eye contact. Another clue? But what did it mean?

He edged closer to the table and took a long sip of coffee, happy to see her do the same thing. She squeezed her eyes closed for a moment before she looked at him. "I know you said we were done talking, but I need to tell you something."

Jake walked on shaky legs to the table, pulled out the chair, and sat down. "Okay." His heart thumped wildly in his chest.

"It's about John." She took a deep breath and eventually sat down across from him, then took another sip of coffee before she went on. "I-I decided not to go out with him again." She blinked back tears. "When I told him, he looked so hurt, like I broke his heart."

Jake gazed at her from across the table as relief flooded over him. "Please don't cry. I feel bad for John. I really do, because he's a nice man. But if you had fallen for him . . ." He gently pounded on his chest with a fisted hand. "It's *mei* heart that would have been broken."

He took a deep breath. "John told me a while back that he had strong feelings for you and that he wanted to court you. It was probably then that I realized I had been taking you for granted, that my feelings were stronger than I realized. But it seemed like the right thing to do, the honorable thing to do . . . to step back and see if you had feelings for him too." It was now or never. "Eva, you have to know that I love you."

He held his breath as he waited for her to respond.

"I know." Eva stared into her coffee cup. "But there are many different types of love." She raised her eyes to his and waited. Was he finally going to tell her how he felt? She could still picture the look on John's face when she'd told him that someone else held her heart and her love. He had guessed that it was Jake right away. Perhaps everyone saw that they belonged together except for her and Jake. But did Jake love her the way she longed for, or as a friend? He'd certainly given her mixed signals.

"*Ya*. There are many different types of love. And you've been the playful little sister type for so long that I guess you grew up when I wasn't looking. By the time I realized you had grown into a beautiful woman who was old enough to date, John confessed his feelings, and . . ."

He stood, walked around the table, knelt down beside her, and reached for her hand. "I'm seeing that grown-up version. Maybe when you went out with John, it nudged me in that direction, but you've also been slowly moving to a place in *mei* heart that is different and new to me."

She stared into his eyes. "And do you like this new place?"

"Very much," he said softly as he kept his eyes on hers. "I'd like for us to be more than friends."

Wow. He'd actually said it, and the way he was looking at her made her think he was going to kiss her, for real. She had waited so long and wanted it to be perfect. He leaned closer, still on one knee, his mouth approaching hers. But she abruptly stood up. "I'm sorry. I have to excuse myself." She held up one finger. "I'll be right back."

She scurried to the restroom, closed the door, then opened the small drawer to the side of the sink. Rummaging through bobby pins, a hairbrush, and loose nails and screws that shouldn't even be in there, she found the breath spray she was looking for—a cool, minty flavor. It would be too obvious to rush to the counter to find the lip gloss and lavender spray Yvonne had given her. But the breath spray would do. She didn't want her breath to taste like the bacon she'd eaten on the way to work.

This was it. Jake had said he loved her, in just the right way, and she was about to have her first kiss. She stood there a few more minutes willing herself to stop shaking. Then she slowly left the bathroom.

Jake approached her as she came into the kitchen. He cupped her cheeks and stared into her eyes. He wanted to kiss her properly, for it to be perfect, but he lingered, giving his pulse a few seconds to settle, if that was possible.

But then something started to happen to Eva. He lowered his hands and pointed to his own lips as he watched hers growing, her bottom lip rounding downward into an exaggerated frown—which it wasn't, because the top lip was doing the same thing in the opposite direction. Within seconds, her lips were twice their normal size.

She coughed and put a hand to her chest. "I feel like *mei* throat is closing up, and it's hard to breathe."

Jake fumbled around in his pocket and pulled out his cell phone, which took forever to power up, then dialed 911. Eva was breaking out in tiny red bumps on her cheeks.

"What's happening, Jake?" she asked as her huge bottom lip trembled and her eyes watered.

As her mouth grew even larger, she began to resemble a big bass. "I think you're having an allergic reaction." His voice trembled as he spoke.

She looked down at the cup on the table. "From *mei kaffi*?" Her watery eyes lifted to his as she blinked back tears.

Jake glanced at the cabinet where Lizzie's love potion was stored, then silently chastised himself, anger bubbling to the surface. He'd wanted to kiss her, not kill her.

His knees were weak as he explained to the 911 operator what had happened.

"You put *what* in *mei kaffi*?" Eva asked through her tears.

"I'll explain more later." He wrapped his arms around her and held her tightly as they waited for the ambulance.

# CHAPTER 18

Jake rode with Eva in the ambulance and held her hand the entire time as her lips grew even larger and more tiny pink spots appeared on her cheeks. The EMS person had given her a shot that he said would help, but Jake was wondering when it was going to start working, and he tried to shake the image of her resembling a fish.

He'd called Eva's mother during the commute to the hospital but had to leave a message on the answering machine in the barn. He prayed all the way there that her parents would get the message. They must have, and acted with superhuman powers, because they were at the hospital even before the ambulance, having hired a driver who had clearly challenged the speed limits to get them there.

Jake had also left a message for Lizzie to find out what was in the so-called love potion. Lizzie had returned his call within a few minutes, then joined him in the hospital waiting room about an hour after he arrived, along with her sister.

"I told you *two* drops." Lizzie had apparently been so distraught by the message that she'd left the house without her teeth.

"I don't think it matters how many drops. The doctor believes Eva is allergic to dandelion." Jake leaned his head back against the wall and sighed.

Lizzie covered her face with her hands. "Then it's *mei* fault."

Esther wrapped an arm around her sister's shoulder from where she was sitting on the other side of her. "It's no one's fault. And the doctor said Eva is going to be just fine."

Lizzie lifted a wadded-up tissue to her nose and blew. "She is for sure going to be okay, *ya*?"

From either side of Lizzie, Jake and Esther both nodded.

They were quiet for a few minutes.

Lizzie cleared her throat. "Did it work?"

Jake slowly turned his head to face her. "We didn't get that far."

"Hmm." Lizzie strummed her fingers atop her knees, then crossed her legs, uncrossed them, then leaned her head back with a thud against the wall. "Ow."

They all startled when a doctor emerged from behind the closed door in the emergency room, followed by Eva's parents.

"She's going to be just fine," the young doctor said. "The shot the EMS personnel gave her in the ambulance was already helping, and we've given her another shot. Her swelling should go down within seventy-two hours. Probably sooner than that."

Eva's parents had stepped to the side and were talking quietly to each other. The doctor glanced at Jake, then Lizzie and Esther. "Any questions?"

"When can she go home?" Jake cut his eyes in the direction of Mary and Lloyd Graber, assuming they would be taking Eva home.

"Within an hour. They're just finishing up some discharge papers." The doctor smiled. "No worries. Really. She is going to be fine. But she'll want to stay away from dandelion."

They all nodded, and after the doctor was gone, Eva's mother approached them. "We will be taking Eva home with us." She glanced at her husband before she looked back at them. "Eva doesn't want anyone to see her right now and asked if you would all leave before she is released. And Jake, she doesn't want to go back to work until the swelling goes down, which, as you heard, shouldn't be more than a few days."

Jake stood up. "*Ya*, yes, ma'am, whatever time she needs, of course."

Esther and Lizzie slowly got to their feet, and the three of them left, already having decided to share a ride home.

Thankfully, Lizzie was quiet on the ride until they pulled up at The Peony Inn. Before she got out of the seven-passenger van, she turned to Jake. "I do know a little remedy that might speed things up. Once when I got stung by a bee, *mei mamm*—"

"No!" Jake and Esther said in unison.

Lizzie huffed. "Fine, then."

After Jake got back to the bookstore, which he'd locked after turning the *Closed* sign to face outward, he sat down on the stool behind the counter, elbows on the wooden top, and rested his chin in his hands. He had been so close to kissing Eva. He was starting to wonder if it would ever happen. He'd told her how he felt, so hopefully when she was better, they could resume where they'd left off.

He had prayed all the way to the hospital, and right now he'd just be grateful to God that she was all right. Giving his head a little shake, he tried to clear the last image of her in his head.

"I look like a fish." Eva held the mirror—the one she'd asked for earlier from the nurse—to her face. "A fish with chicken pox."

Her mother patted her arm. "The doctor said you are lucky that it isn't itching, and it will all disappear in a few days." She chuckled. "I know it isn't funny, *mei maedel*, but leave it to Lizzie to do something like this."

Eva couldn't help but smile, even though it felt like her lips had overtaken her face. "I can't believe Jake actually slipped it in *mei kaffi*."

"Nor can I," her father bellowed from where he was standing near the window. But Eva saw his mouth curl up on one side. Both of her parents had thought Jake was the perfect match for her.

"It really is rather sweet that Jake was willing to go to such great lengths to get you to fall in love with him. Doesn't he know that you already are, and have been?" Her mother winked at Eva.

"*Ya*. I'm almost certain he does. And I think he finally sees me as a mature woman." She rolled her eyes. "Right now, he sees me as a fish."

They both smiled. "Life might be changing for you soon," her mother said.

"I hope so," she said softly. "I still feel bad about John, *Mamm*." She'd told her mother earlier about her conversation with him. "You should have seen the look on his face. But whether or not Jake loved me the way I hoped, it didn't feel fair to put John in second place, hoping I would love him the way I love Jake."

A nurse came in with papers for them to sign, and not long afterward they were able to leave. Eva's father had called the driver, and he was waiting for them at the exit.

Eva reached up and touched her swollen lips, but she was smiling on the inside. It might be a few more days before that kiss actually happened, but Jake was ready to take things to the next level.

After they got home, Eva stood in the living room with

her hands on her hips and allowed the inevitable teasing from her brothers.

"Not just a bass, a largemouth bass." Amos roared as if he'd said the funniest thing in the world.

"That's enough," her father said as he waved an arm to motion them outside. "You all have chores to do."

Eva went upstairs, tired from the day's events. Her mother had offered to bring her some soup upstairs, along with a straw. While she waited, she closed her eyes, fought the sleep that was coming, and wondered how Yvonne was doing. Yesterday had surely been a hard day for her. Eva opened the drawer of her nightstand and took out some lined sheets of paper and a pen. Maybe hearing what had happened to Eva might cheer up Yvonne, or at the least distract her, as she seemed to prefer sometimes. If she hurried, she could get it in the mail today.

By Tuesday Yvonne had settled into a routine. It was mandatory to answer the phone if her aunt, bridesmaids, Trevor's parents, or anyone else called. Otherwise, they showed up at her house to check on her, which was the last thing she needed.

Slouched under her covers and propped up with two pillows, she glanced at the pizza box on the end of her bed alongside an empty container of Blue Bell chocolate ice cream. Prior to Trevor's death, she'd never eaten in bed, much less left empty containers lying around. But this was her life now. Eat, sleep, repeat. And get the mail every few days.

It was nearing dark, so she slipped into her robe, peeked out the window to make sure none of her neighbors were out, then shuffled to the mailbox and retrieved what was most likely all bills. However, she was surprised to find a letter from Eva that had been mailed Saturday. She was glad she'd chosen to get the mail today.

After she was back in her bedroom living quarters, she glanced at her empty food containers in disgust but crawled back beneath the covers anyway and tore open the envelope.

Dear Yvonne,
I am wondering how you are doing, and I can't imagine how hard Friday must have been for you. I am keeping you in my prayers several times per day. Please let me know if there is more I can do.

In some ways, it feels inconsiderate to tell you about my life and what's been going on, but when we last spoke, you said you needed a distraction. So, I'm hoping this distraction might bring a smile to your face. I decided not to go on another date with John Yoder when he asked. It just didn't feel fight. And it was a good decision since it seems as though Jake is ready for us to be more than friends.

Then Eva went on to detail her ordeal with Jake and at the hospital. And for the first time since Trevor died, Yvonne laughed out loud. She didn't recognize the sound of her voice.

Yvonne had known some of her friends for decades, yet an Amish woman she'd recently met had made her feel better than anyone else. Those closest to her had been tiptoeing around her, careful not to say the wrong thing. She had needed a distraction, and Eva had provided just that. Her laughter was short lived, but it was a welcomed reprieve, enough for her to at least carry her empty food containers to the trash can. She kept Eva's letter on the nightstand so she could read it again when life became unbearable.

She climbed back under the comfort of her bedspread and snuggled in. She'd never slept this much in her life, but she couldn't find a reason to do much else. Each time before she closed her eyes, she prayed that she'd feel some sense of Jesus's presence in her life. She hated that she didn't have the faith like the man in the book, and she still had her doubts that his story was true. But she wanted more than anything to believe, to see Trevor again, to know that someday she would.

She wasn't sure how long she'd slept when she heard a knock at the door. As she wondered who would be calling so late, it occurred to her that darkness didn't necessarily mean late. She glanced at the time on her cell phone. It was only seven thirty, so her visitor could be any one of her well-intended friends or family, even though she hadn't missed any calls.

She sighed as she slipped her arms into her robe and shuffled to the front door. Yawning, she came into the living room but stopped long before she made it to the door when she saw something out of the corner of her eye. She began blinking over and over, but the image didn't go away. "Trevor?" Barely any sound came out of her mouth as she spoke, and her heart was growing in her chest. She could feel it expanding. Any minute she was going to explode with happiness.

"Hello, beautiful." Trevor smiled, and Yvonne ran into his arms, halfway expecting him to be a ghost, but he picked her up and swirled her around, clinging to her with as much desperation as she felt. Euphoria filled her from her head to her toes.

She smothered him in kisses—but suddenly backed away. He looked exactly like her Trevor, but unless she'd totally lost her mind, he couldn't be here. He was dressed in white slacks and a yellow polo shirt, and he had never looked handsomer. She breathed in the smell of his familiar scent, gazed into his eyes, and willed herself to stop trembling. Her eyes widened as her mouth fell open. "You're not really here, are you?"

Still smiling, he poked himself in the arm. "It feels like I'm here."

Yvonne walked to the couch and sat before she fainted. Her head was starting to swirl with confusion, and her heart had started pounding so hard that she no longer feared it might explode but instead worried it would give her a heart attack.

Then she pinched her arm as hard as she could and flinched from the pain.

Trevor sat by her on the couch and touched her hand. "What are you doing?"

"I'm dreaming. I'm trying to wake myself up." She squeezed her skin even harder.

Trevor half smiled but cringed a little. "That looks like it hurts. And do you really want to wake up?"

She stopped torturing herself and let go of her bruised skin. "So, I *am* dreaming?"

"You seem to think you are," he said, grinning.

Yvonne had slipped into a nonreality. If this was a dream, it was unlike anything she'd had before. She glanced around the room.

"What are you looking for?" Trevor crossed one leg over the other and twisted to face her, his expression turning sober.

"I don't know." She sighed, but her pulse still hadn't slowed down. "I guess some sort of proof that I'm not sleeping." *Or Jesus.*

"I'd say that big bruise on your arm should be proof enough that you're not sleeping." Trevor brushed hair from her face as he gazed into her eyes. "You're so beautiful."

Yvonne had a thought that caused her adrenaline to spike even more. "Am I dead?" She missed Trevor with her heart and soul, but somewhere beyond her grief, she felt like there were still things she had to do, eventually, when she didn't live beneath the covers in her bedroom.

Trevor laughed, a true guttural chuckle. "No. You're not dead." He leaned over and kissed her with every bit of passion she remembered, and whatever this was, she returned the kiss with everything she had.

"I can't stay." He eased away from her.

Yvonne blinked back tears. "I didn't think you could."

He stood up, reached into his pocket, and plopped a cherry cough drop into his mouth. "Old habits die hard."

Yvonne caught the pun and felt her eyes growing wild and wide again.

Trevor laughed. "Come here and tell me bye properly." He held out his arms, and on shaky legs, Yvonne went to him.

But instead of embracing him, she stared into his eyes, which somehow looked brighter, different. His skin was smoother. His scent enhanced. The color of his clothes more vivid. She wanted to ask him if there was a heaven. And, if so, why was he allowed to come here? Was her faith so weak that God had chosen to send Trevor in a dream so that she would become a true believer? Wasn't that cheating? Wasn't faith all about the ability to believe in the things you couldn't see?

So many questions filled her mind that she couldn't corral them into a sentence that made sense. She finally said, "Will I see you again?"

He leaned closer and kissed her. "I'm counting on it."

A tear slid down her cheek, and he gently wiped it away with his thumb. "I feel . . . something. It's confusing," she said as she searched his eyes. "I've been praying that I would see Jesus. I need to believe. I want to believe. And then there's this book . . . and . . ." She was rambling, she knew.

Trevor gently put a finger to her mouth and smiled. "You don't have to look hard to find Jesus." He motioned around the room. "He's everywhere. In the air you breathe. In every thought you have. He's like a friend you can just talk to. And He is the way to God."

Yvonne began to weep, harder than she thought she'd ever cried in her life. "I'm not sobbing like this because I'm sad . . . I just . . . I don't know what's happening to me."

Trevor pulled her into his arms and kissed her on the forehead, the familiar smell of the cherry cough drop filling the space around them. "Yes, you do."

He made the statement with such conviction that Yvonne was finally able to breathe. "It's the Holy Spirit."

Trevor eased her away and smiled. "I have to go."

"I'm guessing I will wake up and know that I dreamed this entire thing." She lowered her head, only to have him cup her chin and raise her eyes to his.

"I love you, Yvonne."

She could feel him leaving, but instead of sadness, she felt hope. "I love you too."

Then he was gone. Vanished into thin air. And Yvonne was left standing in her living room. But she wasn't alone. And she didn't think she'd ever be alone again as she walked back to bed and got beneath the covers.

"Thank You," she whispered.

When she woke up the next morning, sunlight beamed into her bedroom through the lace sheers layered behind the thick curtains she'd been keeping closed. She didn't remember opening the drapes, but the feel of the sun on her face was refreshing as she stretched, yawning but feeling more rested than she had in a while.

Then, like a stab in her heart, she bolted upright. "Trevor." It all came back to her—the dream, in vivid detail. The way Trevor had looked, how he smelled, the way he smiled and told her he loved her. She was tempted to cry because it wasn't real. It was a dream. But within the same thought, she realized it was also a gift. Her nerves began to settle as she came to the realization she'd been hoping for. She would see Trevor again.

God had gifted her with a special dream. She'd read that the only way to God was through Jesus, and apparently Yvonne must have searched for Jesus in the right place. Or was it like Trevor had said in the dream—that Jesus is everywhere?

She thought about the book and what she should do with it. This morning the author's story seemed more plausible, but something was niggling at her. *Who exactly is the author?* She wasn't sure why that mattered, but it seemed important to find out. Or maybe she just needed a purpose, a reason to get dressed, to go about her life. Her dream should have been enough to motivate her since it had filled her with hope. But she was wise enough to know that the gift, while beautiful in every way, wasn't a part of her reality.

As she stretched again, she saw the bruise on her left arm. Even in a dream, she'd pinched herself hard enough that it should have woken her up.

Smiling to herself, she slipped into her robe and moseyed into the living room, longing for some coffee. But before she made it to the kitchen, something on the coffee table caught her eye, and butterflies filled her stomach.

She slowly shuffled to the table, leaned down, and picked up the cherry cough drop, still in the wrapper. Closing her eyes, she held it to her chest as the same feeling she'd had during the night washed over her. A feeling of peace. Of hope.

Lifting her eyes above her, she whispered the thought that repeated itself in her mind. "Thank You."

# CHAPTER 19

Eva tethered her horse when she arrived at the bookstore Saturday morning, her stomach swirling with anticipation. She'd talked to Jake on the phone, but this was the first time for her to see him since he'd ridden in the ambulance with her to the hospital.

She took a deep breath as she opened the front door, happy to hear the familiar bell ringing. She'd missed work. And she'd missed Jake. He was sitting behind the counter when she arrived, and he quickly stood and came to her. Without hesitation, he wrapped his arms around her, nearly knocking the picnic basket out of her hand.

"I don't look like a fish anymore," she said after the embrace. "And I brought breakfast."

Normally, Jake was practically salivating when she walked in with baked goods, but he didn't even glance at the basket. He cupped her face with both hands instead.

"No, you don't look like a fish. Not at all." He grinned, and Eva's stomach fluttered again. He wasn't going to waste any time. Jake was finally going to kiss her. "You look beautiful." He paused, smiling again. "Beautiful and all grown up."

Eva grinned before she nervously rolled her eyes. "It's about time you noticed."

As his lips drew closer to hers, Eva's heart danced as the basket fell a couple of inches to the floor. Neither of them paid attention. They were consumed and lost in each other's eyes. Until the bell on the door rang, which caused them both to separate and take a step away from each other.

"Lizzie." Eva swallowed hard as she eyed the small woman, whose lips trembled.

"*Danki* to *Gott* that you are back at work and looking normal." Lizzie wrapped her arms around Eva and squeezed before she eased away. She touched Eva's cheek, which was still warm from Jake's hand. "I had to see for myself that you didn't look like a big fish anymore."

Eva stifled a grin. "*Nee.* I think I am back to normal." She snuck a glance at Jake, who smiled, then picked up the basket of baked goods. "I was just getting ready to take this to the back."

Lizzie chuckled. "It looked to me like you were getting ready to do more than that." She raised her eyebrows repeatedly. "But any canoodling will have to wait." She looped her arm in Eva's, urging her to start walking toward the back. Eva felt the warmth of embarrassment filling her face.

"We need to have a quick chat," Lizzie said as they brushed past Jake. Lizzie didn't spare him a glance.

"What is it, Lizzie? Is everything okay?" The woman's timing couldn't have been any worse. Eva was starting to wonder if the kiss was ever going to happen.

"It appears I arrived just in time," Lizzie whispered.

Eva couldn't disagree more, but she waited to hear why Lizzie thought so.

"I saw your *mamm* at the Bargain Center yesterday, and she told me you'd be back at work today, so that's why I got here early before you even opened. I was hoping to catch you before you locked lips with that hunky man."

Eva bit her lip in an effort not to laugh. Lizzie's sister had told her that some of Lizzie's language came from romance books she read.

"So?" Lizzie lifted her palms and her shoulders at the same time, and for a moment, the small woman reminded Eva of a little bird. "Do you have any questions?"

Eva opened her mouth, but it took her a couple of seconds to speak. "Uh . . . about what?"

Lizzie lowered her shoulders, and her hands fell to her sides. "I feel responsible for your trip to the hospital, and even though it's uncustomary to have a conversation such as we're having, I feel it's *mei* responsibility to provide you with any answers."

Eva wasn't sure what the question was. She nervously wrapped the string of her prayer covering around her finger. Lizzie was known to be outspoken, and she and her sister often tried to play matchmaker for members of the community, but this seemed far out even for Lizzie. "Answers to what?"

Lizzie groaned. "About kissing, *mei maedel.*" She folded her arms across her chest and raised her chin. "I read lots of romantic books."

*So I've heard.* Eva was sure her face couldn't be any redder. And the bell on the front door had chimed twice since they'd been in the back room.

"I'm a bit of an expert when it comes to matters of the heart." Lizzie pressed her lips together, then sighed. "So, hit me with any questions you might have about kissing or other related matters."

Eva was barely able to control a gasp of surprise. "Um . . ." The bell on the door rang again. "I-I can't think of any questions," she said, avoiding Lizzie's piercing glare. "But if I do think of anything, I'll let you know."

Lizzie gave a taut nod of her head before she patted Eva on the arm. "Okay. I'm available for any romantic guidance you might need."

The woman was so serious that Eva had a hard time not smiling. "I'll remember that," she finally said, biting her lip again afterward.

"*Gut.* I'm going now." Lizzie did an about-face and scurried out of the back room.

Eva tapped a finger to her chin, grinning and wondering if that conversation had really just happened.

By the time she rounded the corner, she was met by

a flood of people. Over a dozen English women shuffled around the bookstore, and a large van was parked outside. It would be a good day for the bookstore. Possibly because Monday was Memorial Day and lots of folks had a long weekend.

She waited until the women had spread out and she had Jake's eye. He winked at her, then blew her a kiss. Eva laughed. It was as close to the real thing as she was going to get for a while.

After looking around and seeing the women were occupied, she blew him a kiss back. *Good things are worth waiting for.*

Yvonne muted the television so she could completely concentrate on what she'd just read on her computer. The TV was mostly background noise, but if what she'd found out was true, she needed to focus solely on her computer screen without any distractions.

"Wow," she said as she continued to read what was on the screen.

It had taken days of research to find out about the author of the book. *Walk with Me* by Jerry Lance had consumed her thoughts, and finally she knew a little bit about the man behind the story. Even before her research, she'd known that the book belonged with Jake. This only confirmed it.

As she leaned back against the couch, she stared somewhere past her computer, lost in thought. What if things hadn't happened exactly as they had? If Jake had never slipped the book into her suitcase, she would have been left with only the first forty pages in her mind, when there was so much more to learn. What if George had never sent her on a mission to find the book? She never would have met Eva and Jake, two of the kindest people she'd ever known.

She picked up the priceless book that sat next to her on the couch alongside the Bible. Even though *Walk with Me* was special in so many ways, it had ultimately led her back to the Bible. She'd reread scriptures that she had doubted before but now saw in a different light. Often she felt the same feeling she'd felt when Trevor had visited her in what she had to believe was a dream. Maybe the cough drop had always been on the coffee table.

After she'd let her thoughts drift, she looked back at her computer screen and smiled. It was time she returned the book to Jake. She wondered how her two friends were doing, if they'd finally admitted how they felt about each other. Yvonne had called Eva's home phone and left a message. She knew the phone was in the barn, and Eva's mother had called her back to let her know that Eva was recovering well. But she was curious how things were working out romantically for the couple. She would know soon enough.

She printed what was on her computer screen, all twelve pages, then opened the travel app on her computer and booked a plane ticket for the following Friday, deciding not to call but to surprise Eva and Jake.

A trip would do her good, and the visit certainly had a purpose. Yvonne still cried daily, but a new and refreshing hope filled her senses, and somehow she knew she would be all right. And she'd see Trevor again someday.

Jake was having the longest day of his life, even though it was probably his most profitable day so far this year. The English women had browsed for over an hour, and it took almost as long to check them out, each of them paying with a credit card. If Jake was allowed two luxuries, it would be electricity for a modern credit card machine and air-conditioning during the summer months.

His stomach rumbled as he helped Eva bag the women's purchases. He hadn't even had time to sample whatever was in the basket Eva had brought. All the ladies were pleasant and chatty and had bombarded them with questions about being Amish. Jake was grateful for the business, but he couldn't take his eyes off Eva, or her lips that he longed to kiss. But he smiled on the inside as Eva tried to answer questions while also frantically running credit cards. He'd caught her looking at him any time she could. Hopefully, she was as eager for the kiss as he was.

They both waved as the women exited the store, and they were standing next to each other when two cars pulled into the parking lot. More English tourists poured out of the vehicles.

"The store has done exceptionally well today," Eva said, grinning at him. "And it looks like more happy shoppers are here."

Jake scowled. "*Ya*, a great day." He rolled his eyes.

Eva brushed her fingers against Jake's. "We've waited this long," she said, smiling.

He briefly found her hand and squeezed. "I'm tired of waiting." He sounded like a pouty little boy, but it was true. "We could flip the *Closed* sign before they get to the door."

Eva laughed. "*Nee*, we can't do that, and you know it."

"It's my store." He nudged her, grinning. But even as he said it, he knew in his heart that someday it would be *their* store.

"Behave," she said as she let go of his hand and began to welcome the women coming into the store.

Jake sighed. "I'll try."

And for the next hour, they went through the same drill as with the first group, although there were only six of them this time. But they were taking longer, browsing more, and in the end they didn't spend nearly as much as the first group.

By the time Jake had practically rushed them out the door, he knew he couldn't wait any longer. He flipped the sign to *Closed*, then took Eva's hand and dragged her to the back room.

"You can't just close the store at twelve thirty on a Saturday, especially when you are having such a *gut* day." She giggled, understanding his sense of urgency since she felt it too. "Slow down, though." She laughed again.

Jake slowed his stride only a little, and when they got to the back room, he stopped and turned to face her. "If that bell on the door chimes, we are *not* answering. Mr. Maples will know to leave the mail on the counter, like he's done in the past when we were busy in the back. I'm waiting on a refund check on some books I returned, so I hate to lock the door."

Eva wasn't going to argue as the intensity of his gaze caused her heart to flip in her chest. Was it really coming? The kiss? After all the years of waiting?

"You're not going to slip me more of Lizzie's love potion, are you?" She grinned, and Jake hung his head for a couple of seconds before he recaptured her eyes.

"*Nee*. I feel awful about that." He chuckled. "And silly."

Eva shrugged. "I thought it was sweet. Even though *mei bruders*' teasing went on for three days, every time *mei* parents weren't nearby."

He inched closer to her, and Eva fought to control the dizzying current racing through her as a sensuous glance passed between them. There was no doubt in her mind that Jake was seeing her as the woman she'd come to be. She recalled him telling her he loved her before her lips had doubled in size. Would he say it again? She hadn't had a chance to tell him how she felt, although she was sure he knew.

As his hand took her face and gently held her cheek, he felt so familiar. But she found herself seeing him in a new light, too, which surprised her as his lips drew near hers. She loved him. She was attracted to him. But the intimacy, the way his eyes clung to hers as their lips met, him barely kissing her like the soft wisp of a feather at first, then infusing a passion Eva had only dreamed about . . . It was more than she ever could have hoped for in a first kiss.

"How was that for a grown-up kiss?" Jake whispered before he kissed the pulsing hollow of her neck. Eva was so caught up in the heady sensation, fueled even more when he raised his mouth to hers again, she couldn't have answered if she'd tried.

They both jumped when the bell on the door chimed, but Jake shook his head and kissed her again, stopping briefly to say, "They can wait."

Eva wasn't going to argue as she basked in the intimacy of Jake's arms, each kiss more passionate than the last. She'd waited so long for these precious moments she couldn't bear to stop.

Finally, Jake eased away and groaned. "The sign says *Closed*. Can't they read?" He smiled before he kissed her again.

"I can read just fine!"

Eva pushed Jake away and gasped when she recognized the voice. "*Daed*!" She fought frantically to tuck loose strands of hair beneath her prayer covering, which felt lopsided. She glanced at Jake, and the color had completely siphoned out of his face as his mouth hung open.

"Sir, uh . . . ," was all Jake managed to get out as Eva's father folded his arms across his chest. "I *lieb* your *dochder*, sir. This isn't just canoodling."

Eva shot him a sideways glance, grinning a little at the use of the word. Even one corner of her father's mouth lifted in a half smile. *Thankfully.*

"And I *lieb*, Jake, *Daed*." Eva lifted her chin, blew another strand of hair from her face, and attempted again to straighten her prayer covering.

Her father lifted a bushy eyebrow. "*Ach*, well, I should hope so. Maybe lock the door next time you plan on carrying on in such a way." He waved an arm at them. "This canoodling, as you call it."

Eva lowered her head and sighed before she met eyes with her father again. "What are you doing here?"

He cleared his throat. "I . . . I, uh . . . need a present for your *mamm*. She likes books. I thought you could pick one out for her."

Eva thought for a moment. "It isn't her birthday. So . . . ?"

"*Nee*, it's not her birthday." Her father shifted his weight and dropped his arms to his side.

Knowing she might be overstepping, she said, "*Daed*, are you in trouble with *Mamm*?" She cringed a little.

"*Nee*, I am not." He faced off with Eva, then finally

sighed as he shook his head. "Your *mamm* and I celebrate the day of our first kiss. Her idea. I go along with it because it makes her happy." His eyes ping-ponged back and forth between Eva and Jake. "How ironic that we will share this anniversary together. Unless . . . ?"

Eva shook her head. "*Nee*. First kiss, *Daed*."

Her father glared at Jake. "A bit much for a first kiss, don't you think?"

Jake and Eva glanced at each other, then both shrugged, grinning.

Eva's father waved an arm at them again before he rattled off something under his breath that Eva didn't catch. "Just come help me find a present for your *mudder*."

He peered over his shoulder and winked at Eva. Her heart danced even more.

After her father was out of sight, Jake kissed her again . . . and again . . . until Eva's father bellowed her name.

Giggling, she went to go help her father pick out a gift. She'd had no idea her parents celebrated their first kiss.

*I love that idea.*

# CHAPTER 20

Yvonne tried not to go too fast in her rental as she drove from the Indianapolis airport toward Montgomery. It was difficult not to exceed the speed limit since it was lower in Indiana than in Texas, but she was eager to surprise Eva and Jake. With less than forty minutes left to drive, Yvonne's mind wandered, but she mentally landed back on her feet after her thoughts had gone full circle. She would always miss Trevor, but she still had a life to live, and she wanted to make it the best she could—being true to herself, to God, and to those she loved. She'd probably never tell her aunt about her shift in beliefs unless the subject came up, which it rarely had over the years.

She was thinking about her aunt when her cell phone rang. She was surprised to see Eva's number flash on the dashboard display. She was glad she'd taken the time this trip to Bluetooth her phone to the rental car.

"Well, hello." Yvonne smiled. "This is a nice surprise." *And ironic since I'll be seeing you soon.*

"Are you busy?" Eva asked.

"Nope. I'm in the car, but I've got the phone set where I'm hands-free. How are you?"

"I'm doing *gut*. I went back to work last Saturday when I no longer resembled a fish." She giggled. "And . . ."

There was a mysterious edge to Eva's voice. "This must be about Jake. Did you two finally get together?"

"We did!" Eva almost squealed when she spoke. "And Jake asked me to marry him."

Yvonne's jaw dropped. "Wow. You people go from zero to full throttle in a very short time." She thought about how long she'd dated Trevor before he popped the question. "But I am thrilled for both of you."

"Well, we've known each other since we were children, and I guess when you know, you just know. We'll be getting married in November. I know it's a long way from Texas, but it would make us so happy if you were able to attend the wedding. That is . . . if it won't be too difficult."

"I would be honored." Yvonne blinked back tears as she thought about her wedding dress still in layaway. She hadn't quite taken care of everything related to her own wedding yet. "This is wonderful news."

Eva was quiet for a few moments. "How are you doing, Yvonne?"

She pushed her sunglasses up on her head and took a deep breath. "I'm doing good. Really good. The days leading up to Trevor's funeral, and especially the days that followed, were rough, but I feel stronger now and a little more prepared to face the world again."

"I am so happy to hear this. I've been praying for you, and I know Jake has too. I can't pretend to know how you must have felt, and still feel, but *Gott* has a way of giving us comfort during difficult times."

"Yes, He definitely does. Let's just say that things have . . . changed for me." She smiled.

"That's wonderful. You sound better."

And from there, Eva bubbled with excitement as she told Yvonne about her and Jake's first kiss, Lizzie trying to give her advice, and how her father caught them kissing in the back room.

Yvonne laughed as she pictured those scenes playing out, and Eva was still talking when Yvonne pulled up in front of the bookstore.

"*Ach*, a car just pulled into the parking lot. I was taking advantage of some time to myself so I could talk freely. Jake will be back any minute, but I suppose I'd better go and tend to whomever is coming in."

Yvonne dropped her sunglasses back down on her nose, not wanting to spoil the surprise until she was actually walking in the door. "I'm so glad you called, and I am so happy for you and Jake. Please give him my regards." *Or I will when he returns.*

She killed the engine and reached for the biggest purse she owned, which was on the seat beside her. She'd transferred the usual stuff from her other purse, but she'd made sure there was room for the book she was going to return to Jake.

When she heard the *clippity-clop* of horse hooves, she glanced to her right. Jake was pulling up to the hitching post. Yvonne kept her head down, deciding to wait until he was inside the store so she could surprise them both.

He sauntered up to the door, and Yvonne heard the bell ring from her car. He went straight to Eva, who was at the register, and kissed her. Yvonne brought a hand to her chest and sighed. It was so sweet, and Yvonne couldn't have been any happier that Eva and Jake had admitted their love for each other and would be getting married. She hoped she would be able to attend.

Slowly, keeping her head down, she stepped out of the car with her purse, then walked to the door. She waited until she was inside to push her sunglasses up on her head.

"Surprise!" She bounced up on her toes within the pair of running shoes she'd chosen to wear for all the airport walking in Houston and Indianapolis.

Eva's mouth fell open as she gasped. "I was just on the phone with you!" She pointed a finger at her as she rushed around the corner of the counter. "Tricky, tricky!"

"It was hard not to tell you I was almost here," Yvonne said as Eva wrapped her in a giant hug.

"Well, well . . ." Jake walked up behind Eva, and he also hugged Yvonne when Eva finally backed away. "*Gut* to see you."

"Why didn't you tell us you were coming?" Eva was all smiles as she pressed her palms together. "Where are you staying? How long will you be here?"

"I wanted to surprise you both. George doesn't have me on any book hunts at the moment, and neither do any of my other clients. I thought a change of scenery would do me good. And I wanted to see you two. I hope I haven't come at a bad time."

Eva shook her head. "*Nee*, absolutely not. We're thrilled you're here."

Yvonne's stomach churned with excitement. She was anxious to return the book to Jake and to tell him and Eva about the author, how he had led her back to the Bible and ultimately to the realization that there was an afterlife. But she didn't want any interruptions.

"You close at five, right?" she asked. "I was thinking I could take you both to dinner."

Eva and Jake exchanged glances, then Eva said, "Jake is actually having supper with me and *mei* family, and we'd love for you to be our guest too."

Yvonne flinched a little. "Are you sure? I don't want to intrude. Will it be all right with your mother?" She recalled how tasty the food was here. She'd finally started to get her regular appetite back and had given up her pizzas and ice cream.

Eva chuckled. "*Mei mamm* will love having you for supper too. She asks about you often. And have you booked a place to stay?" Eva had the glowing look of a woman in love, and it warmed Yvonne's heart.

"Not yet, but I can stay at Gasthof Inn again. Or, if they're booked, I'm sure I can find a place."

"*Nee*." Eva shook her head. "Absolutely not. You will stay with *mei* family. I know *mei mamm* will insist on it."

"Wow." Yvonne's heart warmed. "If you're sure."

"*Ya*, I'm very sure." Eva smiled.

"It's close enough to five. I'm going to start shutting things down so we can close a little early." Jake walked toward the back of the shop.

After he was out of earshot, Yvonne gazed at Eva. "You look absolutely beautiful, like a woman in love."

"*Ach*, Yvonne. I'm so happy." Eva paused as her smile faded. "Are you sure you're okay with us talking about . . . *us*? It hasn't been long since Trevor passed."

"I am totally fine hearing about you and Jake. It makes me truly happy to see you two together the way you're meant to be."

Eva hugged her again. "I'm going to clean out the register, and Jake should have things ready to go shortly." She smiled again. "I'm so glad you're here."

"Me too." Yvonne was still sad, but there was happiness in her future. She was sure of it.

Eva was ready to smack her three brothers during supper. David was fifteen, Amos was seventeen, and Josh was twenty-one. Apparently, they didn't have the maturity not to drool over Yvonne, even though they had girlfriends. But at least they drooled in silence. Yvonne had mostly spent her last visit in Eva's bedroom, too grief-stricken to do much of anything, and Eva's father had made sure the boys made themselves scarce. So they were obviously making up for lost time. Eva's family didn't socialize much with outsiders, and it was clear the boys needed to work on their table manners when an English guest was present.

Yvonne was eating a lot more than when she was here before. Understandably, she hadn't been hungry toward the end of her last visit.

"You're looking well, Yvonne," Eva's mother said. "And Eva told me you haven't booked a place to stay yet. I insist you be our guest."

Eva glanced at her brothers, whose ears had perked up. She'd get hold of them later.

"Thank you very much."

It would be nice having Yvonne sleeping in the other bed in Eva's room, like a slumber party maybe. But Eva would leave herself completely open to listening to Yvonne and would try hard not to dominate the conversation with talk about her and Jake, even though being his wife was all she thought about.

After the meal, Eva's father didn't waste any time telling his sons either to busy themselves outside or to head up to their rooms. All three of them were gone in their buggies within fifteen minutes. Jake and Eva's father went outside on the porch.

"I must apologize for *mei sohns*, Yvonne. You would think they had never seen an *Englisch* person before." Eva's mother carried a load of plates to the sink. "*Ach*, sorry. That's what we commonly call a person who isn't Amish."

"They were fine," Yvonne said as she picked up two tea glasses and carried them to the counter. Eva was stowing the chow-chow, jams, and jellies in the refrigerator.

"*Nee, nee.*" Eva's mother waved a hand. "I will clean this up. You two go and enjoy your time together."

Yvonne walked to Eva's mother and hugged her. "Thank you for this lovely meal and for having me as a guest in your home." She eased away, blinked a few times. "And I especially want to thank you for . . . everything the last time I was here."

Eva recalled the way her mother had comforted Yvonne.

"*Ach, sweet maedel.*" Eva's mother rubbed Yvonne's arm. "There is no need to thank me. I'm glad I was able to offer you even the tiniest bit of comfort during such a difficult time." She smiled. "Now, you girls go and enjoy this lovely evening."

Eva motioned for Yvonne to follow her outside to the porch. Her father and Jake were sitting in two rocking chairs, and both stood immediately, even though four chairs were on the porch.

"I'm going to leave you three to visit." Her father scowled as he shook his head, then turned to Yvonne. "*Mei sohns* are gone, presumably off to see their girlfriends, which they will possibly deny later. But I hope they didn't make you feel too uncomfortable with their ogling."

Yvonne smiled. "Sir, they were fine. I'm just happy to be here."

Eva's father tipped his straw hat before he went back into the house.

Yvonne put a hand over her stomach. "What a wonderful meal. I am stuffed."

"I'm sure *Mamm* will leave desserts out on the table." Eva motioned for Yvonne to sit in one of the chairs. Then she and Jake sat on either side of her. Smiling, Eva glanced at Jake. "I *know* Jake will want dessert later."

He chuckled. "*Ya*, I'm not known to turn down anything sweet."

"When my food settles, I'm sure I'll be scanning the offerings also." Yvonne stood up. "I left my purse on the couch. Actually, it's more like a small suitcase." She grinned as she rolled her eyes. But I need to go get it." She looked at Jake. "I have something for you."

Jake rubbed his chin. He supposed Yvonne could have brought them a gift from Texas, but he suspected it was something else. And when she walked out carrying the book, he realized his hunch had been correct.

"I'm returning this." She held out the book, and after hesitating, Jake took it.

"You could have sold it, you know." He ran his hand across the worn leather, happy to have it back in his possession, but he'd meant what he said about her keeping it.

"I know you said I could, but Eva probably told you that I read the book." Tears formed in the corners of her eyes before she sat in the rocking chair again. "I never knew a book could be so transformative. Some of it was super hard for me to read, but it challenged me to look at things in a new way. It even led me back to the Bible."

Jake was glad to hear that because in his mind and way of thinking, the Bible was the only real book to rely on.

"Anyway"—Yvonne dabbed at her eyes with her finger—"it's clear to me that this is a book to be shared with others, those like me who are on the fence about God or who don't believe in Him or possibly just don't think there is anything for us after this life." She glanced back and forth between Eva and Jake. "I know that I'll see Trevor again. I know that if I live a good life based on the teachings of the Bible, through prayer and communion with God, I will go to heaven."

Jake looked at Eva when she sniffled. Then she said, "*Ach*, Yvonne. This news makes me so happy, and I'm thrilled that you came to share it with both of us in person."

His future wife was beautiful even when she was crying, but he knew these were happy tears.

"Those first forty pages were hard to read, but when the author finally found his faith again, I wasn't able to put the book down. His words touched me in ways I don't know how to explain, except that the book led me on an inner quest to really search my beliefs. God showed Himself to me through this author's words, and He guided me to Him. I will be forever grateful that you snuck that book into my suitcase." She paused and looked down before she locked eyes with Jake. "This is a book that should never be sold, only shared. For its content, yes. But there is another reason that you should never sell the book, Jake."

He sat taller, his hand still on the book in his lap, his chest tightened from trying not to cry along with Eva. Yvonne's news brought forth all kinds of emotions. He almost hadn't put the book in her suitcase. If he hadn't, would she still not believe in an afterlife? Or would God have still led her to Him via another path? Jake made a promise to God that he would read the book, especially if it served some sort of divine purpose. He waited for Yvonne to go on.

"It took me a few days, but I was so curious about the author that I began doing some research online." Yvonne took a deep breath, unsure how Jake would respond to her news, but he needed to know about the author. "I've been chasing down rare books for so long that I have a few tricks up my sleeve. I'm in some groups on Facebook. I know people who know more about books than I do." She waved a hand dismissively. "Anyway, the author embellished on his name a little."

Jake and Eva exchanged looks of confusion.

"He wrote under a pen name. I don't know why, but I can only assume that at the time, he didn't want anyone to know he was the author. It took me some time to trace the book all the way back to its roots since it was published in 1875 by a small publisher who hasn't been in business for over a century." She paused, hoping Jake didn't find this news upsetting, but the author had found redemption, and it felt wrong not to share what she'd discovered.

"Jake, what was your grandfather's name?" She needed to be completely sure she was correct.

"Benjamin Lantz," Jake said, eyeing her skeptically.

"And he was named after your great-grandfather, correct?" Jake nodded, and Yvonne took a deep breath and waited to see if Jake made the connection. After a few seconds, she said, "The author's name is Jerry Lance, but that's the name he wrote under. His real name is Benjamin Lantz. Your great-grandfather."

Jake's eyes widened. "*Mei urgrossvadder* wrote the book? That would explain why *mei grossdaadi* didn't want me to sell it, at least partly."

Yvonne nodded. "If that's the word for *great-grandfather*, then yes. It's a very raw retelling of how he lost his faith, then found it again. Any idea who MAC is? That's who he dedicated it to."

He shook his head. "I have no idea."

Jake, I truly believe the book should never be sold but only loaned out to those who might need it. The average person will never know that it has a financial worth that far exceeds most books, but always be careful whom you loan it to. I feel like God will guide you in that effort. I know the three of us believe the Bible is the ultimate reading guide for truth and guidance, but if *Walk with Me* leads someone onto the correct path—the way it did me—then I believe it is meant to be shared."

"I will make it a point to read the entire book," Jake said as he stared at it in his lap. "Maybe Eva and I will read it together like we originally planned."

"I'd like that," Eva said softly.

Jake stared at Yvonne. "*Danki* for learning about the author and for bringing it back to me."

Yvonne blinked her eyes as she tried to keep from crying. "No, Jake. Thank you, for knowing in your heart that I needed it in some way." She swiped at a tear that slipped down her cheek despite her efforts. "It helped to change my life. It helped me work through my grief by knowing that I will see Trevor again someday."

The three of them were quiet for a while, each lost in thoughts that probably varied in many ways.

For Yvonne, she could sum up her emotions in one word: *hope*. And she would be forever grateful for God's perfect plans. For her. For Jake and Eva. And for all those who reached out to Him in an effort to do His work and to be their best person.

Smiling, she stood up. Despite being emotional, Jake and Eva were aglow with newly acknowledged love for each other. Yvonne kissed them each on the cheek, then excused herself to go to bed so they could enjoy some time by themselves. So many nights Yvonne had been uncomfortable being trapped with her thoughts, but tonight she felt a peacefulness that she was sure would only get stronger with time.

Eva stood up when Jake did, and they glided toward one another like skaters on ice until they were fully embracing. He held her tightly before gently easing her away, kissing her tenderly. Eva savored his touch, the way he smelled, held her, and continued to show her how much he loved her.

"I think Yvonne is going to be okay," Eva said when they'd finally separated a little more. "And if I had a *schweschder*, I would want her to be someone like Yvonne—smart, compassionate, and maybe even just a little bit worldly. Someone older than me." She gazed into Jake's eyes. "It's nice that she took the time to find out who the author of the book is and that she made the trip here so she could tell you in person."

"All part of God's plan for her. I suspect she is wondering where life will take her from here." He stared into Eva's eyes. "I can't imagine losing you. My heart hurts for her."

Eva's eyes grew moist as she locked eyes with her one true love. "I don't think we can really understand how she's feeling, but I know that I can't stand the thought of not being with you either. At least now Yvonne believes she will see Trevor again, and she'll carry that belief with her, helping her to heal. And you played a part in that."

Jake pointed upward as they stood underneath the porch awning, stars glistening in the distance. "*Gott* gets credit for that." He twisted his mouth from side to side as he often did when he was thinking. "I really am going to read the entire book, like I told Yvonne. It feels more important than ever now that I know *mei urgrossvadder* is the author. And *Gott* might use me again to make sure the book gets into the hands of the right person. I wish I knew who MAC was, but something in my heart tells me I'm not supposed to know."

"I think you are probably right. Do you still want to read it together?" Eva's hand slid down to her side and found Jake's, their fingers melding together into a natural fit.

"*Ya*, I would like that." He squeezed her hand as he placed a gentle kiss on her forehead before he found her eyes. "I would like to spend *mei* life doing everything together with you. Forever."

Eva's eyes widened. She'd never grow tired of hearing that.

"Would that be okay with you?" He kissed her again, something else she'd never tire of.

"I think that would be lovely."

He turned her around until they both faced the starlit sky, and he wrapped his arms around her waist just as a falling star shot across the sky.

Eva closed her eyes and made a wish. Then smiled at the man she planned to spend the rest of her life with.

# EPILOGUE

**Five months later**

Yvonne couldn't believe her eyes when she pulled up to Eva's parents' house. There had to be almost a hundred buggies tethered to the fences that surrounded the house, along with about a dozen parked cars. She wondered if she would be able to find Eva before the ceremony. Her flight from Houston had been delayed, and she hadn't arrived at the airport until almost dark the night before. Then she'd had a two-hour drive to a hotel. Eva had offered repeatedly for Yvonne to stay with her at her parents' house, but Yvonne knew the chaos a wedding brought on, and she didn't want to be in the way. She'd kept in touch with Eva over the months since she'd returned the book, and she was happy that her friend's big day was finally here.

She made her way down the road from where she'd had

to park, careful not to twist an ankle on the gravel. Flats would have been a better option than the three-inch heels she wore. Smiling, she took in the scenery. Three huge white tents were set up in the yard with tables covered in white linen, and women bustled around everywhere. Yvonne was looking forward to seeing Eva and Jake get married, although she wasn't sure how she'd feel about a three-hour worship service—seated on wooden benches. And the ceremony would be recited in a language she wouldn't understand. Eva had told her in a letter that everything would be in Pennsylvania *Deutsch*.

As she continued her trek to the house, the sun was still rising. She couldn't believe everything started so early in the morning—and Eva had said it was an all-day affair that went on into the night. The ceremony was scheduled to start in thirty minutes, and as she weaved through the crowd outside, she was surprised to see how many non-Amish people were there, although at least three-quarters of the crowd were Amish.

She pulled open the screen door to the living room, which had been totally transformed the way Eva had described to her. Complete walls had been removed, revealing bedrooms where furniture had been removed or was pushed back against a wall, opening up the space so it was one giant room. Apparently, like many Amish homes, the old farmhouse had been built that way over a hundred years ago to accommodate weddings and worship services. The walls were literally removable. Each family had to host a church service every ten months, give or take, Eva had told her.

People were sandwiched in the room like sardines in a can. Some older women and pregnant women were seated in regular chairs toward the back of the room. Backless wooden benches filled the space between them and an open area in the middle, where Yvonne assumed the ceremony would take place. More benches were on the other side of the open space. Eva had told her that the men sat on one side of the room, women on the other side.

It was a unique and intriguing setup, and obviously a lot of people had helped with the preparation. Yvonne inched her way into the room, then felt a hand on her arm.

"Hi, Mary." Yvonne smiled at Eva's mother. "Today's the day." She wasn't sure whether to hug Mary in front of all these people since public affection was generally frowned upon. But Mary embraced her.

"I'm so glad you're here." She kissed her on the cheek. "Eva and Jake were thrilled that you were able to come." She waved an arm over the area. "Find a seat anywhere."

Yvonne took a seat toward the back of the room. It had been months since Trevor died, but she wasn't sure if a wedding was going to cause a flood of tears. She could escape easier if she sat in the back row.

The ceremony began right at nine o'clock. People were standing all along the walls, and the benches were full. When Yvonne saw Eva, she shed her first tear, and it had nothing to do with Trevor. Her friend glowed, and even though she was clothed in attire like she would wear every day, her dress was perfectly pressed and shone from the newness of the fabric. How many times had Yvonne seen Eva or her mother with flour on their wrinkled black aprons? But today Eva looked beautiful in a dark green dress with a white apron. She'd told Yvonne that it was the same dress she would be buried in when she died.

As Yvonne settled into a ceremony she wouldn't understand, she fought the images of her and Trevor standing together and exchanging vows. Everyone had been right. Time did heal, but it would take a long time before Yvonne didn't find herself sensitive about everything that reminded her of Trevor. And she still missed him. Maybe she always would.

She managed to make it through the ceremony without full-on crying . . . until Eva and Jake took their vows. They were different from the traditional vows Yvonne was used to, and it was hard to hear them. But Jake and Eva's eyes said it all, and Yvonne said her own prayers for happiness for the couple. She loved the part where the bishop gave Jake a Holy Kiss on the cheek and his wife did the same with Eva. It felt so sacred, and it was a custom that had been passed down for generations.

Even though she hadn't understood the language during the ceremony, the fellowship filled her with love just the same. She was surprised that she hadn't taken more notice of the time, but when it was over, her stomach was rumbling, and she was sure the food would be amazing. Eva had told her that women arrived as early as five in the morning to start the food preparations.

Yvonne wished she could have arrived sooner, a day or two before the wedding. Maybe she could have helped with preparations and spent time with Eva and Jake. But George had had her on another book hunt, her third one since Trevor passed, and it had kept her occupied. She would have to leave on Sunday, but when time permitted, she hoped to travel back to this peaceful place to spend more time with her friends.

For now she stayed off to the side and out of the way, outside near one of the tents.

"You look a little lost."

Yvonne turned quickly to her left. "No, not really lost," she said, smiling. "Just trying to stay out of the way."

The man smiled at her. He was considerably taller than her . . . and handsome, with dark hair and blue eyes. He looked familiar somehow, but she couldn't place him.

"You're Yvonne, right?" He gestured toward his body, clad in black jeans, a crisp white shirt, and black loafers. "You might not recognize me. Last time we met I was in uniform at the bookstore."

Yvonne snapped a finger. "The police officer, the one who arrived after the bookstore got broken into."

He nodded. "Abraham Byler."

"Nice to see you again," she said as a wave of guilt washed over her, threatening to drown her. It was much too soon to be attracted to another man.

"Are you in town for long?" he asked, trying to sound casual, but failing.

"No, I actually go home tomorrow." She shrugged. "Work stuff. But I didn't want to miss the wedding."

"Was it difficult to sit through such a long service without understanding the language?" He tipped his head to one side.

Yvonne remembered Jake telling her that Abraham had grown up Amish before he decided not to be baptized in the faith and instead joined the police force. "You know . . . I thought it would be. But there was a sense of fellowship that filled the void. It was . . . lovely."

"There you are!" Eva rushed across the lawn, dragging her new husband along with her. "I'm so sorry we didn't get to see you before the ceremony."

"You look gorgeous." Yvonne hugged Eva then Jake.

"Do you remember Abraham?" Jake nodded toward the man standing next to Yvonne.

"I didn't at first, without his uniform . . ." She glanced at the man next to her, convincing herself that it was okay to think he was handsome. Most women surely did. "But he reminded me about our meeting at the bookstore."

"I know you're leaving tomorrow, and I hate that." Eva rolled her lip into a pout. "Today will be such a busy day, we won't have much time to spend together."

Yvonne reached for both of Eva's hands and squeezed them. "This is *your* day. And I am definitely coming back when I have more time."

Eva looked over her shoulder, then back at Yvonne. "I have to find *mei mamm*. She had a question about one of the cakes. There are four of them." She hugged Yvonne again, then laughed. "Remember when I told you that our weddings are quite the affair?"

Yvonne nodded. "Yes, I do. And you need to go find your mom and enjoy everything about this day." Her thoughts drifted to Trevor, but when Jake hugged her again, she snapped back. She smiled as Eva dragged Jake with her, never letting go of his hand.

"They make a cute couple," Abraham said, also watching and smiling as Eva and Jake skipped away toward a future Yvonne prayed would bless them abundantly.

"Yes, they really do." She stepped sideways when a woman carrying a large tray filled with olives and pickles almost caught the side of her head.

"Whoa, it's getting crowded out here." Abraham chuckled.

"Yeah, lots going on. I think it's always that way at weddings, Amish or not." Yvonne's bottom lip began to tremble, and she couldn't seem to get it to stop. She would have already been married almost a month if Trevor hadn't died. It was harder than she'd thought to separate this wedding from the one she would have had.

Two more women slid by her, carrying trays of food, causing her to bump into Abraham. "Oh, wow. I'm so sorry."

He put a hand on her arm until she had her balance.

"No apologies. These women function like a well-tuned machine when it comes to getting food on the table, even for this large of a crowd."

"I bet there are four hundred people here." She sighed. "Wow."

"It'll be a while before they have all the food out, but it will be a plentiful feast." Abraham stared at her as her lip started to tremble again. Eva and Jake had probably told him about Trevor. Or maybe not. But his compassionate expression seemed to say that one of them had.

"Do you want to take a walk, get away from this crowd until they are actually ready for people to sit down?" He kept his eyes on her, an all-knowing expression on his face, as if he knew she needed saving right now, before everything caught up with her and she melted into a sobbing mess.

Yvonne cast her eyes on the fall foliage for as far as she could see, bursting with red, orange, and purple hues. Fall in Texas wasn't nearly as vibrant and colorful. "Uh, I probably shouldn't . . . I mean, I don't know . . ." She bit her bottom lip, then looked up at him.

"I think we should sneak off, breathe in the season, and step away from this crowd for a few minutes." He smiled. "Walk with me."

Yvonne stared at him for a long while. *Walk with Me.*

Was it a sign? Merely a coincidence?

But when he smiled, she leaned down and slipped out

of her heels, tucked them under her arm, and welcomed the tickle of the plush green grass between her toes.

"I'll walk with you," she said to him before she looked up at the cloudless sky and smiled.

# ACKNOWLEDGMENTS

As always, God gets the glory for every story He lays upon my heart. But it doesn't hurt to have a fabulous publishing team onboard also. Much thanks to everyone at HarperCollins Christian Publishing, especially my amazing editor, Kimberly Carlton.

Natasha Kern is the best literary agent a gal could have. Thank you for your constant encouragement and support both professionally and personally. I'm blessed to have you as my friend.

Janet Murphy, what can I say that I haven't already said over the past decade? What began as a casual business relationship morphed into a lifetime friendship. I love and appreciate you!

I also have a fabulous street team—Wiseman's Warriors—some of whom have been with me from the beginning of my writing career. Thank you so much for all you do to promote my books.

As for my writing career, there wouldn't be one without my readers, so a huge thank you for traveling on this wonderful journey with me.

Much love to my family and friends for understanding about my deadlines, but for also dragging me out of the house when I've been isolated for entirely too long, lol. 😉

# DISCUSSION QUESTIONS

1. This book is a work of fiction. In real life, do you think that most people would have kept a promise the way Jake did, or would they have taken the money offered for the book?
2. In the beginning of the story, did you see Yvonne as a threat or competition for Eva? Or did you read between the lines and recognize that she was just a friendly person trying to do her job?
3. At what point in the story does Jake realize that his feelings for Eva have matured and developed into more than friendship?
4. Did Jake do the right thing by choosing to be honorable and stepping aside so that John could court Eva? Should Jake have shared his feelings about Eva as soon as he realized he loved her as

more than just a friend? Or did everything play out exactly as it should have?

5. Yvonne is clearly on a journey when it comes to her faith, and we see her slowly evolving throughout the book. What are some examples of her spiritual growth?
6. Yvonne is older than Eva and seems to fall organically into a "big sister" type role. What are some examples of Yvonne giving Eva advice? And, after Trevor dies, the tables are turned. What are some examples of Eva providing Yvonne with exactly what she needs at the time? (Hint – Eva provides several distractions for Yvonne during her grief.)
7. What did you think about the scene when Yvonne dreams about Trevor? Or was it really a dream? Do you think God sends messengers to help us with our grief? Have you ever had dreams about loved ones who have passed? If so, how did you feel?
8. Who was your favorite character? Who did you relate to the most? It might not even be the same person. If you could have dinner with any of the characters, who would you choose and why?
9. The book—*Walk With Me*—is a large focal point in the story. Do you believe that a book, fiction or nonfiction, can change your way of thinking when it comes to spirituality and matters of the heart? Examples?

10. If you could secretly drop yourself in the middle of any scene like a fly on the wall and just observe, which scene would that be and why?
11. Did you ever suspect that one of Jake's relatives might have written *Walk With Me*? Were you surprised to learn that his great-grandfather was the author?
12. What do you foresee in Yvonne's future?

# The Amish Inn Series

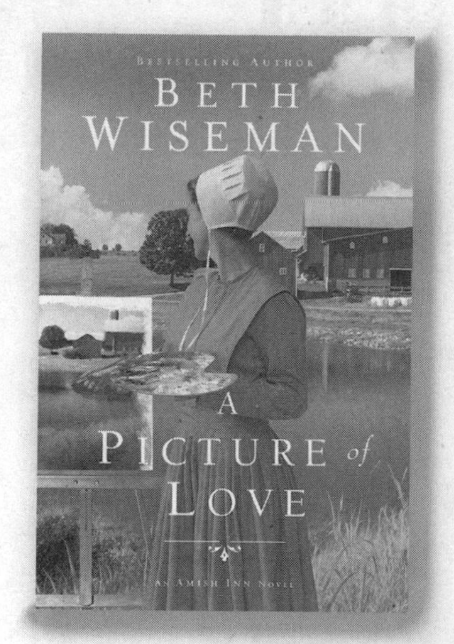

**AVAILABLE IN PRINT,**
**E-BOOK, AND AUDIO**

# ABOUT THE AUTHOR

Photo by Emilie Hendryx

Bestselling and award-winning author Beth Wiseman has sold over two million books. She is the recipient of the coveted Holt Medallion, is a two-time Carol Award winner, and has won the Inspirational Reader's Choice Award three times. Her books have been on various bestseller lists, including CBD, CBA, ECPA, and *Publishers Weekly*. Beth and her husband are empty nesters enjoying country life in south-central Texas.

*Visit her online at BethWiseman.com*
*Facebook: @AuthorBethWiseman*
*Twitter: @BethWiseman*
*Instagram: @bethwisemanauthor*